SUNNY G'S

series of

RASH DECISIONS

Navdeep Singh Dhillon

DIAL BOOKS

Dial Books
An imprint of Penguin Random House LLC, New York

First published in the United States of America by Dial Books,
an imprint of Penguin Random House LLC, 2022
Copyright © 2022 by CAKE Literary

Dial & colophon are registered trademarks of Penguin Random House LLC.

Visit us online at penguinrandomhouse.com.

Library of Congress Cataloging-in-Publication Data is available.
Book manufactured in Canada
ISBN 9780593109977

10 9 8 7 6 5 4 3 2 1
FRI

Design by Mina Chung • Text set in Carre Noir Std

For all the brown nerds, especially Shaiyar and Kavya.
This book would be terribly dull without you.
May you keep writing fanfiction, be as intense and
passionate about your fandoms as Sunny and Mindii,
and never let any ullu da pattha mispronounce your name
or ask for your nerd credentials. You are my favourites.
Please don't start a heavy metal sorcerer band.

To Navreet, Mum, and Pappari: Sorry for swearing in
all the languages you tried to instill high culture.
You brought this on yourselves, innit.

CHAPTER 1

THE LIFE PROMTASTIC

Ever look in the mirror and think to yourself: *I look fan-tastic. My face, my nose, my eyes, the blond streak in my hair, my body, these clothes. Everything is lit.*

Yep. Me neither.

I'm in the gender-neutral bathroom at prom, where an alarming number of people are not washing their hands. I'm staring at my phone, unable to commit to pressing the "add to story" button on this post. I hit delete and take more photos from several different angles, experimenting with various facial expressions ranging from *Oh, I didn't see you there* to *I am Sunny Gill Rebranded: Hear Me Roar.*

It's a little jarring looking at this new face in the mirror. I've been in here for eight minutes and counting, trying to regroup. I was ready to do this thing, make this my big night. Then I find Stefan sitting front and center at the table I was randomly assigned to. Of all people, it had to be him, the dude who made my life a fucking nightmare from seventh grade on. So I bolted straight to the bathroom, and now I'm reassessing all the grooming choices I've made since Thursday. Including the blond streak I had added at Super Cuts, hoping for a bit of whimsy.

It's not that I don't like this new face. It just feels like a stranger staring back at me—the beard and turban gone, replaced by gelled-up, wavy, shoulder-length hair. My beard was never a sexy Jason-Momoa-as-Aquaman beard, or wild and dangerous like Dafydd the Feeble's from the Jamie Snollygoster series me and Ngozi are obsessed with. Not as cool as my brother Goldy's manicured designer dari, with the twirled-up mustache, or as intimidating as the rough bristles of Papa's salt-and-pepper beard. But it was uniquely mine: a sparse, soft layer of black sprinkled over my cheeks.

Almost all of the older warriors and sorcerers in Jamie Snollygoster have beards, a sign of wisdom and courage, hard-won from a lifetime of wielding magic and battling baddies. Or maybe they don't have time for grooming? A good ten pages of book one was spent on the first years contemplating their future beards. That's what initially drew me to Dafydd—his magnificently wild I-don't-care beard.

The summer before ninth grade I made the transition from wearing a patka—the kid version of the turban—to the one adults wear: the pag or dastaar. I was excited. My beard was lightly coming in, I could recite a respectable number of pauris from the opening sacred composition of our Holy Scriptures, the Guru Granth Sahib. I'd had enough of the childish patka. I was ready to man up and claim the dastaar. Plus Goldy thinks anyone who has a beard and is still wearing the patka deserves all the ridicule they get. He calls it the Sikh toddler look.

Before I committed, I spent hours researching turban styles, watching Sikh TikTok stars, Punjabi singers, and vloggers on YouTube. I even uncovered some fun facts. For example: The word *dastaar* comes from the Farsi *daste-yār*, meaning "the hand of the Divine." And the word *dolband* became *turban* thanks to the terrible pronunciation of the French and English.

An eternal optimist, I thought I would glide on in to my first day at Barstow High, the most badass ninth grader wearing dollar store sunglasses, a turquoise dastaar, tied patiala shahi style. I walked in with the swagger of a Punjabi singer or Bollywood star ready to defend the honor of his girl/family/village with a dramatic AF preamble before unleashing The Thappar of Pain #ttp. I had high hopes. No more bullying. Reverence. Awe. Girls swooning.

It took one terrorist comment from Stefan to unravel it all.

I wish I had Papa's confidence. His pag has always been one style that takes him ten minutes to tie: mildly creased and pointed, super wide and loose. Hair is one of the fundamental outward physical characteristics of being a Sikh, and the one that Papa says is the easiest thing to do: "You don't even have to do anything. Let nature take its course!"

My brother, Goldy? His confidence is on another level. Never a planner. No research, no watching turban-tying tutorials, nothing. Probably woke up every morning and rocked whatever turban style he felt like. For his prom, he wore a ridiculous silk teal peacock dastaar. He got drunk that night and needed me—his little brother—to once again cover for him. Yet he's the one Mama and Papa talk about like he is the most amazing son that ever existed.

My hand instinctively pats the journal inside my bright orange-and-red skull-on-fire crocheted pouch—part of my Dafydd the Feeble cosplay. Biji—my grandmother—and I sell the pouches, among other things, on Loom the Fandom, our Etsy store. Well, technically the store is on Etsy—that's where you have to go to actually buy things. But my social media business presence is on Instagram, where I answer questions and post pics. The pouches do pretty well. You'd be surprised by how many people design amazing pocketless costumes and forget to make matching accessories. The mark of a beginning cosplayer: a kickass cosplay ruined by a fucking tote bag from Trader Joe's. My pouch is a lifesaver. It holds all my manly essentials: breath mints, hand sanitizer, phone, money, cards, a small set of keys, and of course, Goldy's journal. Which is kinda mine now.

I'm glad nobody else from our Bramble-core heavy metal band, Unkempt, is here, because they would all be taking shifts telling me how anti-canon it is to wear my crocheted pouch without a kilt or armor. Especially Ngozi, my best friend and the lead singer. She thinks she gets a say in everything about my life. Do I get a say in hers? Not bloody likely. She's British. Says weird shit like that all the time. But when I say anything, suddenly it's "Sunny, you plonker." Or "Leave it out, Sunny." Which are not even legit Britishisms, they're from some obscure Brit TV show she and her mom watch.

Every year me, Ngozi, and the rest of Unkempt play at the Snollygoster Soiree, an annual shindig dedicated to the world of Jamie Snollygoster. Even though Jamie has millions of fans and is the star of the Snollygoster series, me and Ngozi never liked the entitled fucker. Maybe he just reminds us of Stefan with his "jokes" about people's weight and the way they speak. Or perhaps it's that Jamie couldn't just sit his ass down and memorize some fucking spells instead of looking for illuminated maps by opening doors nobody told him to open.

Plenty of other fans feel the same way, which is why the heavy metal Bramble-core subgenre is even a thing. Me and Ngozi immediately loved the two minor characters, Dafydd and Safia Brambleberry, father and daughter sorcerers who lived at the unnamed tavern just outside the grounds of Malmesbury Academy. We started writing about them in our fanfiction, which quickly turned into songs. We both felt like Safia should have been the real hero of the books anyway.

Aside from his beard, I liked Dafydd because he was a solid friend to Jamie and loyal, like tragically loyal even to shady-ass people who had a vendetta against him. And he didn't give a shit when people tried to ridicule him for only own-ing one style of armored cloak for every single occasion. Soirees, battles, serving mead at the tavern. Unbothered. The way I pretend to be online and wish I were in real life. I look up at my face in the mirror and sigh. It would be nice if Ngozi had just come here to Normal Prom. But she definitely won't; this is as far from her scene as you can get. There's no way she would stand for this dress code, which has no restrictions on what the boys wear, but the girls can't even show their shoulders or ankles, like we're in Victorian England. Still, I wish she were here. Even if she was scowling silently at the table, mocking the suit I'm wearing and my face.

Maybe I should text her?

Ngozi just doesn't understand that this year I want to do something different, that there's a world of magical possibilities even here at Normal Prom.

She probably thinks I'm here because of a girl. But alas,

there is no girl. Just a lifetime of watching rom-coms in Hindi, Punjabi, and English. I wish there were someone I could make a grand declaration of love to. But it's just me and my tanhai, aka angst. Terminal.

Like Ngozi's one to talk anyway. She's just as awkward around girls as I am. Plus, she's hardly the only one annoyed with me tonight. I'm also supposed to be at home for Goldy's barsi, marking the anniversary of his death. Like he'll miss me or something.

Everyone is constantly telling me what I'm supposed to be doing. Goldy made it out of Fresno, fucked it all up, and now he's gone. And even though Mama and Papa have never said anything, there's no way I can leave now. They probably, definitely expect me to stay in Fresno for the rest of my life under their watchful eye. I don't even like alcohol. The smell, the taste, the idea of not being in control of your own body and thoughts? No fucking thank you. Even in death, Goldy manages to be a dark, stinking cloud looming over my head.

Goldy's the reason I'm here at Normal Prom in the first place. Kind of. A few months ago, I found this notebook behind a bookshelf in his room. A journal from when he was at rehab It was a real mess, kind of like his approach to life: unorganized, completely unfettered by consequences, reaping all the benefits.

I loosen the tassels and flip open the pouch. I remove

the notebook and look intently at it. When I found it, I re-covered it with a simple crochet sleeve using three different colored wools: teal, green, and yellow. You can still see Goldy's original, tattered cover underneath: a picture of a peacock with faded teal feathers.

I flip through the notebook, hoping something insightful will suddenly come tumbling out. But it's the same as it was when I first found it. Inside is pure chaos: some journal entries, blank pages, doodles, artwork, random poems, words in large letters. My eyes land on the word *rahao*, which I learned about at Khalsa School. It means to pause and think deeply about the central message of a shabad— a sacred musical poetic composition.

On a blank page after all his gibberish, I've written out a heading for a new list: *Sunny G's Series of Rash Decisions*.

It comes right after Goldy's final almost-entry: *Goldy's List of Ways to Be a Better Dude*. Dated a few days before he died. But no actual list accompanies it. Just blank pages upon blank pages, a sea of nothingness. The finality of the blank pages kind of freaked me out. That's why I started the rash decisions list.

No more obedient Sunny G who does whatever everyone tells him to do. Time for Sunny to make reckless life choices.

The first and so far only entries in my rash decisions notebook:

1) *Change face*

2) *Go to prom*

I close up the notebook and place it back in my pouch.

I look at the draft of the Insta post on my phone. Creating hashtags and captions is much easier for my Loom the Fandom account. Those I can come up with in seven seconds flat. They're usually inspirational quotes, along with a photo of something I crocheted available for purchase. The latest: a cup of masala cha wearing a crocheted tea cozy, sunset in the background. The caption: "Don't just let life pass you by wondering what if. BE the IF."

I'm fucking profound on social.

But I need a better shot for my personal Insta. I pause and lean over the sink, angling my chin upward. That's when I notice it. An out-of-place nose hair. Things quickly spiral out of control because it goes like this: You notice the nose hair, you destroy said nose hair, and think that's the end of it. But there's a plot twist. More nose hairs. You question whether these really are new or they've been here this entire time. You realize the futility of destroying them all after the fourth one. By then your eyes are a watery mess, making it look like you've been crying five fucking minutes into prom. Blasted. Nose. Hairs.

I make another attempt at a selfie, pinching two fingers together to zoom in close. I gasp as I notice my meatloaf-sized sideburns. I don't remember why I thought it would be a good idea to do them myself. They look uneven. Am I overthinking? Perhaps it's my posture, I rationalize. I cover my face with my thumb and index finger, like there's a secret carpenter's level pulsing through my veins. Sure enough, the results are clear. Fresno, we have a problem: One sideburn is slightly lopsided. I notice the nose hairs again. Like arrows being shot from my Nostril Army of Archers.

I consider tucking them back inside, but WHAT IF I SNEEZE? Or there's, like, a gust of wind just as I am saying something super insightful? I'll tell you what: It will send all the nose hairs tumbling out and I will become a goddamn meme. That's what.

I glance back at this new draft. I look like a dude carrying the weight of the world on his shoulders. I type: *Time for Prom! #SunnyAtProm #AwesomeTime #PromBathroomSelfie #NewFaceWhoDis #WeDidIt.*

I zoom in close on my phone camera. My hair is a mess. This angle makes it look like it's been elf-locked even though it's tangle-free. I could use one of Safia Brambleberry's spells right about now, even though Ngozi thinks the whole idea of an anti-frizz hair enchantment is some white supremacy bullshit.

Mama would probably just tell me to use baking soda and vinegar on my hair. She thinks those two things alone can fix all the world's problems: hair straightener, beard regrower, oven cleaner, skin exfoliator, toilet bowl freshener. If Mama were a doctor, instead of working at the video store, I bet ninety percent of her remedies would involve baking soda and vinegar. The other ten percent would be turmeric, which she always cooks with. "It is antiseptic," she says. "You should always be prepared for calamity."

Baking soda, vinegar, turmeric, knots, and spilling the latest tea in Bollywood. Those are the things me and Mama talk about. We don't talk about Goldy. Not even in euphemisms.

You'd think a year would be enough time to accept that my brother is gone, to learn to start using the past tense. I still feel a lump in my throat when I use the words that feel so final: *dead, death, cremation, alcoholic*. No more playing video games with my brother, getting yelled at for following him around everywhere. It's just so definitive. Gone.

The bathroom door flings open, and I can feel my left buttock twitch before I even see him. Chiseled White Boy Face Stefan. That's what Ngozi and I call him because he looks like the Eurocentric vision the author—E. B. Goyle—probably had in mind when she described Jamie Snollygoster's face in the books: "They had never seen a boy so handsome. His cheeks were chiseled as though the Gods Themselves had come down to do the work, his nose, slender and ending at an angle, lips as red as roses, a beautiful sharp dimpled chin." Our beloved series has got plenty of problems. That's the reason we started writing fanfiction in the first place.

Stefan doesn't look all that. His dimpled chin looks more like a chin-with-two-butt-cheeks trying real hard to pretend they're not butt cheeks. But he does have that face that they love to cast on TV shows: the hazy blue eyes, and pale skin, like he hunts vampires in his spare time. Uses the phrase *chai tea* non-ironically, thinks telling racist jokes about a variety of races makes him an equal opportunity offender and not just . . . racist squared.

He brushes past me, handles his business, then sidles up next to me and turns on the faucet. My face is still turned upward from the nostril viewing and I'm frozen there, so as not to look like a doofus. And in so doing, feel like a much bigger doofus. Of the million universal nerdy things he could mock me for, he always goes for the lazy racism, with geographically and culturally inaccurate jabs that have surprisingly not gotten more complex over the years. Five years in, and it's still terrorist, ISIS, jihad, with plenty of microaggressions thrown in. You'd think I'd have some comebacks by now. You'd be wrong.

I'm ready for the blow, but he just checks himself out in the mirror as he lathers up his hands, rinses them off. Then shakes his head in annoyance at something on the wall as my face lowers to a normal elevation. "Hand dryers, man," he says, catching me off guard.

I suck my teeth at the hand dryer like it's been talking shit about my family, and inhale deeply in an attempt to avoid stuttering. "S-spreads more g-germs than paper towels." I watch Stefan's face to see if he noticed the stutter. "But what you gonna do?" I add, like I'm a gangster from the 1940s. "C-can't wipe your hands on your pants."

The sound of the hand dryer stops. He laughs. "See ya back at the table."

I nod as he makes his way out of the bathroom.

Surreal. I have never had an encounter with Stefan that didn't involve some kind of humiliation. My very first interaction with Stefan was in seventh grade when we had to introduce ourselves, which is a really stressful activity for any kid, double for a kid who stutters and looks the way I do. And then Stefan happened. I was in the middle of stuttering on the first syllable of my name when Stefan muttered "t-t-terrorist," and some of the other kids started laughing, which completely threw me off and I started stuttering like a machine that's short-circuiting. Until the teacher interrupted me, finished my sentence, then told me to sit down. In high school, it evolved into a cruel strategy just for laughs, where Stefan would constantly interrupt me, just to make me stutter and feel like shit. He made school hell. I got a little reprieve when Ngozi entered the picture in the middle of ninth grade, bringing along all kinds of other things: the Jamie Snollygoster series, the joy of fanfiction, and the Bramble-core heavy metal scene that we discovered together.

I take a deep breath and exhale as quietly as I can. I hate that I'm so predictable. But those days are behind me now. And in a few weeks all of this is going to be over. Maybe this plan is working after all.

I wash my hands. As the hand dryer loudly spreads germs all over them again, I feel a giddiness. Is this what happy feels like?

As I exit the bathroom, I finish up my post. *Sometimes*, I write as the caption, *you gotta stop saying Fres-No, and start saying Fres-Yes!*

CHAPTER 2

THE PROMTASTROPHE

I'm sitting at the table watching Stefan not notice me. I quickly realize it's not just him, it's everyone here. Just carrying on with their conversations, paying no attention to me at all. So this is what it feels like to blend in. I could get used to this.

I don't know the names of everyone at the table, but recognize some of the faces from middle school or elementary, others from classes or rallies. Maybe some of them feel that way about me, like I look vaguely familiar, but without the beard and turban, they don't realize I'm me?

I'm surprised Jasmine isn't saying anything about my face. She never actively bullies me, but does occasionally join in the yuk-yuks with Stefan and his minions. Jasmine's not especially religious, but we have occasionally bonded over the delicious glory of muttar paneer and jalebis at Sikh functions. I glance at her hair. It's dark red, almost maroon, and falls neatly to the tops of her shoulders. Her prom dress is a deep shade of green, matching her eye shadow. An odd choice, but definitely in line with this year's prom theme: nature.

I clear my throat and wait for a tiny lull in the conversation to dive in.

"Th-this ambience is interesting," I say. The stutter is barely noticeable—nice.

"Ambience is a good way to put it," Stefan replies, looking up briefly from his phone. It's still jarring to hear him speak to me like a human.

"It's like the Green Goblin exploded all over the gym," Pushpa says.

"You w-would think someone would b-be like, this is too much green, man," I say.

I bite my lip to refrain from adding, "YES. I have just started a conversation!" Out of habit, I lift my hand and my fingers clasp my now nonexistent beard.

The Prom Committee interpreted the theme of nature as making everything green instead of actually *going* green. And not like an elegant hunter green or whatever. I'm talking plastic terrible-for-the-environment bleh-green tablecloths, plates, cups, cutlery, and trees made out of crumpled-up brown paper stapled to the doors, with green paper serving as foliage.

Even the centerpieces are green jars filled with fungus-topped pebbles, meant to resemble some kind of otherworldly moss. Green streamers flutter as the exhaust fans in the corner of the rooms go full blast. I love the cheesiness of it all.

Life doesn't have to look as extravagant as the Hvede Gala from the books. I look around the room and my heart swells as I look at all the hideous décor, the clamor at all the tables around the room, the dinky dance floor. This is lit. It's what I imagined prom would look like, from all the years watching old teen movies, like *Sixteen Candles* and *Ten Things I Hate About You*. The magic is here. Most of these kids don't realize it because they don't speak rom-com as well as I can, but this is it. After tonight, nothing will ever be the same.

I know why Ngozi is annoyed with me. This decision doesn't involve her. That's what she's mad about. Meanwhile, she's leaving for Berkeley over the summer to study neuroscience or some shit. Don't remember her consulting me about that. So this night is it. Literally everything changes. After this, it's just formalities and paperwork: settling accounts before graduation, ordering our caps and gowns, making sure we're doing superficial meaningful things with our friends, that kind of busywork to distract us from the fact that everything is a fleeting moment, high school is a blip, our friends, our family, none of it is as important as we think it is.

The kitchen staff bring pitchers of water over for each table. I'm surprised they trust us with glass. I look down at my phone. I'm kinda glad everyone has their phones out and that this is how people communicate. Makes it so much less intimidating when you run out of things to talk about. I can't imagine the days when you had to just stare at a person the entire time and come up with things to say.

I think about some universal things to enter into the conversation. Weather. Food. Skin. You'd be surprised how versatile of a talking point that last one is. Who would not want to be complimented on their skin? If someone said something like, "Hey Sunny, nice skin, yo," I'd be like, "Much appreciated, braah. Let me walk you through my morning and nighttime skincare routine. I have just switched moisturizers and no longer use beard oil on account of not having a beard." Then I'd pause, giving everyone enough time to chortle, possibly even guffaw.

Another reason I'm glad Ngozi isn't here is because I know what she'd probably say. "You're off your trolley. What the donkey bollocks sort of chat-up line is that? Why don't you just tell people you think their skin is soft and you want to wear it like a blanket?" Just because she's British, she has the audacity to claim my Dafydd accent and syntax are not quite cutting the mustard. Like she would know. My accent is fucking flawless.

I sit in silence and concentrate on not sucking my teeth, a habit I picked up from Ngozi. Not sure if it's a Nigerian thing or a Ghanaian thing or just an Ngozi thing. Her dad is Nigerian and her mom is Ghanaian, which she claims means she is the ultimate authority on jollof rice, and can define the perfect rice to tomato ratio.

Jasmine does have lovely skin. It looks lighter than usual, though nothing competes with Stefan's vampire aesthetic. Fluorescent lighting? Extra layer of concealer? Skin-lightening cream from the desi store? Uhhhh. No. I should probably stay away from anything that could be construed as "your face is looking rather fair and lovely today, much whiter and more beautiful than usual." I could talk about the shape of people's skulls. Okay. This is definitely venturing into creepy territory. I see Ngozi's point.

Besides, the conversation at the table has already shifted to their usual adulation of gods and goddesses of star-spangled spandex, aka superheroes in comic books. Way out of my depth. Fortunately, there is internet on my phone. I glance down at the tabs I've opened. Which ones are the Avengers again? Are they DC or Marvel? Is Ms. Marvel the blond lady or the desi girl? There's so much to consider, I might as well give up. I focus on figuring out how to contribute, perhaps a compliment on someone's ensemble? That's when I notice Jasmine's dress again. She has Jasmine-ified it all along the sides and the trim and places where nothing all that exciting happens. I look closer and see that not only are there comic book panels sewn into the fabric (which looks like polyester or cotton, maybe?), there are some kind of light-up tracks strategically placed all over the dress.

I wonder what she used for the lights. It looks like an updated version of a Tron-dress she wore at NerdFest a few years ago. It can't be LED strips. Way too much light diffusion. Dressmaking is not really my forte, although I do dabble. The girl sitting next to her, Paola, is wearing a flowing white prom dress with a large gold necklace and matching white hijab. I don't know her that well, but has she Paola-fied her dress too?

Stefan catches me looking at the ridiculous purple vest he's wearing. He rises and waddles exaggeratedly toward me. Oh, no. I don't know why he's waddling. Is he mocking me again? Or maybe an injury? He's not an athlete. Unless chess club has suddenly become a contact sport.

Stefan gestures to the vest. "Ordered it from Italy three months ago."

Satisfied, he starts waddling back, then pauses. "I got my umbrella in the car," he adds, talking to nobody in particular.

This seems like an odd thing to say, even for Stefan.

I slowly piece things together. They're all in cosplay! All of them. Superheroes. This is going to be one wild night. Apparently, I have something in common with everyone here, even Stefan. Who knew!

"Y-you're that villain plant woman from Batman," I say to Jasmine.

The table roars with laughter.

"Poison Ivy, yeah," Jasmine says as she squints at me, like she's trying to place me. "Stefan is the Penguin."

This shit is clearly against school policy. I'm the only dumbass wearing straight-up school-sanctioned Prom Attire with zero alterations: an expensive, uninspired black tux I rented from the place listed on the school website like a rule-abiding hobbit. I don't believe this. For once, I'm the only one not in cosplay. Only I am. I'm dressed as boring-ass-guy-in-tight-suit-at-prom instead of my usual Dafydd the Feeble cosplay: this crocheted pouch, plus my armor and a chain mail helmet with custom-made mustache and beard combination because it's canon.

These pants are much tighter than I anticipated.

My nostrils flare, and I feel the nose hairs expand, my sideburns flopping, my newly cropped and streaked hair rising up. Stefan is making his Thinking Face, which requires a lot of concentration, a puckering of the mouth, a squinting of the eyes. It's the face he makes when he's about to say something terrible, usually about me, for a cheap laugh. Or perhaps it's the face he makes when he's constipated and needs to go to the bathroom.

"Holy shit!" Stefan says, leaping up from his chair again.

"What happened to that whole ISIS garden on your face?" Stefan says loudly, inches away from me, running a hand slowly over his face, his eyes searing into mine. "ISIS garden or not, I'd recognize that sss-sssss-tutter anywhere," he says, then looks around the table and laughs. He's probably been sitting here this whole time coming up with what he thinks is a hilarious joke. Nobody laughs, which is worse than people actually laughing because they're just sitting there quietly and letting him get away with it.

"You look a million times better," Stefan says, like I did it for him. "Why'd you do it?"

Everyone is staring at me. I realize they're waiting for me to speak, but the words aren't quite coming out. "W-www-ww." I'm in the dreaded perpetual mid-stutter zone. I feel the muscles in my face tense as I try to just get out this sentence, this word. As fleeting as I know this moment is, it sure is taking a long fucking time to end. My fingernails dig into my palms as the stuttering increases rapidly, even though I'm attempting to control my breathing with a hand on my diaphragm—a technique I learned in a YouTube video about stuttering. It's a lost cause.

As much as Goldy struggled with everything else in his life—coming out as gay, admitting to being an alcoholic, thinking he was bigger, smarter than what life had in store for him—he never seemed to question his dastaar. I have no clue whether or not he struggled spiritually with his faith. Aside from Biji, nobody in our family is super religious, but we go to the gurdwara on most important Sundays. Mama and Papa mostly like to socialize, while Biji gets to eat sweet parshad or extra syrupy gulab jamun without anyone monitoring her sugar intake. Shortly before Goldy died, he would occasionally join Biji with reciting path in the evenings. Dude volunteered ONE TIME to serve food at the community kitchen and Mama and Papa won't stop bringing it up like he cured world hunger or something and didn't relapse a couple weeks later. Everyone is still staring at me. I want to tell Stefan, "ISIS is geographically and racially inaccurate." I wish this new face would give me more authority and the power to really put him in his place. Why can't I stand up, smash a glass on the floor, look right at Stefan and everyone at the table and be like, "Foul-smelling swamp demons! A curse on all your lafunga houses!" Followed by a hush, and a flurry of videos of the showdown being uploaded to social media. #TeamSunny #SunnyDestroysStefan.

It doesn't matter. They've moved on. Everyone zones out as my voice moves from a stuttering stuck record to a low mumble that trails off. I take a deep breath when I realize it's over. I've never understood why my stutter is so frustratingly illogical.

Jasmine looks up from her phone. "Stefan." Her voice

sounds dangerous. Maybe she's going to let him have it? Finally, after all these years.

"'Sup," he says.

"Remember when I told you to be careful not to put the keg in Amy's garage or her parents would find it and totally freak? And then you were all, 'Whaddya think I am, some kinda idiot?'"

"That's not what I sound like."

There's a pause.

"I had to use so many hookups to get that keg," Stefan says.

"I swear to God, if you talk about the fucking keg . . ."

"Torpedo keg," Stefan clarifies.

"ONE MORE GODDAMN TIME." Jasmine lets out an exasperated sigh. "Because of your keg. Sorry, your torpedo keg." She looks up to glare at Stefan. He bites his lower lip. "The after-party is canceled. Amy's parents are staying home. Now what?"

There is a moment of complete, mournful silence at the table.

"Well," Stefan says sheepishly. "That sucks. But the plan was to wait for the photo booth to take photos and video for the 'gram anyway, then bounce. So same plan except instead of going to what's-her-face's house, we'll just go to the Snollygoster Soiree. They prolly got alcohol. Maybe not a torpedo keg." He shrugs. "We're dressed for it anyway."

"Oh, what a good idea. Let me just get on that," Jasmine says, dramatically punching in numbers on a gigantic imaginary phone, simulating logging on to the site for tickets. "Looks like it's sold out. Who could have predicted that, on the night of prom?" Jasmine is steaming mad. "FYI. It's been sold out for two weeks."

"Don't worry," Paola says, her voice diplomatic. "We ain't staying here for five hours listening to this goofy-ass music and looking at these people all night."

I must admit, this scenario has not occurred in any of the prom-themed movies or novels I've watched or read. People sometimes go through a bunch of obstacles to arrive at prom, but no matter whether they're drunk and happy or drunk and sad or drunk and mad, they still stay at prom. That's what's supposed to happen. What is this leaving prom shit?

"Don't Fannypack Gill over here got a hookup?" Stefan says, pointing at me like I'm a menu item. Wait, is he talking about Dafydd the Feeble's custom-designed pouch? Did he just compare this carefully crocheted sporran—a warrior's pouch—to a mass-produced cheap piece of junk American tourists wear in Europe so they get mugged quicker?

This. Mother. Fucker.

I curl up my fists, like I'm going to start a prison fight.

"Oh yeah, you doing poetry or something at the Snollygoster Soiree?" Paola says.

"Sorcery metal," I reply. "The subgenre is Bramble-core, b-b-but our band is Unk-k—"

"Sounds fucking dangerous," Stefan interrupts me like a shithead. "Isn't bramble like a jam or a soap or something?"

"Hello. Safia Brambleberry?" Jasmine says, lilting her voice upward but still not happy with Stefan or the situation at hand. Still, she's the only relatively rational one in this group. The rest of them give me blank looks.

"B-brambles are thorned trailing vines that g-grow in the countryside in the Petrichor F-F-Fiefdom. Bramble-berries grow on the bramble, so brambleberries are the general name for things like thimbleberries, gruffleberries, angleberries." I realize, aside from thimbleberries, none of these juicy berries exist in real life.

"Oh," Paola says.

"You're talking about the book about that one dude who falls through a toilet?" Stefan says, unimpressed. He doesn't say it in a mean way, just in a totally dismissive, clueless way, which is five times as annoying. I am at a loss for words. Such an oversimplification of *The Ballad of the Boy Who Fell Out of the Tesco Bog*, the first book in the Jamie Snollygoster series, where, yes, he does fall through the toilet, which, it is very clearly explained, is a fucking portal, so he ends up thousands of miles beneath the surface of the Earth we know. It's like if I said, "Oh yeah, Spider-Man, that one comic book about the boy who gets bit by a magical spider." Bet that would make everyone at this table mad.

I frown mightily because when I think of the perfect thing to say to him, boy is he gonna be sorry.

"Well, they probably hooked you up with extra tickets, right?" Stefan says, looking right at me. Then everyone else turns to look at me too.

"Oh. Uh," I say. Sweat trickles above my eyebrows. It's an exhilarating yet nauseating position I'm in. So much perceived power. And no actual power. I kind of have an extra ticket. It's my ticket, which I'm clearly not going to be using. E-ticket, rather. But it's nontransferable because I'm a performer. Says so in big, fat, bold letters.

Of all the ways to shut this down, I choose to go with "Yuppers," smacking my lips loudly as I pat my crocheted man-bag.

All eyes remain on me.

"It i-is. It is going to be a very awesome party," I say. "Th-the awesome . . . est."

The lights dim. Ah, Mr. DJ. A fast track to get the kids on the dance floor. But no one moves. Except me.

"Well," I say, standing. "I'm going to go urinate." And with that, I briskly walk away from the table, in the opposite direction of the bathroom, out of sight.

CHAPTER 3

THE GIRL IN THE
BRAMBLEBERRY DRESS

I'm sitting by the snack table in the dark, shoveling handfuls of dry tortilla chips into my mouth. I wish I'd added salsa, but it's too late now. I am way too committed to eating these dry tasteless chips. This is my life now.

I stare out into a big blur of people descending onto the dance floor. Dance floor. I use the term very loosely. It's basically a large rectangular space near the back wall. The basketball hoops are raised toward the ceiling and covered with streamers and balloons to try and make us forget we're in the gym. Stefan and the rest of the table are probably out there gyrating and selfie-ing it up. Everybody has their cell phones out, a sea of bright flashes as they take photos and videos and snaps and gifs and boomerangs to add to their stories in an attempt to manufacture the joy of prom. I should post a selfie of me in the dark by the snack table alone to really capture what it is like.

On the other end of the gym, they've started setting up

the photo booth, which already has a huge line. Maybe that's where everyone is at. Or they could still just be sitting at the table, waiting for me so they can get the tickets I don't actually have. Even if I did have one hypothetical ticket, who am I giving it to? Stefan? Over my cremated body.

I still don't get it. Why bother spending all this money and energy coming to prom, renting a limo, getting all decked out, asking someone out with an over-the-top Promposal, if you got plans to bail as soon as possible? Stefan's Promposal involved getting his cop brother to stop Jasmine as she pulled out of her driveway, just so he could bring a pizza to her with the words *Pizza Come to Prom With Me* spelled out on it in pepperoni.

Ngozi thinks that's a terrifying thing to do to a person of color, and she's right. There's nothing charming about it.

I take out my phone and play Mama's voicemail on the speaker, since it's just me and the tortilla chips anyway. It's simple and to the point: "Hi, beta. It's me, your mom. Anything you need from the store? Lucky Mamaji is picking up some Haldiram's and a crate of Limca for the barsi. Okayyyy. This is your mom." She always signs off with that, like I'm going to mistake her for a telemarketer calling me son and asking me to do errands.

Papa, on the other hand, has sent ten text messages in the past half an hour or so. None of them seem to indicate

29

he knows I'm not actually at home, although he doesn't use text messages the way normal people use them, so who knows. They're both busy over-preparing for everyone coming to the house. We've never actually talked about Goldy being gone, can't use the word *death* or *alcoholic* or *cremation*. But here we are having a barsi, a commemoration of his death. Which I'm expected to attend.

Papa only texts me about technical issues. I glance at the last several he sent:

"Your chacha emailed a pdf file but I can't download it on my phone???"

"Also how to upload a photo to whatsapp?"

"ok figured out how to get pdf still don't know how to upload photo to whatsapp?"

"What's my apple id?"

"Chacha told me how to upload photo. Is password same for apple id and facebook?"

"Urgent response requested at convenience."

Texting Papa back is a bad idea. But I do it anyway.

"Password is different. Your Facebook password is tandoorichicken65. Why do you need password for Apple ID? Don't download any more apps."

This is the kind of interaction me and Papa have whether I'm in the house or away, and most of our face-to-face conversations aren't any better. In a parallel universe, I could have just told Mama and Papa I'm going to prom and not coming to the barsi. But we don't do that in my house. We contort ourselves into all kinds of positions to avoid saying what we're really thinking or feeling. I couldn't even cry at Goldy's cremation because of the usual idiotic reason: Makes me look weak. Papa's favorite expression: "Stop acting like a pajama." Translation: Man up. Like the rest of my aura projects old-school Punjabi film hero Maula Jatt and The Rock levels of masculinity.

I really wish Biji had a phone to text. I bet she'd love SnapChat. We can sit and crochet for ten minutes or all day, talking or in silence, and I always feel lighter. She doesn't give a shit if I cry or want to tell her in my not-so-perfect Punjabi that I simultaneously hate Goldy and I love and miss him. With Mama and Papa, there's always a lot of busywork to keep us distracted from talking about Goldy or anything else real. Reality is overrated anyway.

I look at my Insta and Snapchat and TikTok. Nothing. Just a couple random views, no reactions, no emojis, no likes. Like I don't exist. I put my phone in my man-bag and consider the situation. Plus point: I'm here at prom on my way to making memories! Not a plus point: Stefan is going to come asking me for the tickets I said I have. Plus point: Stefan and his table of dweebs plan on leaving. Now the dilemma: How do I dig myself out of this lie? Maybe if I stay hidden long enough, they'll just leave on their own and I can see who else is here. *Pretty in Pink* wasn't all roses either, and it's been like fifteen minutes. I just gotta give it time.

I take my phone out again.

"Hey Siri," I say. "Tell me a joke."

I don't remember when I started talking to Siri like she's a real person, but it's comforting having someone there whenever you need them, even if she just googles everything. She booms through the speaker of my iPhone:

"Mr. Spock actually had three ears: a left ear, a right ear, and a final front ear."

I laugh loudly. "Oh, th-that was a good one, Siri. I'm going to use that one tonight."

Under normal circumstances, I would be texting Ngozi. But what do I text her after bailing on her and knowing she is leaving for Berkeley? "Hi. Night going well? GREAT. Me? Oh, everything is fucked. Can you hook up tickets for the Snollygoster Soiree? Oh yeah, no, I'm still not coming. It's for Chiseled White Boy Face, and his terrible friends. Yes, he still thinks All Lives Matter."

"Hey Siri," I say. "I c-could just lie to Stefan again and t-tell him he can pick up the tickets at Snollygoster Soiree. Or that I'll have my people text the tickets over, and then just not do it. Right?"

She's in the middle of telling me she doesn't understand the question when I rudely interrupt. "Hey Siri. Send message to Ngozi."

32

Siri makes her usual ding sound. "What do you want it to say?" she says. Another ding for good measure.

"So, a slight pickle. Send," I say, dictating into the phone. Siri sends the message with a whoosh.

I wait.

Nothing.

I try again:

"Do you have extra tickets to the Snollygoster Soiree? Paper or e-ticket is fine. A friend needs them. Two friends."

First I get those ever-irritating ellipses. Then she finally texts back:

"You should listen to your heart."

Such a petty move. I'd be impressed if she were doing this to someone else. Instead of ghosting me, Ngozi is replying with gibberish, perfunctory American fortune cookie–style non sequiturs. To me. To me!

I furiously tell Siri to text back: "Prom is awesome. Real great music. Food is top notch. Connecting with a lot of people I haven't seen in years. Some people I friend-zoned that are trying to rectify that situation. You know how it is."

I see the three dots appear, disappear, reappear.

Her message arrives: "Oh, why didn't you just say so. No problem. I'll leave 200 tickets with the butler next to the charcuterie in the foyehhh. What friends?"

I can't say Stefan or Jasmine. *Hate* may be a mild way to describe her feelings for either of them.

I respond: "You wouldn't know them."

And then it comes: "Well. I barely know you."

I shake my head and put the phone away.

I feel that familiar heavy sensation in my chest. I close my eyes, willing it to be something it's not: gastrointestinal issues, tortilla-chip-induced heartburn, syphilis. Okay, not syphilis. Definitely not syphilis. It sounds so frivolous, especially when there are people all around me. Loneliness.

I pause for a few seconds, leaning against the table as the debilitating sensation pulses through me. My heart is beating fast. I close my eyes, run a finger over my kara, and breathe. I pull the phone out, hoping for the best. My thumb cramps up as I scroll through all my social media feeds again.

I look around the room and all I can see is potential for a magical night. Almost all of the movies I've grown up watching have a small hiccup in the opening. That's all this is, right? A hiccup? Before I know it I will meet a girl who wants to break out of the friend zone with me. Or maybe there's someone here tonight who I want to break out of the friend zone with. My eyes widen as I scan the room. I don't recognize many people.

"Siri," I beckon as I stretch my thumb and readjust my palm. "How do people get out of the friend zone?"

"Here's what I found on the web," she says, and lists

some articles, including one with eight specific strategies from *Men's Journal.*

I've seen so many Bollywood and Hollywood movies about this very premise. I look around the room, at the dance floor again, the weird bright light on the other side of the snack table, and touch my face as I consider my options. I reach into the bowl to scoop out more of the tortilla chips. There's something in there. Something alive.

"Actually," a voice—definitely not Siri's—says as the warm and fleshy thing removes itself slowly from the bowl. I'm relieved it's a hand, a human hand, a human hand attached to a living human body. But the voice continues: "The friend zone doesn't exist. Kinda like the magical experience you think you're gonna have at prom."

I snatch my hand from the chip bowl in a panic, sending tortilla chips flying. A few Tostitos hit me in the face as I narrowly save my phone from death, and quickly place it back in my pouch for safety. How long has she been standing here? It occurs to me she's not standing. She's sitting.

"This is what you do?" I sputter at the girl. "This is what you do?" I repeat. "Spy on people like, some, some kind of . . ." I struggle for the right word. "Badger. Or, like, another quiet woodland creature . . ." I trail off. *Badger.* I don't even know where I was going with that analogy.

With that, I am out of outrage, although I have plenty of involuntary flaring of my nostrils.

The girl's head turns and a bright light shines right in my eyes, obscuring her face. She switches the light off. I realize the light isn't from a doorway or a spotlight. It's coming from her head. She is wearing a headlamp, the kind you wear when you go camping, only a much lower wattage. In her hands is what looks like a book. A friggin' book.

Her face comes into focus. Now I recognize her. Mindii Vang. I don't *know her* know her, but I know her. You know. Like I've seen her around at different cosplay events. She hangs out with Ngozi and the crew sometimes. She was probably in a class with me at some point. I know she's in the anime and manga clubs, solely because she's always at the booth looking for people to join during club week.

"Are you," I say incredulously, "reading? At prom?"

"No," she says. "I'm trying to read, but some fool keeps distracting me with his addiction to his bright-ass phone and very loud existential crisis."

"Oh boy," I say. "And I thought I was having a shitty night."

"You are having a shitty night. I am eating chips and trying to read a particularly riveting study called 'Spirits Are Real: The Relationship Between Hmong and Japanese Spirits in Contemporary Anime and Manga.'"

"So friggin' wordy," I say. "Like what spirits?"

"I don't know. I didn't get very far because some fool is being real loud. I'm right in the middle of this section on

36

the complex nature of Hmong Dab and Japanese Yokai."

"I don't even know what to say if you think that sounds like a non-shitty time," I say. I don't tell her that I used to watch the *Yo-Kai* anime with Goldy as a kid. Or that the study sounds intriguing. There's nothing intriguing enough to hide in the dark at prom with a friggin' flashlight on your head, though.

"Why are you even here?" I say. "And talking nonsense about things you just don't understand? Like the friend zone of all things. You should read a study called 'The Friend Zone is Real.'"

"I can see you've spent hours of research on this with your phone. Sorry, I didn't mean to offend your girlfriend," Mindii says.

"S-S-Siri is not my girlfriend! The friend zone is a fact. Movies center on its existence. Novels rely on it. I'm not gonna debate facts. What's next, we gonna debate climate change?"

"Well, it was kinda cold last winter, which means global warming is definitely a hoax," she says. There is a moment of quiet as I realize it's a joke. "I bet the term *friend zone* was invented by some dude named Chad who poured his heart out to a girl and she rejected him," she says. "So then he's all, 'does not compute. I need a way to not feel bad about being a shitty person and gaslighting my friend into having feelings for me.' C'est voila. The term *friend zone* was born. Better term to use would be *predator zone*."

The music has shifted into a slower-paced song, drowning out whatever response I would have had. I do see her point. But not a chance I would admit that. I blame the patriarchy. "Is Chad even a real name?" I say over the music.

"Or it's the name of a very expensive cheese."

"Sounds like a fungal infection."

"Do you have Chad and don't remember where you contracted it?" Mindii booms loudly. I realize she's pretending to do an ad. It's pretty funny. She's pausing. Oh. She's expecting me to finish.

"Then take this . . . uh . . . medicine, m–motherfucker," I say, ruining the joke.

Only she's laughing.

There are a handful of kids still on the dance floor, but most of them are making their way back to their seats.

"What's the deal with the Snollygoster Soiree? Just go," Mindii says. "Prom is a big bore. Trust me, I came here last year too. "

"You know nothing," I say. "And who goes to prom two years in a row? You're like that guy in *Sixteen Candles*."

"Is that a boy band? Wait, why am I like someone in a boy band?"

"It's a cult classic. It's like one of the quintessential prom movies."

"Sounds like I really missed out on not watching that obscure movie so I could understand this one reference. If you must know, I came here to chaperone my sisters. Not by choice. I'm always getting roped into doing shit that I don't want to do. You wouldn't get it."

I would totally get it. I do get it. Of course, I'm not going to tell *her* that.

"Oh," Mindii says.

"What?" I say.

"The deal with the Snollygoster Soiree tickets. And everything else. I got your number. So very interesting," she says, sinking back into her chair, turning the headlight back on.

"N-no. No," I say eloquently. "I got your number. You don't got my number. Wait. What do you mean?"

She laughs. "You don't have the tickets. So now you're a headless chicken."

"You're so weird," I say. "A headless chicken? Because I'm dead?"

"Do you know anything about chickens? Headless chickens run around panicked trying to fix things and be on their way, even though they are fucked. Because," she explains very slowly, "they have no heads."

"No," I say being instinctively argumentative. Even though she does apparently have my number.

I'm about to say something to cut her to the core,

ridicule her for reading in the dark alone with a fucking camping headlight, not having a date, being a dorkus maximus. If only I could come up with something.

The double doors to the gym open, letting in a burst of ugly fluorescent light as Mr. Graham, the economics teacher, steps into the hallway.

Just as my brain is about to unleash some witty insults in Mindii's direction, I hear Stefan's voice. Jasmine is behind him.

"Ayy yo, if it ain't the urinator," he says, running a hand through his very blond hair. I attempt to do the same. So awkward.

"So," he says, unwavering. "I need those tickets to Snollygoster Soiree. Like now."

There is no logical reason I couldn't have just said "I don't have the tickets" five minutes ago. And no reason I can't say it now. I don't owe him anything. I don't owe Jasmine or anyone at that table anything. In fact, in two weeks, I'll probably never see them again.

But instead of all that, I nod my head, and say, "Word. Word. No doubt. No doubt."

Mindii knows there are no tickets. I know there are no tickets. I have a feeling Stefan knows too, but he wants Jasmine to clearly see that I am lying so when he starts humiliating me in front of her, it'll seem totally justified.

I'm gonna become the number one trending laughing-stock in about two seconds flat.

I make a big show of unhooking the pouch from my belt.

I see Mindii stand up, the big, fat dissertation she was reading in her hand. "Those tickets are mine, actually," she says.

"What?" Jasmine says.

"What?" Stefan says.

"Hain?" I say. When I'm surprised, Punjabi comes out first.

"I SAID THOSE TICKETS ARE MINE, ACTUALLY," she screams at both of them, and grabs the pouch from my hands. All four of us are suspended in time. I'm mesmerized by Mindii's dress, a pale, shimmery blue, but it's probably weird to say something about it now. She moves in closer and is looking right at me. It's unnerving, yet I'm not averting my eyes like I do with Stefan or most people. It feels strangely comfortable. It might be the dorky head-lamp still attached to her forehead. Her eyes are large and brown, her hair twisted into a knot in the back, two braids in front with blue beads keeping them from unfurling, her face an imperfect circle.

Stefan has this dumb expression on his face, like he's calculating a math problem.

"Peace. Mindii out," Mindii says, my pouch in hand. With that, she throws a peace sign and casually pushes past the double doors and walks out of the gymnasium.

Holy shit, I think. That's no simple blue dress.

"Was that dress brambleberry?" I say out loud. "Like a floaty, brambleberry blue? Like the color of the berries found in the wild inverted forests on the outskirts of the Malmesbury Academy? I thought it was just blue this whole time."

Is she in cosplay? As Safia Brambleberry?

Jasmine stares at the door in disbelief. "What the hell just happened?" Her eyes bounce between me and Stefan.

Focus, Sunny.

"Mindii just stole the extra tickets I was going to give you," I say.

We all stare at each other for a beat.

"Well," I say, my voice rising a little more. "I'm going to go urinate."

"What is with this guy and his bladder? Didn't you JUST go?"

"Interesting thing about urine," I say, "is that it contains high levels of salt, which is why the Army Field Guide recommends you not drink it if you get stranded in a desert."

Stefan looks at me, flaring a very quizzical nostril in my direction. They both look at me. Stefan looks at Jasmine because he desperately wants to say something.

"Because of the salt," I reiterate.

It's not the best exit line, but I am ecstatic that for once I'm not humiliated at the hands of Stefan. That he got his ass handed to him. That usually happens in Act Three of most movies. And we're definitely only in Act One. Now I just have to get my pouch back from Mindii.

Why on earth did she save me, though? And where did she go with my . . .

I gasp as I remember my life is in that crocheted pouch. My phone, cash, student ID card. I take another gulp of air. My series of rash decisions notebook. She didn't save me. I just got jacked. A blast of that hot Fresno heat smacks me in the face as I sprint to the parking lot in my tight pants.

CHAPTER 4

ESCAPE FROM THE PARKING LOT
OF DOOM

That dress was definitely brambleberry blue. It's unmis-takable. It's not like a normal blue and it's not purple. It's smack in between the two, and what, it just "happens" to be the same style of dress Safia Brambleberry wears to the Hvede Gala in the books? Inconceivable.

But I've got more important things to worry about. I'm in the parking lot, alone, resting from all that running, and thanks to Mindii, phoneless. Also thanks to Mindii: pouch-less. But more importantly: notebook-less. I guess I have two more rash decisions to add to my notebook. If I ever get it back.

It makes no sense that Mindii Vang isn't still here in the parking lot. We lost sight of each other for all of six seconds, between my brief hesitation and her committing Grand Pouch Theft. I bet that's a felony. Maybe she wasn't just being nice and saving me from humiliation. I bet she knows that Loom the Fandom is about to blow up and she's been following me and this whole thing was a ruse to get my pouch so she could sell it. Or worse: She's gonna wait until it really blows up and then blackmail me for it. She better not snoop in my notebook.

I stand up and do more sprints to try and catch this girl—but I don't see her anywhere.

What was I thinking? It's June. In Fresno. 102 degrees out. I'm roasting. I pause, trying to catch my breath, a thick layer of sweat soaking through my formerly pristine dress shirt.

Where else could she have gone? I wince as I run my nails across my cheek, forgetting for the millionth time I have no barrier between the world and my face.

I bite my lip as I realize on top of everything, I won't get to eat my goddamn rubber chicken cacciatore, included in the price of the ticket. That's the one thing Mama and Papa and Biji would agree on: Such a wasteful boy, this Sunny is. Then Goldy would return from death, reincarnated into the body of a billionaire—pretty sure that's how reincarnation works—just to jump on board the Let's-shit-on-Sunny train because that's just the kind of supportive brother he is. Was. I'm already in phone withdrawal. This is hell, being alone with my thoughts.

I kick the dirt in front of me as I think about this mighty pickle of a situation. I could just go back to prom, pretend like nothing happened, let absent-Mindii take the heat for the whole ticket fiasco. But my friggin' phone—and the only photo I posted the whole time is of me in the bathroom!

I sit down on a patch of grass a few feet from the actual parking lot and blink real hard. I have to find Mindii. The sun has just gone down and the sky is a beautiful deep crimson.

"Foibles!" I say, looking angrily at the sunset, the trees lining the fence just outside the parking lot.

Did I really just let a weird girl steal one of my only meaningful mementos of Goldy?

I'm trying to figure out my next move when, out of nowhere, two bright lights come rampaging through the parking lot. I freeze in a panic. As I catch my breath, my ears recognize the tune: an awful home-studio mashup of Punjabi rap and instrumentals with 1990s West Coast hip-hop beats. Separately maybe it would count as music. And there, looming, is Goldy's ancient, rickety ice cream truck. About to run me over.

It takes me a minute to realize I'm not being haunted. Not by Goldy at least. It's Raj, one of his alcoholic friends. He went to rehab a few months before Goldy did, but as far as I know Raj just went the one time and that was it. He didn't need a frequent visitor card like Goldy. I don't know the extent of Raj's recovery, but unlike Goldy, Raj is not dead. So it seems to be working. I guess I should give Raj props for convincing Mama and Papa to send Goldy to rehab in the first place, which they were reluctant to send him to because of the money and the usual "loki ki kehn ge"—what will people say—worries. Less than a month after the cremation, Mama and Papa gave this sabji-for-brains Goldy's ice cream truck. I'm not mad. I never wanted the thing, but still, I should have been consulted.

I used to think there was only one kind of alcoholic, someone who couldn't go without a drink for a single day. So I'd believe Goldy when he'd stay sober for weeks and months, and tell me that he was in control of the "situation," as he put it, not the other way around. That it was just a matter of free will and self-control, that he just needed to stop after two drinks. Simple. But of course stopping after two drinks never happened and it became a big awkward embarrassing scene when anyone tried to help him enforce his own fucking rule. I didn't really understand that he wasn't just being a dick until he came into my room one evening under the pretense of borrowing something and quietly told me that he was an alcoholic. Like, I know he had an illness, an addiction. If we were raised to be different kind of men, I would have hugged him, cried with him, told him I loved him, asked what I could do, listened to some of his dumb fucking poetry.

Goldy was alone in his room the night he died. I found him passed out, a motionless body on the bed, three empty bottles of whiskey next to him. He probably bought them from one of the million Punjabi-owned liquor stores all over Fresno. No chaser. You have no idea how often that image enters my brain. There was no smell of death, no vomit, just the usual funky smell of Goldy's room. Mama and Papa said very little during the whole thing. No crying. Made me call the ambulance, talk to the paramedics, even though their English is perfectly fine (thanks, colonialism). At the hospital the doctors managed to revive him long enough so he could incoherently tell us that he didn't want to die, and by 3:23 a.m. he was pronounced dead. Alcohol poisoning. Like he's a fraternity bro and not a professional fucking alcoholic. What a pointless way to go.

Raj steps out of the truck, wearing large, mirrored sunglasses, and is finishing up the last few bites of what looks like a Klondike Bar. He extends his hand. "Raj. Naam toh suna hoga," he says, in a thick raspy Punjabi accent, willfully slaughtering the famous dialogue originally spoken by Shah Rukh Khan's character, Rahul, in *Dil Toh Pagal Hai.*

"That's not the line," I say.

"Pretty sure it is. From like *DDLJ* or something," Raj says, licking the wrapper like an overgrown kid.

"Are you being serious right now? He doesn't say the line in *Dilwale Dulhania Le Jayenge.* He says it in *Rab Ne Bana Di Jodi* as a NOSTALGIC JOKE! Shah Rukh Khan plays Raj in like f–five movies," I screech. "In everything else he's Rahul. The line is 'I'm Rahul. Naam toh suna hoga,'" I say, getting really agitated. I've explained this shit to him a bunch of times. The actual line is one of my favorites, but it sounds so dopey in English: "I'm Rahul. You probably already know my name."

In any case, it's not Raj. None of Goldy's friends even watch Hindi films properly.

"Well," he says, tossing the wrapper into a nearby trash can, "let's just agree to disagree."

I want to rub the ice cream right into his beard and snap a photo. Maybe launch a social media shaming campaign, #IceCreamBeard.

"First person out of prom," he says. "Pretty damn impressive."

"Nice pag," I say. My standard ultimate insult. It's the opposite of a nice pag—he knows it, I know it. It's a blah-colored, mediocrely tied pag.

"Nice face," he says, and I immediately recoil. My insults used to carry a lot more weight when I rocked my beard and turban, complete with crisp, sharp folds and a wrinkle-free larh.

"Why are you here anyway?" I say.

"See this?" he points his beard toward the ice cream truck. "This is an ice cream truck. And see that?" He points the beard to the sunset. "That is Fresno heat."

"Okay," I say, before he points his beard toward prom. "I get it. You're here to sell ice cream."

"Very good, beta," he says. "Surprised your mummy-papa let you come here to this night of paap and debauchery. Good you're leaving prom like a good Punjabi munda. Shaabash puttar. Good job."

"I'm still *at* prom," I say, defiant. "I just came outside for some fresh air." I peer at the front of the ice cream truck. "Still didn't fix the windshield wipers, huh?"

The windshield wipers didn't work when Goldy owned this thing either. It's one of the things Papa and Goldy constantly argued about.

"No, I didn't fix the windshield wipers," Raj says, just as indignant, "because we live in California. In case you ain't heard, we in the middle of a drought. If I was driving an ice cream truck in Africa, I bet you'd be like, 'Yo man, how come you don't got snow chains. That could be hypothetically dangerous.'"

"Africa is not a country," I say. "I bet it snows somewhere."

"This is why you're going to community college. It's hot as balls in Africa. You apply yet?"

I hate this town. Everyone knows your business before you know it. You can't even fart in peace without random aunties and uncles offering you homeopathic anti-flatulence medicine. If my phone hadn't been jacked by Mindii, I could look this snow in Africa shit up. I have an overwhelming desire to prove him unequivocally wrong. I would settle for one tiny image of a dude pausing during a road trip anywhere in Africa with snow chains visible, or maybe a snow-capped mountain in the background, just so I could be all, "See. You are the donkey."

But Raj takes this moment to turn into a walking encyclopedia.

"Some of the mountain ranges in countries like Chad or Libya or Algeria or Tunisia only get snow every seven or eight years," he says. "But you were obviously not talking about them, right?"

"Obviously not," I say, quickly trying to find a way to change the subject. He's gotten into his I-know-about-all-this-shit-and-am-gonna-unleash-it-now mode. I keep forgetting his short-lived major at Fresno State was International Politics, which apparently encompasses knowing the snow situation in Africa.

"It does snow in South Africa. But not enough to warrant snow chains on tires."

Before I can snap back at him, I'm distracted by a low roar in the distance.

Raj is still spouting data about African nations and precipitation, but I can't even hear him as the roar grows closer.

I turn to see a motorcycle passing us in slow motion. It zigzags through the parking lot. Sequins sparkle in the sun. My pouch! It's Mindii. She pauses, removes her helmet, shakes her hair, puts the helmet back on. Then she's off again in a blur of helmet, hair, bike, and brambleberry-blue dress. The warm gust of air mixed with the gray of the exhaust, the smell of fumes—all of it oddly relaxes me.

Raj hasn't been paying attention to any of this shit. His eyes are on me like he's asked me something. Did he ask me something?

"Follow that girl," I say, racing toward the passenger side of the ice cream truck.

"Slow your roll, Scooby-Doo," he says, not moving. "I got a business to run."

I walk back and squint at him in my sternest, most intimidating look. "It's a life-or-death situation. I need to get something back."

"If it's your dignity, I think you left that at the store you rented that suit from."

"It's a life-or-death situation," I say, trying to look non-panicky.

Raj makes his let-me-think-on-this face as I rush again toward the passenger side of the truck and lift up the door handle, open it, sink into the familiar, uncomfortable seat. He moseys toward the truck incredibly casually.

The truck is still just like Goldy left it. But Raj is DJ Dangerous, complete with a lion as his logo, so by God does he have his sound system set up like it's a club. Speakers, woofers, subwoofers, tweeters, black lights, even a setup for karaoke in the back. Meanwhile, nothing that is supposed to work inside or outside the truck works. Passenger airbags, seat belts, windshield wipers. His freezer is barely functional.

Raj slowly gets into the driver's side and adjusts his beard, his turban, and his massage cushion. Finally, he puts the keys into the ignition and rumbles off like the world's slowest getaway driver.

Fortunately, there is only one direction to go out of the main gates: right.

"So who's the girl on the bike?" he says as we pick up speed. Meaning, like, twenty miles per hour.

"Just some girl," I say. I don't mention Goldy's notebook. I mean, my notebook.

A few moments pass as we drive. The heavy bass of Punjabi music—cut with an obligatory rap portion that sounds like Raj did himself—causes my eye to twitch.

"There!" I say as we spot her in the left-turn lane heading toward Bullard Avenue.

"This girl is pretty damn slow on that fast-ass bike," Raj says as we putter along behind her. "Kinda like she wanted you to catch up to her."

The light turns green and she takes the turn, Raj behind her. Another car gets between us, and for a minute I think we've lost her. But then I hear that low roar again, and see her weave through traffic and into a parking lot.

That's it. We've got her. There's no escaping now.

CHAPTER 5

MINDII VANG, POUCH THIEF

We pull into the Denny's half a mile from school, across the street from the Walgreens that used to be a car wash. It usually isn't very busy, so the waitstaff don't care if we only buy one soda to share and spend hours here.

"Pull up next to her," I tell Raj.

I frantically try and roll down the window to yell at her, but I'm fumbling around so much, I look like a jackass.

Raj smirks and says, "Oh yeah, window still don't work." She's already halfway inside.

I get out and Raj gets out too. I give him two quick manly taps on his shoulder and brush past him. Raj leans against the ice cream truck with no intention of leaving.

"O-okay bro," I say.

"Okay then," he says.

"I can take it from here. I got the situation under control," I add, trying to sound like I actually believe this to be true.

"No doubt," he says. And then follows me inside the Denny's.

I grit my teeth. This place tends to get packed in the wee hours of the morning or in between parties while people fill up before figuring out where else to go. It's fairly empty right now. I see Mindii sitting down at a table. Instead of looking embarrassed or terrified at the wrath I'm about to unleash, she waves me and Raj over.

"There she is," Raj says. "She's sitting at the—"

"I. F-f-friggin'." I take a deep breath. "Know," I say as we move toward her table.

Mindii is living it up, sitting at the table with fat cushion-y benches, booth style. Her bright yellow motorcycle helmet is placed on the floor. As we get closer, the other three people already sitting at the booth come into focus. The rest of our sorcery metal band minus Ngozi. The two Georges are stuffing themselves with snacks. They rarely participate in conversations unless it's about music or nuanced plot points of Snollygoster-related things. Shirin is blowing on her nails.

So weird to think this is our final performance. Right now, with this tux and this face I'm feeling the same way I felt the first time I publicly went out in cosplay: like a pakhandi. A phony.

The two Georges are in an incomplete hydraulics-based cosplay. They're both cosplaying different components of the Agan-Panchi-Muj, a class of terrifying fire-breathing Avian-Bovine enchanted beasts who protect Malmesbury Academy. Cambodian George looks up at me. She is wearing a crop-top for now because who wants to be wearing hydraulics while chilling out at Denny's? Japanese George is also in relax mode. He is wearing shorts and a short-sleeve button down. Their mechanical wings are probably in the Bramble Van outside, along with all our musical gear: amps, guitars, drums, harp. Did anyone bring my seven-string electric guitar?

For as long as I've known the Georges, they've always cosplayed together. They started calling themselves the Georges when Mrs. Ward refused to even try and pronounce their names in ninth grade because of reasons all of us in the band know too well: the caucacity. She started with the usual pause, half-hearted attempt at pronunciation of their actual names, then said, "We'll have to give you nicknames so I don't butcher your names." Like she was doing them a favor. In response, they started a parody Tik-Tok account (@thetwoGeorges), which they only planned to mess around with once. Cambodian George wore a wig and pretended to be Mrs. Ward, who pronounced all the white-sounding names perfectly, then gave the brown kids, all played by Japanese George, ridiculous nicknames like Toast, Mayonnaise, and Unseasoned Meat. At the end the catchphrase was: "I'm just gonna go ahead and call you George. All of you." The thing went viral, so they kept going, and now they've got a pretty huge following.

Shirin isn't in her full cosplay either. "Well, this land sure is strange!" she says overly dramatically at me. I already know she's crossplaying Jamie. I helped her pick out the chain mail material for her dress. Her commitment to the Jamie accent mingled with her natural Farsi-tinged English just makes all the irritating things Jamie says sound more fun.

I've rehearsed the things I'm going to tell Mindii and don't want to give up my position of power by sitting down, so I remain standing. Like the churlish fucker he is, Raj takes a seat.

"You don't look too comfy in those clothes. And what's with the pouch. Can't just wear that without Dafydd," Shirin says.

"H-heyyy, Jamie," I singsong and wave, attempting to still look stoic and intimidating.

I control my breathing and look right at Mindii. "The p-p-pouch you have, you better return it or legal things will be taking place!"

Not exactly what I had in mind, but it makes sense— more or less.

My jaw is tense as I wait for Mindii to respond. I'm expecting her to be defensive, to say no, to claim it's hers, or worst of all—to return the pouch without Goldy's notebook. My notebook.

Instead, she reaches into her purse and tosses it onto the table.

Raj looks at it all judgy. He gets up. "So anticlimactic. I'm out."

"Drop me back at prom," I say.

"You wanna go back there? To do what? Wash the dishes?"

"You wouldn't understand," I say, like I'm trying to explain the intricacies of Mughal architecture to a gerbil.

"By the time you get there your homies are gonna be gone. You think they're just waiting for you?"

This thought had not occurred to me. Who else do I know there? Am I gonna be at the table by myself? Still, I'm committed.

"Can I get a ride or not?"

"Your boring night. What do I care. I'm going back regardless to sell those fools ice cream."

I unzip the pouch to make sure the notebook is there. "This all seems to be in order, Safia," I say, like we're making a deal for diamonds. I turn and start walking away.

"I'm not Safia," Mindii says.

"What?" I say, pausing mid-step.

Mindii laughs.

"Did you miss the braids?" She showcases them.

I smack my forehead. Katara from *Last Airbender*. Of course. I used to watch that show all the time with Goldy.

"That's such a Sokka thing to do!" she says excitedly. "You should totally tie your hair up in a Sokka bun."

Goldy loved that show, spent almost a hundred bucks on a fat hardcover book on the extended backstory of the Kyoshi Warriors, who didn't even get a cameo in the M. Night Shyamalan movie adaptation. Oh yeah, he ranted about that for days, weeks, months, years. I glare at her as I start walking toward the exit with Raj. I casually flip through the pages of my rash decision notebook and see writing in purple pen.

"You wrote," I say, aghast, "in purple pen?"

"Red is very unlucky," she says.

Purple pen is bad enough, but it gets worse: The words *Not really rash decisions* are scribbled above my list.

My eyes widen in horror. Has she a) actually made notes on MY rash decisions? And b) dismissed them as NOT rash decisions?

"How f-friggin dare!" I say, my voice cracking. I close the notebook and tuck it carefully back into the pouch, fuming.

"Yo!" Raj says impatiently. I turn away and take a few more steps toward the door.

"I was just offering you some honest feedback," Mindii says. "You know people pay a lot of money for good editors."

I turn back.

"This is not a writing workshop! This is MY journal. And y-you just . . . you . . . know nothing."

I raise my hands up. I have no words for this girl.

I look back and see Raj has left. Fuck, I'm stuck.

Mindii just stares at me blankly, half smiling.

And of course, right on time, I hear the dreaded sound of a Cockney accent. "Well, well, well," she bellows from behind me. "After all that donkey bollocks, the Head Plonker of Plonkertown wants to come to the Snollygoster Soiree after all."

As much as I'm not feeling Ngozi or any of these people right now, her Chur cosplay looks fantastic. Thanks to me. I helped her with some of the needlework and provided valuable feedback when she asked whether she should go full West African traditional and wear a round colorful gele head wrap, or her usual large Afro. I told her, "You gotta do what you gotta do." Words she clearly took to heart. Her Afro looks great, bright red lipstick to match her gray fur-trimmed maroon gradient dress with bright-colored ankara fabric, eyes winged out in gold with turquoise eyeshadow, and huge golden hoop earrings.

"W-w-were you waiting in the back just so you could make th-this dramatic entrance?"

"Yes, I was. Glad you noticed." She turns to Mindii, smiling. "All right?" This is how she asks someone how they are. It's another weird British thing.

"I'm cool," Mindii says.

I look at Mindii. Then I look at Ngozi. Realization dawns. "Were you and f-f-fake Safia here conspiring this whole t-time?" I say, my voice lilting upward.

"Umm. I'm not fake anything. I'm Katara. From the greatest TV show ever made. Don't make me bloodbend you."

I'm much too befuddled to respond.

"If by conspiring you mean did I mention that you'd be sulking around at Pedestrian Prom in this idiotic getup that looks even dodgier than I thought it would, instead of coming to the spectacularly decorated Snollygoster Soiree, performing with the most amazing Bramble-core sorcerer metal band to ever exist . . ." Ngozi takes a deep breath. "Then yes. That's exactly what happened."

"Why are you even here? Aren't you supposed to be chaperoning your sisters??"

She pauses.

"Oh, okay. Did I just make that up in my head?"

"Kind of. I said I was at prom to chaperone my sisters. Which was true. Last year."

I piece things together.

"S-s-so the whole time you were sitting there, you had planned to kidnap me?" I look accusingly at Mindii.

"Kidnap? I rescued you from the most boring night of your life."

"What if I hadn't come to the snack table? Then what was y-your plan?"

"Would have figured it out," she says matter-of-factly.

Mindii is . . . bananas. Who goes to prom to steal a boy without a plan? That's so incredibly . . . rash?

And yet . . . an interesting development. Mindii Vang wants me to come to the Snollygoster Soiree? Why? What's in it for her? Anyway, my cosplay is at home. Even my beard. I blow a strand of blond hair out of my eyes.

Ngozi catches me looking at Mindii and she knows she's got me. "You bloody well better not show up wearing this drab prom attire. People will think you're cosplaying a beardless pencil."

"Well, I can't just get Dafydd," I say. Cosplayers have a tendency to name our cosplays, like how bakers name their sourdough starters or normal people refer to their friends and family members. We do not, under any circumstances, call it an outfit or costume, like we're casual dresser-uppers on Halloween. "Dafydd is at the house." Along with my entire family and a giant memorial for my dead brother. It's going to be Mission: Impossible to get it, even if I did have a ride.

I look at Ngozi. "Aren't you supposed to be at the roller rink?" I say.

Ngozi sighs loudly. "Yeh." She looks at Mindii. "Engagement party for my cousin, innit. She's twenty-seven and is acting like she's having a sweet sixteen party. Such inconvenient timing. I barely managed to sneak out long enough to come here for a nibble."

It's kinda sweet she took the time to coerce me into leaving Normal Prom in the middle of all her hectic-ness. Also pretty damn shady. At least her Chur cosplay looks Nigerian-ish, so she can wear that to this engagement party without it turning heads.

Ngozi's face straightens up. "Might as well tell me. You have that face."

"I do not," I say.

"You bloody well do."

"N-no. I d-don't."

Ngozi stops. "Not even going to use your totally pants British accent? Now I know something is off."

"It is not pants," I say irritably. "I am great with accents. When I do Dafydd, people think I sound like I'm really from Petrichor."

"Leave it out, Sunny," Ngozi scoffs. "Nobody thinks that. They just think you're talking with a gob full of food. Like a hamster."

"Better than your American accent."

"Whelllll," she says drawing out every single grating syllable of what she thinks is a Southern accent. "Aaaaaa beg to difffferrrr."

I look over at Mindii, who is enjoying this a little too much.

"Don't be a plonker, Sunny," Ngozi continues. "I'll be at the soiree by eleven, right after the jollof rice competition. You just worry about yourself and be there. Or you're a fucking dead man."

"I'll have to figure some things out. I don't have a ride anymore."

"As luck would have it, I just happen to be free," Mindii says.

Ngozi smirks.

"Sorted," she says.

I roll my eyes.

"Go get Dafydd. You can leave that poxy accent at home and just use your garish American one if you like."

"It is not poxy. It's lit."

With that, I follow Mindii outside, a giant cloud over my head.

She pulls on her little yellow helmet and hands me a bigger black one, then throws one leg over her motorcycle, a Yamaha. Hmm. I always thought they only made keyboards. Nice to see they've branched out to non-musical machines that can potentially kill people.

I strap on my helmet warily and then take a seat behind her, a man without options.

CHAPTER 6

SUNNY IMPRESSES THE GIRL BY TELLING HER ABOUT YARN

Maybe, like Normal Prom, I'd built up a much more glamorous image in my head of what it would be like zooming through the streets of Fresno on the back of a motorcycle: the freedom of being on the open road, a fresh breeze gently caressing my skin. Instead, I'm getting hot, smog-filled air slapping me in the face, my brain filled with constant thoughts of death by splattering. I didn't think the ride would be this bumpy. My ass feels like it's been repeatedly kneaded.

We park in a tiny open space near the fence to the back-yard. There are four cars already parked out front. The entire neighborhood is composed mostly of Mexicans, Punjabis, and Hmong, so it gets super loud on the week-ends and random evenings when people just want to have an impromptu party or get-together.

I really don't want to be at the house because of the barsi. Death anniversary. It's going to be so weird. I'm just hoping I can stealthily sneak in, get Dafydd, and sneak out, undetected. But mostly I just don't want to be reminded of Goldy for so much sustained time. That's literally what a barsi is, a remembrance. They're going to be serving Goldy's favorite foods, like muttar paneer, and because this is Mama and Papa we're talking about, people will be reciting and singing poems, making overly dramatic speeches about the amazing Goldy Gill. I really don't want to explain my face to anyone. Mama and Papa have seen it, of course. She touched my face with sadness and Papa muttered "Fittey mooh," then threw a chappal at my bedroom door. But since those first reactions, they've mostly said nothing. Biji's only reaction was to say nothing too, but it's a different non-judgy way of saying nothing.

The sounds of the barsi are slightly muffled from this side of the house. It's dark now and beautiful, the sky filled with stars and constellations, and on clear evenings, the moon looks so close, you could jump up and take a great big bite out of it. When I was six or seven, me and Goldy and Papa would hang out on his lawn mower tractor— you know, for the half an acre of garden in the back—and it would be such a thrill feeling the ground beneath us vibrate, listening to Papa talk about how amazing soil is over the loudness of it all.

Mindii hoists herself off the bike in one smooth motion.

Her dress is unsullied, not one speck of dust on it. I get off the bike clumsily, my shoes covered in dirt, the bottom of my rented pants dusty. I take a step and realize a pebble has made its way into my sock. A mosquito comes and bites me on my hand and another one gets me right on the forehead. I can feel the bites swelling slightly. Mosquitos, fruit flies, bees, annoying house flies. Goldy rarely got bit when he'd go outside. Me, I'm a sweaty, swelling mess.

"So," Mindii says. "What's the plan?"

I pause to take off my shoe and remove the offending stone, then look up at the sky, hoping for some divine intervention. A bolt of lightning, a flood, a bunch of scary-ass birds prophesizing the end of times.

"You know we don't really have to go through with this." I straighten up and dust myself off, a futile effort since the entire area is dirt and dust. It's like trying to stay clean in a mine. "We c-could just say we *tried* to get D-Dafydd. Also, my parents are very traditional. It will bring great dishonor on my family if anyone sees me bring a girl in the house," I say somberly. "Could get very tense."

There is silence as the weight of this fills the air.

She starts laughing riotously. She has to grab my shoulder to keep from falling over. It's kind of offensive. I mean, sure, nobody's going to arranged-marriage me or bust out swords, and neither Papa or Mama is going to disown me for bringing a girl to the house. Or for anything, really. But still, Mindii could act a little concerned. Because I'm not entirely wrong.

Papa's already embarrassed enough, between my very public love of crochet and Goldy's very public alcoholism (and yes, for Papa these offenses are equally embarrassing). We've got a big family, and everyone's probably here, all the thayas and bhuas and chachas and mamas. How am I supposed to explain Mindii's presence to everyone related to me by blood, not to mention the family friends who have inserted themselves into our lives so we have to call them auntie and uncle?

"Fine. Let's go. If I get sent to work at a call center in Jalandhar tonight, this is on your head."

"Just make sure there's mango lassi at the wedding reception. I mean, we're here to pick up your cosplay so you can play in a Brambleberry tribute heavy metal band at a Snollygoster-themed party. I don't think I'm going to be the biggest threat to tradition in this house tonight."

"My cosplay has a name. Dafydd. And the musical subgenre is called Bramble-core," I snap.

She's already walked over to the Raat di Rani plant, with its gorgeous tubular white flowers cascading up the fence.

"What's that aroma?" Mindii says. I'm trying to strategize the best way to sneak into the back of the house, toward the craft room.

"Aroma?" I say, distracted.

"Yeah. You know, smell?"

"I friggin' know what *aroma* means!" I say sharply. "Sunny can spell. Sunny know big words." I immediately bite my tongue because I don't know the English word for the plant the aroma is coming from.

"It's called Raat di Raani. The English word is . . . uh . . . Queen of the Night," I say, literally translating the Punjabi phrase Mama uses.

She pauses to look at the tiny white flowers and takes a deep inhale. "Night-blooming jasmine. I'd know the smell anywhere," Mindii says. "My niam tais—my grandma— used to grow it and would make me a small necklace with it every Hmong New Year."

I glance over at her and breathe in the jasmine too. "How do you pronounce the Hmong word for grandma? Is it nitai?" I venture, attempting to mimic the pronunciation.

"Na-tai," she says slowly.

"Na-tai," I repeat.

She nods her head, but I already know it's not quite right.

We walk along the perimeter of the fence and enter through the side. I open up my pouch and take out the keys.

Inside, we walk past the sunroom, where all three of us—Mama, Biji, and me—sit and gossip and crochet.

Sometimes aunties or relatives come here during birthdays or on Diwali and Bandi Chhor and Vaisakhi and, well, any reason to knit or crochet and talk smack while the men watch cricket or football or play cards, which used to turn into whiskey and poetry sessions.

When Goldy came back from rehab his third and what ended up being his final time, we were all determined to make sure he didn't fuck up. Papa emptied out the whole house of alcohol, and I really thought it would fix things. I monitored Goldy like a hawk to make sure he didn't even think of drinking. I still remember the autopsy report we received weeks after he died. Most of the words were gibberish, like cyanosis, lung bases, alveolar space. But then there were little spots of normal English: "he voluntarily consumed alcohol," and "alcohol toxicity." Like yes I understand it's a disease, but man—it's hard to really feel that when the word *voluntarily* is stuck in my head.

Biji's bed is here too. My parents tried really hard to get Biji to sleep in an actual room, but she enjoys being close to an open window and in a wide-open room. So the sunroom is her room.

The lights are all on, but Biji is most likely outside, hanging with all the old people or sitting around listening to the poetry.

We go down the narrow hallway and Mindii pauses in front of the door to my room and the crafting area. She briefly looks at the wooden sign that says "Loom the Fandom," and the photo of yarn taped underneath. "This has to be your room," Mindii says, posters of colorful yarn, a giant poster of Kajol and Shah Rukh Khan from *Kuch Kuch Hota Hai* on the wall. "I like this movie," she says. "I used to watch it with my niam tais all the time."

I have so many questions, starting with her knowing one of the major films of the 1990s Hindi film industry.

But then I scramble toward my desk to hide the stack of books on alcoholism that I just don't have the energy to move. Thankfully she changes the subject and brings up my other great love: indoor gardening.

"So. Gardening, huh?" she says, which is a nice way to comment on the mess. Herbs and flowers are scattered everywhere, in bottles, tin cans. There are clothes all over the floor, even though there's a laundry bin right there. A record player sits on a table in the corner, with vinyls of Punjabi songs—many of them glorifying "manly" consumption of alcohol; it's kinda unavoidable—*Star Wars and Other Galactic Funk*, a ton of limited edition Bramblecore metal, and some regular metal bands I've picked up over the years.

"I dabble," I say as she looks around.

"Every apartment we've ever had," she says, "we always planted things. It all goes in our food. My niam tais"— she pauses—"hustled big-time to get seeds and cuttings of things from the old country. I still don't know what they're called in English. We use a thousand herbs for our chicken soup, and you can find all of them in our garden. Even Si Toj. Fun fact about Si Toj: It's used to induce menstruation. Me and my sisters use it all the time. Great for regulating flow too. Menstrual flow."

"Oh. That's grrrreeeaaaat," I say, nodding as fast as I can to indicate just how cool I am with the words *menstruation* and *flow*.

"Okay," I say, pausing. "I don't get it."

"What?"

"All of this," I say. "This." I wildly gesture with my hands because I don't even know how to express what I'm trying to say.

She steps in close. She knows what I'm asking.

"Isn't it obvious?" she says, looking at me.

I tilt my head.

"I like you. For secret reasons."

I blink at her. Is this sarcasm? Or what do you call it—being facetious?

I don't know what to think or feel. Should I laugh?

She starts walking out of the room, toward the craft room.

She already sees the Dafydd cosplay and is heading straight for it. It's hanging next to the mannequin head I use to size things. Yes, like fake beards.

"This is fucking incredible," she says, examining the crocheted black-armored vest, chain mail helmet, crocheted beard, a little steam-punk telescope for the eye with a crocheted eye-telescope . . . uh . . . cozy.

"You made this?"

"I did," I say, happy that she's excited. "But can we rewind like eight seconds?"

She does a really bad enactment of time reversing.

"To the part where you said you like me. Like . . . like me . . . like a . . . uh . . ."

"Spiky and pungent durian?" she says, smiling.

"Uh," I say.

"Ngozi mentioned you weren't coming to the Snollygoster Soiree, so I thought, this guy clearly needs rescuing. And lucky for you, there I was."

"But it wasn't just there you was. You came for me."

"Sometimes people need rescuing. I came to rescue you, Sunny Gill."

I feel my heart flutter; an awkwardness envelops me.

I must look confused, because then she says, "You don't recognize me at all, do you?"

Of course I recognize her. "English class? Anime Club? Denny's? The Snollygoster Soiree? Did I miss something?" I say.

"Comic-Con. My niam tais's soul had been gone a couple days at that point." I look at her. Her eyes look far away.

That's such a great way to think about it instead of someone just being dead. "My entire cosplay had come apart. And there you were, with your amazing beard and flowy turban and that funny sign."

I'm floored. "C-cosplay d-doctor for all your sewing needs. My parents would prefer I fixed humans," I say.

"Dafydd looked different then," she said.

"I've been cosplaying him a while and keep adding things to make him look more precise."

The cosplay doctor is arguably the most important person at a con. The person who carries around supplies for when people inevitably tear their dresses, shirts, pants, capes, horns, armor, or their masks come unglued. I have a kit I wish I could fit in a pouch, but sadly I need to bring a furry backpack with pretty much everything needed to fix things.

I don't know what to say or how to react. Without skipping a beat she changes the subject. "How'd you make the beard?" she says. "It's so soft."

"Trick is to use crepe wool," I mumble.

There are very few people who would have a beard large enough to pull it off without making or buying one. I use crepe wool, which I routinely use to make the hair and beards for my online store. I could do the motions in my sleep: Remove the twine, extend the wool, pull firmly, untwist fiber, cut small pieces, use spirit gum. Poof. Beard.

"So what's your problem? You got this whole tricked-out cosplay and you're sitting here wearing a tux and a little while ago you were wasting time at the most boring prom ever.

"Well, let's see it."

I slowly put on Dafydd and feel a tingle of joy and sadness. I love Dafydd the character so much because he reminds me of me, but also who I wish I were. I wish I could be confident in exactly who I am, and loyal, and just owning my flaws and virtues. While Dafydd suffers because of his truthfulness, I can't even be truthful to myself.

I hear slow footsteps and panic. Biji yells, "Kaun ya?" *Who's there.* She's changed into a comfortable salwar kameez to sleep in, and is wearing one of my crocheted Hufflepuff hats. The barsi has just started and Biji loves to socialize, but can only take so much before she needs a break. She needs to recharge, and likes to spend time by herself. She'd been doing self-care before the phrase was even coined.

Biji walks up to where we're both standing next to the sewing machine.

"Sat Sri Akal, Biji," I say, and lean in for a big hug. She pauses to look at me and laughs loudly. She always laughs whenever I wear cosplay.

She notices Mindii, but doesn't ask any questions

75

other than whether we've eaten. She stops to adjust her fat brown-rimmed glasses. After crinkling her nose, she squints up at me—she's pretty short at five feet exactly. She looks at Mindii, and opens her mouth to smile a big gummy smile, her teeth in a glass by the sink. I bend down as her soft bony hand reaches for the top of my head. She pats it. She looks over at Mindii and her eyes light up.

"Pani?" Biji says, looking right at Mindii. Mindii smiles. Biji nods and very slowly heads back down the hall toward her bedroom.

"She asked if you wanted water, but what she's really asking is if you want ice from her fridge with an ice machine. Yes is the only correct answer, so either way you're getting ice."

She comes back to the room, carrying a tray with three glasses filled to the brim with ice. We stand around awkwardly attempting to drink essentially a glass of ice with two teaspoons of water. Every so often, Biji looks intently at Mindii.

Mindii points to the crochet cover for a tissue box, which I'll be honest, is kinda overkill, and says, "Did you make this? It's lovely."

Biji laughs. Then she takes out a bag from under the table and lays out its contents. It contains all kinds of crochet patterns and some phulkari, floral work with intricate motifs and shapes.

"Incredible," Mindii says. "Can you tell me how this is made?" She looks right at Biji and Biji looks right at her. I like that Mindii isn't looking at me for help, even though I still need to translate. I tell Biji what Mindii asked and then translate what Biji says, while they just look at each other and talk. I don't usually see Biji this energized, unless she's sneakily eating jalebi or dishing out some juicy gossip.

"When I was little, my mother would invite neighbors and relatives to our courtyard and I would join them. That's how we learned. And we'd sing folk songs. Now it's difficult. Life is so busy," she says, waiting for me to translate.

I translate.

Biji continues looking directly at Mindii like I'm not there, and shows her a piece she only shows people she likes. It's stunning. The stitching is so intricate and delicate, the shapes jagged, handmade.

"Back in the old days," I translate, "women used to start making these as soon as a daughter was born, creating these majestic, gorgeous phulkaris for dowries."

"It looks beautiful," Mindii says. "But screw dowries and bride prices."

"Yeah, n-no. Word."

Mindii reaches over and looks at the design, then traces her fingers over it. "The pattern reminds me of what we do in paj ntaub."

I know the Wikipedia version of what she's talking about. It's like how I know about African Americans using quilting techniques in the Underground Railroad, passing down coded messages and family history through shapes and symbols. I find anything involving some kind of thread and needle fascinating.

"What does *phulkari* mean?" she says.

"*Phul* means flower. *Kari* is work. So flower work. Basically, it's embroidery with all kinds of shapes. Not j-just flowers."

Mindii's eyes sparkle. "Get out! That's just what *paj ntaub* means. Flower cloth."

"Pan . . uh," I say.

"Pan. Dow," she says slowly.

I attempt to repeat it.

She moves closer to Biji and shows her the bottom of her dress. "I made this with my niam tais."

Biji looks at it intently.

"There's all kinds of symbolism in this," Biji says.

Before I can translate, Mindii looks at her and says, "Embroidery is such a great language."

Biji offers Mindii a gummy grin. She slowly gets up and takes out another box, and out comes this mesmerizing phulkari work on what looks like a men's atchkin. I've never seen it before. It's black with a beautiful shape of a peacock on the front, with gold-patterned geometric shapes, dark blue and green silk thread to look like peacock feathers, unfinished gorgeous scenery in the background. Like, truly phenomenal.

"And this," I continue live-translating, even though I'm a little weirded out, "is for the boy when he gets married. Goldy is always doing things uniquely." Biji lets out a laugh. I take a breath. Goldy. Maybe it was a slip of the tongue?

"Well, you are amazing . . ." I hear Mindii saying as everything blurs. Biji is in the middle of saying something when I stand up, kiss her on the cheek, and abruptly start walking out of the house.

CHAPTER 7

THE INTERESTING THING ABOUT
ALMOND TREES

I'm standing by the side of the house near the small walnut tree that signifies the beginning of Mama's garden,
just out of sight of the Kavi Darbar setting up on the back
lawn for Goldy's one-year barsi. It feels extra surreal being
here in my Dafydd cosplay because if a single person sees
me, I got a whole lot of explaining to do. Probably starting with the fake beard, then moving on to my actual face,
although I'm pretty sure every Sikh in the entire world
knows what I did. Probably broadcasted on all the news
channels and radio stations.

For as long as I've been alive, we've always had a Kavi
Darbar—Mama and Papa's go-to gathering no matter the
occasion, a mehfil of Punjabi poetry, pageantry, and the
careful handling of egos when poets inevitably went over
the time limit.

I used to love the more joyful Kavi Darbars when I was
a kid and they were small gatherings inside the house.

Everyone used to sit around in these large circles, sprawled on the floor or across couches, with me and Goldy right in the middle with makeshift instruments to provide the taalam, the rhythm: usually a pair of spoons and the floor or a chair. When we were younger, Mama would sit with us, briefly explaining what the words meant. But you can't explain poetry one word at a time.

Mama would start things off by asking if anyone had any ailments they needed remedied. And people would say things like lost love, general sadness, or specific funny things like who would win in a fight between lassi and cha. She had this knack for being able to prescribe poems to the small crowd, singing in tune, and recalling poetry in their entirety, some of them bawdy, some melancholy and beautiful, all from memory. Most of the poems she sang were in Punjabi, with occasional nazms in Urdu and Hindi. By the end of the night, the uncles were drunk enough to sing their own improvised poetic forms of the sher and kavita and believe they were making profound social and political commentary. There would be the occasional Drunkle—me and Goldy's term for Super-Drunk Embarrassing Uncle— but for the most part it was a fun end to the night until the next time. I'd refuse to go to bed and would end up snuggled up with Goldy, who would let me fall asleep in his arms, Mama's phulkari shawl wrapped around me.

Tonight the Kavi Darbar has a much more serious vibe, the speakers and chairs and podiums all outside. So clinical. The lopsided podium is all the way on the far side of the house in front of Papa's small section of slowly growing sugarcane stalks.

The atmosphere is somber with people sitting and milling around. Having the barsi outdoors is a good strategy that Mama probably came up with to make sure people don't show up too early or stay too late unlike our usual indoor Kavi Darbar where that kind of thing was encouraged, expected. Fresno's summer weather acts as crowd control with daytime temperatures reaching cozy furnace levels, and by seven p.m. it starts getting breezier and the mosquitoes come out to feast on anything remotely natural. By eleven p.m. you could almost describe the weather as pleasant.

There's no escaping the fact that the entire purpose for this Kavi Darbar is a poetic subgenre I didn't know existed: "Maut Shayari." Death poetry.

Any second now, Mindii's about to walk out and yell at me for leaving Biji and her like that. I got nothing to tell her that makes any sense. *Rushed out to save a baby. Saw a small squirrel about to be eaten by an eagle.*

I could hot-wire her ride and make a run for it. Rub that rash decision in her face. "Siri," I say, "how do you hot-wire a motorcycle?" The quintessential rash decision:

life as a fugitive on the open road. But who knew it would be so complicated? According to one article, all I need is a friggin' "wire lying around" and a wire stripper. "Sure. G-great," I say.

"That's what I thought. It's nice to be appreciated," Siri responds. Sigh.

Another, "easier" method just requires a flat-head screwdriver and an optional hammer. I let out an exasperated sigh. Why can't life be like a 1980s Bollywood film where the keys are always in the ignition just when you need to make a quick getaway?

I wish I had a flat-head screwdriver and a wire stripper. I'd so be out of here on Mindii's bike. Then I wouldn't need to explain myself. Second time I've left like that tonight. I should put that on my résumé under special skills: "Expert in extremely awkward, abrupt exits." I'd hire me.

I look over at the gigantic pots in the pop-up outdoor kitchen a few yards away from the podium. My stomach growls. The volunteers are serving classic langar: dal, sabji, chole, and deep-fried orange jalebi for dessert, made with pure sugar and ghio. They are speedily throwing roti and naan in the requisite heat-blasting tandoor.

It's definitely not breezy yet, but it's heading in the direction of pleasant.

"Yum!" Mindii says, coming up behind me and giving me a good scare. I let out a manly scream, and quickly giraffe my neck to make sure nobody saw or heard me.

Dafydd's armor is sturdy, the little steampunk telescope a little uncomfortable. My chain mail helmet is thin enough for my hair to slide under and the bike helmet to go on top. I hope this doesn't look like I'm wearing a chain mail chunni. Probably should have thought this out a little more, and it doesn't look like it would protect me properly in battle. Not like me or Dafydd are one of those people in Petrichor who get excited about warmongering.

I catch my breath as I watch Papa walk toward the podium in his beige suit and beige dastaar, rather than the brighter colors he usually wears. If he turned around and squinted real hard, he could theoretically see me. But in my Dafydd cosplay maybe he'd just think I was a really dark, sweaty, furry tumbleweed and continue with what he's doing anyway. Mama stands by awkwardly, adjusting her chunni and looking vacantly into the distance. She hates formal wear and socializing. She would much rather be gardening in one of her tie-dye skirts and tops.

I look at Mindii for a long moment and preemptively explain myself. "Look. F-fine. I know. I-it's. It's just. You know, y'know?" I eloquently rationalize my behavior with Biji.

I don't want to tell her all the things, like that these scribbles in Goldy's notebook are all I have left of him. But I do need to explain to her that she is completely wrong about my rash decisions not being rash decisions just because I research them . . . slightly. "The p-peacock phulkari," I say instead. "I just wasn't exp-pecting it."

The speaker sputters as Papa hits a high note almost as soon as he starts singing. The sounds of the barsi are getting under way, crickets are chirping loudly, a gentle buzz of conversations punctuates the air, and I want to be somewhere, anywhere else.

There will be no poetry prescriptions tonight.

Mindii moves closer to me. I'm dreading follow-up questions, pity, scorn, anger, awkwardness.

"Dude," she says, "are those speakers?" It takes me a second to register she's not talking about the speakers from the Kavi Darbar. She points toward one of Goldy's old speakers from his ice cream truck now sitting in Mama's garden, filled with dirt and flourishing with chrysanthemums.

"Yeah, it's a speaker," I say, hoping that will be that.

She starts walking toward the garden and I quickly catch up. Mindii hovers over a broken freezer.

"It's my mom," I say. "Every time anyone tries to throw something away, she grabs it and uses it as a planter. Broken toilets, sinks, microwaves, toaster ovens, shoes, chappal, nothing is safe from Mama and her fifteen-year-old rusted pruner." I point toward random sections of the garden, where all of these things are used to grow everything from chives to cucumbers.

"Absolutely amazing," Mindii says.

Papa's voice becomes a low rumble as he slowly sings the line of his original poetry "Ki rakhiye naam iss alam da." Mindii quiets down as we listen. "That's your dad?" she asks. I nod. She walks toward an almond tree, where we can kind of see the podium behind some large bushes.

"Such a beautiful voice," Mindii says, and glances at me, a little confused about what's happening. "But so sad. Is this a religious poem?"

"No. It's just a depressing poem."

"Okay," Mindii says, not really convinced. I don't have the words to tell her what this is. It's not exactly something you can guess. Ah, is this your dead brother's one-year death poetry anniversary? Thought so. The muttar paneer gave it away.

"The poem is . . ." I say, about to translate it badly.

"Don't," Mindii says. "Let's just listen for a bit."

We stand there listening to the sounds of Papa's poem, the garden humming.

"This poem isn't religious, but there will be religious-themed poems tonight. And some might even be directly from our Holy Scriptures—the Guru Granth Sahib—which have a lot of poetic hymns in different languages. And they're always sung in a specific raag, so like a musical scale to set the mood according to the composer of the shabad."

"If it's in different languages, how do you read it?" she asks.

"There's one unifying script: Gurmukhi," I say.

"Mmm," she says, taking everything in. "That's so wonderful. You have your entire history and literature and belief system at your fingertips. Like whenever you want it, it's just there."

"I never th-thought about it like that. But yeah," I say.

"My niam tais used to tell me stories about why we don't have a written history. One of them is that horses were so hungry, they ended up eating all our literature."

H-h-h-h," I say, and immediately regret embarking on the letter *h*. "H-hor-horses," I finally say triumphantly. I realize I haven't asked a question, or made a statement. Might as well have said "Cabbages." I'm really hoping I don't have to say it again in the form of a question or statement.

Mindii purses her lips, like I just asked something really personal.

"Niam Tais tells the story much better in Hmong. Mine is not gonna be that good. But basically thousands of years ago my people lived in the Hmong Kingdom in China and had like literature and art and all that. Then there was an attack and some Hmong escaped on horses with our books. So they get to a riverbank or something and take a nap and wake up to find the horses ate the books. It's like way more dramatic when she used to tell it. And she would change things up, like add a queen and three sons. Or was it two? So, yeah.

"I don't know if this is the same thing as what is going on here, but my niam tais was one of the last people to do Kwv Txhiaj. Hmong song poetry."

I try to repeat her pronunciation and fail.

"Kooh Zee-ah," Mindii says. She shrugs. "It's a tonal language. The written language is kinda recent, but it's spelled *K-w-v T-x-h-i-a-j*."

My eyes widen.

"This spelling is for us, not for you all to mangle the pronunciation by what you think it's supposed to sound like." She laughs.

"Okay," I say. "Fair enough."

She pauses to pick a soft almond cocoon straight off the tree and crack it open with her teeth, then proceeds to scoop it out and eat it.

"Poetry," I say. "Poetry is . . . nice."

She doesn't say anything about my dorky response.

The moon shines down on Mindii, her face glowing.

"Interesting thing about almond trees," I say, and stop for a moment, "is that you have to be careful about the variety. Bitter almond, for example, contains cyanide."

"They should call it killer almond," she says, deadpan.

I laugh, an embarrassingly loud snort at the end of it.

I used to spend so many hours here in the garden,

whole summer afternoons, really. It used to be me and Goldy raking the leaves, helping Papa lay down fertilizer, or helping Mama with planting and weeding or whatever weird gardening hack she heard or read about. Laying down cardboard to kill weeds. Decreasing acidity in soil with baking soda to produce sweeter tomatoes. Spraying plants with vinegar for the hell of it.

I got really into bugs. Analyzing, categorizing, documenting. I found out the hard way that almond trees attract spiders. And unlike other bugs, like bees near our rosebushes or the crickets in the grass, spiders are silent. One time this spider scared the shit outta me, so I told Goldy to kill it. He takes off a chappal and says, "I'll kill it if you want me to, but let me holler at you real quick. What's the spider doing? Nothing. Just doing spider things that got nothing to do with you."

Of course I'm like, kill that bastard spider with your chappal anyway. But he wouldn't do it. I got real mad at him, and he said, "Stop wanting to kill something just 'cos it exists in a way you don't understand."

I don't know if he was mad about the spider. Or something else. Couldn't just be easy with this guy.

"This is my b-brother's journal," I say, touching the pouch. Even to my own ears my voice sounds different. Heavy, thick.

I wish Goldy wrote sensical journal entries or even

just left a letter for me. Instead I get a notebook filled with gibberish. Nothing that tells me anything about who he really was, how to unravel his story. Maybe I watch too many white people shows, because that's really what I thought would happen at some point after the cremation. There'd be a box of his belongings, and a lawyer would read words written by him, for me, about me, to me, and then there'd be a specific object of sentimental importance he'd leave me. There was none of that. He didn't even leave me this journal. I just found it. And it's still a mess. I'm still a mess.

"This party is a barsi, a d-death anniversary," I say quietly, "for my brother. Goldy."

She says nothing. Literally nothing. It's oddly comforting. No *I'm sorry for your loss*, no expectations of me to say something deep and meaningful. I look down at the soil, a spider crawling away, minding its own business.

"The song poetry is part of the barsi?" Mindii says eventually.

"It's Maut Shayari. Death poetry," I say. "It's basically poems dealing with loss or grief or sadness. That kinda thing."

"Sounds pretty metal to me," Mindii says.

I smile sadly.

"This whole thing is pointless," I say, that familiar suffocating feeling rising in my chest. "The cremation was the

Antam Sanskar, which should be The End. Soul Departs. Reincarnation Process Begins. And yet . . ."

"People are still human," Mindii finishes.

"Yeah, people are annoying," I say, even though I know that's not what Mindii means.

Papa finishes singing his poem and someone else is starting to say a few words. Probably about Goldy. The voice is muffled because of the sound system, but I'm pretty sure it's something along the lines of "Goldy was so amazing. He was such a perfect person, always destined for greatness."

It's only been a year, but when I close my eyes, I don't see his face anymore. Just the suspension of time as I pressed the cold, metal button for the incinerator at the cremation.

"Spiders are cool," I say, in the world's worst non sequitur.

"Sure," Mindii says, stepping closer.

"We think spiders are quiet. But they have very complex communication through vibrations. Imagine, even without eardrums they know when a person is screaming, crying, or laughing." I feel myself getting squeakier, my pitch really high, like I just took a swig of helium. "There are things about Goldy I will never know. He wrote nothing in here that makes any sense. And I can't even make one rash decision properly. I just . . ."

I'm in the middle of my sentence, and she slides her arms under mine and pulls me close. I fight my instinct to flail around and extract myself from her, but then I feel her close her arms tight around me, and realize it's a hug. I feel my breathing slow down; a sense of calm falls over me.

"Maybe you were right," I say. "Neither of the things I wrote about were rash. Except following you out of prom. At least I have a few more things to write about in my rash decision notebook."

"Well," she says, and pulls away. "Those aren't your rash decisions either. They're mine. I like you, but you can't have my rash decisions."

I blink real hard at her.

"I'm the one that took your pouch, that's why you came after me. You still haven't actually made a single rash decision yet."

I let out a groan.

"So what now?" I say. "We don't have much time before the Snollygoster Soiree."

"Somebody's got Destination Fever," she says.

"Is that?" I say. "From *Last Airbender*?"

She smiles. I can't tell if she's impressed. I only know it because I used to watch the show with Goldy.

"We got plenty of time. Four hours. It's your book," she says. "You wanna fill it up, you decide."

"Oh cheese and crackers," I say. "That's a lot of time."

"That IS a lot of time!" she says excitedly.

"We should establish some rules."

"Yeah, of course. That's how rash, crazy, impulsive decisions work. Through a set of rigid rules."

"How about I'll choose one thing, you choose the other. And no backing out." I look at her to see what she thinks of these rules, which are pretty simple. Maybe too simple?

"What's your first rash decision. Quick!" she says.

My eyes dart around.

"Uh . . . I'm hungry." My stomach growls on cue. "Let's g-go to a restaurant you like," I say.

She doesn't even pause. We start walking toward where the bike is parked.

CHAPTER 8

THE NIGHT MARKET

My arms are clasped around Mindii's waist as we veer onto Highway 180. It's a really strange feeling not having a clue where we're going, kinda exciting, but also terrifying. I don't remember the last time I didn't have at least a little help from my phone.

I stroke a hand over the thin chain mail chunni-helmet overflowing from under this bike helmet. I wonder how I look in it. In an alternate universe where I still have my kes—my hair, what color turban would I be wearing right now? What did Sikh warriors battling the Mughals and the East India Company wear to protect their heads? Couldn't have been just their regular ole turbans. Goldy would have researched this stuff already. He loved things like that. Couldn't tell you the names of the Panj Piare, but could easily list the top five battles in Sikh history. In the midst of my deep thoughts, I am served a mouthful of polluted, dry Fresno air, which does feel breezier than earlier. Still not at pleasant yet, but it's getting there.

Mindii takes the exit and drives through the parking lot and onto the grounds of the flea market. The first time Biji and Mama brought me here to go yarn shopping I found the words *flea market* so funny and translated it into Punjabi for Biji, who thought it was just another weird American thing, like drive-through coffee, or figuring out how to make roti on an electric stove. Makhi mandi. A market for fleas.

It's always popping early in the morning on Sunday with stalls for everything imaginable, from car parts to yarn. Right now it looks like an emptier, more spread out, non-cobblestone-y version of Langley Green, that sketchy place just past Honeysuckle Lane in Petrichor, where all the immigrant gangster elves, curse-makers, and predatory wand and broomstick scammers operate.

"Well, this has been s-super," I say, not moving an inch off the bike. "But it's getting pretty late and I would p-prefer not to be eaten by a boar tonight."

She gets off the bike, my fingers reluctantly unclasping her body.

"That's a very specific death. Anyway, that's ridiculous, there aren't any wild animals here. Unless you count mosquitos. There are spirits, though. But they're not the kind to eat humans."

She says this very matter-of-factly. My eyes dart around

and I sprint to catch up to her. We cross over to the field opposite the makhi mandi, which has a handful of lights strung up on trees and fences. In the distance there's a lit-up trailer.

"You want some of the best Hmong sausages in the world, this is it."

I take in the aroma of sizzling meat as my heart returns to a normal-ish beat. "Ah," I say. "It's a food truck."

"I didn't know you had such a powerful sense of deductive reasoning. Yes. That is a food truck. This is a tree. Those are birds," Mindii says, pointing up toward the sky, a smirk on her face.

"Sausages," I say, pondering this very questionable rash decision. "H-how do you know that's not against my religion?"

"I don't," Mindii says. "But I've seen your feed and it's mostly filled with burgers, cupcakes, and yarn. Also you plagiarizing other people's deep thoughts."

"They happen to be original," I say as she walks on ahead before I even have a chance to explain the complexities of consuming meat in diasporic Sikh cultural and religious life.

The line we're standing in is not huge, but it's still a line.

My nose takes in a whiff and damn, it smells really good.

"Okay," I whisper. "So what's in a Hmong s-sausage?" I say as we get to the front.

"It's a rash decision is what it is," she says. "For you anyway."

The dude serving is wearing a Nirvana T-shirt and a bandana. There aren't any photos of the food or anything. I don't even know if I should bother asking for a menu. I look over at the plates people are eating. Barbequed ribs. Sticky rice. Humongous, juicy sausages, some kinda sauce.

Dude smiles and speaks animatedly in Hmong to Mindii, looks over at me, and says, "You can't handle Hmong sausage. I got ribs, though. Purple sticky rice? Wanna try some crispy pork?" He turns back to her and says something else in Hmong.

This is looking mighty suspicious.

"I want the sausage," I say adamantly. I am willing to die for this sausage now that he has not-so-subtly insinuated he thinks I can't handle it.

"Just FYI, it's Hmong-level spicy," he says. "You should have some boba."

Son. Of. A . . .

I control myself and scoff. In my calmest authoritative voice, I add, "I'm Punjabi. Spicy is in our genes." I'm not actually sure how true that is, but we do have lal mirch in our masala tin that Mama sprinkles into everything.

"I will not have a boba, as a matter of fact," I say, overstuffing the sentence when I could have just said "Nah."

Although I love boba, in this moment I am asserting

my status as alpha male just like they do in the jungle.

"What kind of fool don't want boba?" he mutters to himself. He makes a lot of noise with his metal spatula and then serves everything up in disposable containers loaded on a plastic tray.

"Tiger bite," he says, pausing to look at me, "sauce?" he finishes ominously.

"Yes. I love tiger bite," I say, looking right at him.

He places a small container filled with . . . uh . . . trailer-made dipping sauce onto our tray and we start walking around to find a place to sit down. Mindii takes a sip of her gorgeous creamy boba-layered Thai iced tea. "My niam tais loved boba. I uploaded this one video of me and her drinking boba to YouTube years ago and it's crazy how many people have seen it."

"What's the video called?" I say.

"I forget. *Niam Tais Likes It*? Something like that."

Of course I find the video. I click on it and it starts with a close-up of Mindii and her niam tais with a whole host of nibbled pastries lying on a table, looking at the camera as they loudly slurp their boba. She breaks into a smile and says something in Hmong as she picks up a colorful, cute, circular pastry with some kind of filling, and chomps down. Then they both start dancing to a Justin Bieber song. Mindii is watching the video with me, her face close to mine.

"Little hamburger pastries," I say.

She laughs too.

Then stops smiling when she realizes I don't actually know the name of the pastry. "Macarons. They're macarons. Are you telling me you don't know what friggin' macarons are?"

"No, yeah," I say after a very long pause. "Of course I know. O-obviously."

My eyes focus on the views.

"TWENTY-SIX THOUSAND VIEWS?" I scream.

"So weird, right?"

"Dude," I say supportingly.

I sheepishly look at the table, then at her. I'm about to ask her.

"So," I say. "Do you use other things? Like Insta. Or something."

"You asking my handle?"

"A little. I mean, yeah."

She smiles. "Take my number instead." She grabs my phone to type it in.

"Now I'm super curious."

"Okay," she says. "Don't say I didn't warn you." She types in her Instagram handle. Thousands of followers. I scroll. The photos are nice—sunsets, close-up of flour, those burger pastries. More baked items. Her grandmother. Another sunset. Then I let out an audible gasp as

I see gaps of weeks, months in her feed. I tap the top and zoom up to see not even a single story today or yesterday, or the day, week before.

"Dude," I say.

She nods.

"How do you have so many followers when you don't post that much? What's your problem with Instagram?"

"Same problem I got with YouTube. It's like this. You're living your life. You're happy. You're sad. You're lazy. Whatevs. You're living it. You get on Instagram. Or YouTube. Or Twitter. Or TikTok. You stop living your life. Now you're living your life for likes. Getting all upset 'cos your life don't look like the bullshit other people are posting. Getting all kinds of stress for a fucking heart."

"What a load of shit," I say. She makes a good point, but on the other hand, if I had influencer-level views, I would peddle it all. "Hi guys, so a lot of you have been asking what toothpaste I use to get my teeth so shiny. It's manjan, motherfuckers." One night a year people recognize me at the Snollygoster Soiree as screaming guy with guitar. Other than that I don't have much social media clout. Sunny G, Influencer has a nice ring to it. Her whole "I've seen your feed" thing, citing very specific trends in my posting habits is not something I expected.

"It's been three years since Niam Tais died and there's just this space that's always going to be empty."

I say nothing this time.

"You know, I don't know if she even liked any of the pastries." Mindii laughs. "She was always a good sport, though. And loved hamming it up for the camera."

I smile. "Your parents own a bakery?"

Mindii nods. We spot some makeshift boxes near some trees with a plastic table next to it and we sit down. She lays out all the food on the table, slowly opening up each container. She pours some tiger bite sauce over her sausage. I do the same as she sips from her boba and raises an eyebrow at me. The provided plastic butter knife is definitely not strong enough to cut into the sausage. I give up and just bite into it. The juices explode all over the box as I take several ravenous bites. Mindii is eating her food delicately, pausing to take sips of boba every few minutes. She waves at The Dude as my eyes immediately start to water, my tongue is on fire, my entire body set ablaze. I take some huge gasps, like a fish trying to breathe on land. I look pleadingly at her. I can't tell if I'm dying from the sausage or the tiger bite sauce. Is it both? How many Thai chilies did I just inhale?

Mindii gives me some of her boba as The Dude walks on over.

"Oh," he says in full gloat mode. "Now you want the boba. What happened to I-am-the-Bionic-Punjabi-Man? I already prepped your boba."

"Oh my days," I sputter, steam escaping my eyes.

"Is that an expression?" he says.

"It is." I take a deep breath. "In." I take another deep breath. "Petrichor." The Dude places the extra boba on the table.

"And that's why it's called tsov tom," he says as he goes back to his food truck.

"It is pretty spicy," she says.

"I can usually handle . . ." I say, and take a massive gulp. "Who am I kidding? I can't handle anything spicy," I admit. "Wait, what's jaw the thaw?" I say, approximating what I think The Dude just said.

"Tsov tom," Mindii repeats, which sounds similar to what I just said, but she says it with much more musicality, almost no breaks. Kinda like jawd'jaw, but much prettier. I guess not that similar then. "It means tiger bite."

"The name of the hot sauce that almost ended my life?" I say, confused.

"Tigers, for some reason, are like really evil in Hmong folktales," Mindii says. "My niam tais used to tell me all kinds of stories, some scary, some very pointed that involved a lazy granddaughter, who would talk back, and the girl would get bitten by a tiger and die or become a spirit or something. I don't know how legit most of her stories are," Mindii lets out a laugh. "So basically," she continues," If you're a dumbass and go up to a tiger, you're gonna get bit."

"So not really like going up to The Dude and calling him a bottle of Tabasco then?" I say.

"You should totally try that. Nobody eats Hmong sausage the way your maniac-ass did. We go easy on the sauce. It was pretty entertaining though. I just wanted to see your head explode a little. Not completely. Here, have some more purple sticky rice," she says. I scarf the entire plate down, sausages, sticky rice, and all, cut with sips of boba.

"So?" Mindii says.

"It hurts less," I say as I swallow the last few pieces of sausage. "And I can feel my face again."

"A good sign."

"Holy shit." I don't believe I didn't even take a photo of the food. I quickly take out my phone.

"Addict," she says.

"I'm not a fucking addict," I say, putting away the phone and locking eyes with her. She looks like I just slapped her.

I look away. "Look, I'm sorry. My brother is. Was. An addict. Well, an al-alcoholic."

I feel a rush of blood go to my head as the word is out there. Things are weird now. You can't go back to normal after a word like that is out. Can you?

"I'm sorry. I should have chosen my words more carefuller," she says.

She smiles.

"Carefuller," she repeats, and laughs.

I laugh too. She grabs the paper plates and struts on over to the trash to throw them away.

"C'mon," she says, pointing across the empty grounds. "Something I wanna show you."

I don't move for a second because this is really weird territory. The awkward phase in my house lasts at least a couple hours and as long as, well, I guess we're still in the awkward phase.

We're on the other side of the food truck, on the grounds of the makhi mandi. We stop at a random spot, empty, dark, unmarked.

"Our stalls," she says.

"Wait, did you say stalls?"

"Yeah," Mindii says. "One is me and my parents. Baked goods. Croissants and stuff. The other one is me and my niam tais. Was."

"What did you sell?"

"Handmade jewelry. And two kinds of paj ntaub. The flower cloth and story cloth."

I nod.

"We embroider the flower cloth on all kinds of stuff. Paj ntaub jeans and shirts are our hot sellers. Niam Tais used to make the story cloth in the refugee camps. So she kept doing that here too out of habit or something, or maybe the money. A couple days before she died, that's what she was in the middle of doing."

We let the moment sit.

"What kind of designs for the flower cloth?" I ask.

"All kinds. I don't even know what some of them look like in real life, but I can stitch them. Like the nplooj sua leaf or the kalia, a caterpillar cocoon."

"What happens next?"

"That's a question for tomorrow," Mindii says.

"What happens tomorrow?"

She doesn't say anything.

I feel a sharpness in my chest.

"It's been three years since my niam tais died and I still get upset and angry about her death. I can't even imagine you losing your brother to a disease."

"I guess," I say. "But he chose to put that in his body."

"I know you're angry and hurting," Mindii says. "But he probably had all that pain too."

I look away and don't respond.

"You ever talk to your grandma like she's still there?" I say. "I talk to my brother sometimes. Mostly yell at him. Not him exactly. His words and drawings in his notebook. Sometimes it'll just be me in the garden yelling at the rose-bush like I've been sipping the cactus juice."

She lets out a squeal. Cactus juice is a reference from *Last Airbender* I didn't realize I'd used. Friggin' Goldy. I'm surprised I'm telling another human being all this information.

"We argue about a lot of things, but traditional Hmong belief is that everyone's got three souls. One gets reincarnated, one watches over us to protect us, and another goes to the spiritual realm. That's why I love *Last Airbender* the TV series so much. It"—she pauses—"speaks to my souls."

I groan at the cheesiness. She smiles.

"I talk to my niam tais all the time. Maybe your brother's spirit is in that garden or the notebook. I don't know how it works. I'm not a shaman or some scholar. What do you think happens after a person's soul leaves?" Mindii asks.

"Oh. Uh. Um. Well. Sikhs believe it's just a part of the soul's journey toward whatever happens next. The physical body is just a temporary home for the soul. That it's nothing to be sad about, it's a celebration," I say like I'm reading from a PowerPoint.

"Yeah. But what do you think?"

"I don't know," I admit. "You?"

"I don't know either," she says.

I look around. In the morning the market will be full of life, but for now this place is just a vast emptiness.

Mindii and I stare into space for a few more minutes. Then she starts walking quietly back toward the motorcycle, our shadows playing as I follow.

"What does *Mindii* mean, anyway?" I say, wanting to get out of my thoughts.

"Guess."

"Mindy Kaling?" I say.

"You think my Hmong parents named me after an Indian comedian?"

"Could be." I take out my phone and look it up. "A freshwater pipefish. Found in coastal rivers and mangrove estuaries. Eats small crustaceans. Okay, that sounds more like it."

"Your first guess was closer," she says. "It's from a show with Robin Williams from the late '70s called *Mork and Mindy*. They used to watch it when they first moved here and I guess liked it so much, they named me after the character." She shrugs. "I think they just wanted a first name that sounded white, which they thought would bypass all racism, and *Mork and Mindy* just happened to be on."

I laugh.

"Yeah, sometimes things aren't that deep. Maybe my parents just looked outside, saw it was Sunny and that's how they named me."

"You could have been named Cloudy with a Chance of Rain Gill. That would suck," Mindii says.

"That's a mouthful. It's funny to me when parents name their kids white names, like some racist is about to say some racist-ass shit to me and then b-b-be like, hold the fucking phone, I apologize my fellow White. Here are the privileges we owe you."

Now Mindii laughs.

"Hang on, why's your name spelled with two *i*'s at the end, though?"

She shrugs.

"Probably because English spelling is super inconsistent with limited vowels. Hmong parents especially love extra vowels. I can see my parents thinking putting the two *i*'s at the end was making it clearer for white people instead of more confusing. I love it, though. Wouldn't change it for anyone."

"Yeah, I love how *Dafydd* is spelled. Much better than boring ole *David.*

"You ever think," I say, looking up at the night sky. "Your whole life would be so much more different if your parents . . ." I pause to look at her. "Had named you Mork."

Mindii lets out a snigger.

"Oh, boy. Mork Vang."

"My actual name is Sh-Shamsher. Shamsher S-Singh."

"It sounds so majestic."

"It means brave as a lion," I say sheepishly. "But I've always been just Sunny. I mean, look at me. I'm no lion. They should have just named me Freshwater Fish."

Mindii looks right at me.

"Don't underestimate fish. They may not have vocal cords, but they can communicate just fine with grunts and growls and hissing. Your name is your name. You don't owe anyone anything. Niam Tais was really irritated when my parents named me Mindii. She just thought, 'This doesn't sound Hmong, doesn't sound Lao. It's a nothing name.'"

Don't ruin this moment by opening your mouth.

I open my mouth.

"It's not a nothing name. It's a . . . uh, something name."

"Corn. Ball," she says.

"It's nice," I say. "Being real . . . with . . . uh . . . y-you."

I watch the color in her cheeks turn red.

I made her blush.

I did not ruin the moment.

CHAPTER 9

A FINE TIME FOR A ROLLER DISCO QUIZ

It's my turn to choose the next rash decision and a sense of excitement comes over me, like it's not even noon and someone just baked me a decadent chocolate cake. It quickly turns to dread because this hypothetical baker just dropped my hypothetical cake, but there's nothing hypothetical about my anger. We've barely started and I'm already out of ideas.

"To th-the highway!" I say grandiosely, a ploy to buy some time as Mindii starts the engine. Despite this sturdy helmet, the wind is blowing a lot of hot air into my face; sweat pools at my neck and back. Nerves. I see the exit for Ashlan and tap her shoulder, then mutter expletives at myself inside the confines of my helmet and loud fluttering wind at this decision. Ngozi's cousin's roller rink engagement party. That's where my brain is taking us. This is going to be awkward. I don't even roller-skate.

We park in front of a boxy beige building. Mindii pulls off her helmet and peers into the side mirror of the motorcycle, adjusting her hair so the large hoop earrings are fully visible. I keep looking at her face, fascinated by the way she carries herself. Why am I looking at her face? Am I looking at her face? Yes. Yes. I sure am. I quickly pull my face down to the other mirror and adjust my . . . uh . . . . Dafydd's beard. Angling. Re-angling. Angling again. I really wish I'd spent more time on it: used a different type of wool, changed up my crochet pattern for a more realistic look.

I miss my actual beard, even if it was much too short to angle, let alone re-angle even if I wanted to. Goldy spent so much time and money using overly expensive beard oil, beard shampoo, conditioner. Even had special mustache and beard brushes. A hundred bucks he named his beard. Some Sikh warrior. If he had been alive during any of the historical periods where Sikhs were fighting off powerful empires like the Mughals or the harami British, Goldy would have missed the entire battle because of his complicated beard-grooming regimen. Would have come onto the battlefield in his tie-dye dastaar and twirled-up mustache being all, "Bole So . . . where everyone at?"

Papa used to have an elaborate routine once a week, on Saturday morning: putting mehndi on his beard, which turned all his grays a bright orange. Like that was somehow better than leaving the beard alone. But he hasn't had that routine since Goldy's death, so it's all gray now anyway.

Despite not doing as much drama as these two fashion

models, I always felt a sense of pride walking down the street with my beard. Now it's like I'm disconnected from my people.

"Hair behind the ears like this, or like this?" She moves the hair falling over her ears into different positions as we start walking.

Oh God. This is one of those situations where I wish I could just blurt out the first thing that comes to mind. But there are a thousand thoughts already flooding my brain. Option 1: If the hair is behind her ears, the earrings are visible, but her ears will stick out. Option 2: If the hair is in front of the ears, then it looks fine, but no earring visibility. Wait, how long ago did she ask that question? Hasn't been over a minute, has it?

"I suppose what it all boils down to . . . is your r-relationship with your ears," I say, choosing my words with care. "But irregardless, your ears look c-c-cute." I pause to think about my use of *irregardless*.

I feel my face go warm as I watch Mindii burst out laughing, reckless and loud.

"Thanks, cute nerd," she says.

I let out a giggle. Like a full-on giggle. Definitely not on purpose. And strangely I don't feel the need to abruptly stop or cover my mouth or deepen my voice, expand my chest, and pretend that sound never came from my body. Not about to wear a T-shirt that says *I am Sunny Giggler,* but it feels good not having to pretend. Only person who calls me cute on a semi-regular basis is Ngozi, and it's more like, "Oh, you think you're so cute. Well, you're about to die," when we'd play video games together.

Me and Mindii head over to the entrance to the roller rink. Such a fancy term for an enclosure. Roller coop. Roller cage. That's what they should call it. I can't say I've ever had the desire to fasten wheels onto my shoes and hurtle toward my death.

Until tonight, that is, because right now I'm Rash Decision Sunny. Yep, gonna put on some skates and ride around in circles hurtling forward at unsafe speeds.

Any minute now.

This is going to be so embarrassing if they don't let us enter. Ngozi is going to be surprised to see me, that's for damn sure.

"You know, for someone named Sunny, you have a very dour face right now," Mindii says, giving me a gentle push on the shoulder as we make our way toward the entrance.

I gasp with fake outrage.

There are balloons tied to the doors, the banner disappearing into the darkness. Our shadows look tall and ghoulish.

"If this is a kid's birthday party, the cake better have rainbow sprinkles."

"If it doesn't?" I say.

"Well." Mindii pauses to think. "I'm gonna have to cut a bitch," she says, and starts walking inside.

"Sounds reasonable," I say, following behind.

There is an overdressed woman sitting on a plastic chair who I immediately recognize as Auntie Iyabo. Only reason I know her name is because she's Ngozi's actual auntie—her dad's sister, as opposed to the countless unrelated older Nigerian and Ghanaian women she calls auntie as a sign of respect. Punjabis make it less confusing because we have super-specific words. Like your dad's sister is bhua vs. mom's sister is massi, so anyone we call auntie is definitely not related.

Auntie Iyabo's complexion is a gorgeous dark cedar. She raises her eyebrows and distractedly waves a hand at us. She doesn't recognize me. Because I'm Dafydd? Before I can mention my name, she booms, "Who are you?" Her accent sounds like the bass of a heavy drum, every letter enunciated. I used to think there couldn't possibly be Nigerian stutterers because of how all of Ngozi's family spoke, enunciating every letter with such confidence.

So one day I asked Siri and found a video for the Nairaland Home for Stammerers based out of Lagos after a whole series of awful clips featuring stuttering preachers as the butt of the joke. I looked up Indian stuttering foundations too and finally saw brown people who stuttered and I felt so seen. It was reassuring to see there were people everywhere like me, and that I'm not broken. This is just a part of me.

Auntie Iyabo looks very distraught in our direction.

"You are very late. You missed the opening prayer and presentation of the kola nut!"

"Oh," I say, attempting to convey I understand the gravity. Auntie Iyabo stops to inspect the Hmong embroidery on Mindii's dress and points with her lips to indicate approval. Then she examines me in my Dafydd cosplay.

"I'm S-S . . ."

"Sunny. It's you under all this drama, ehhhnnn? Why you no dey say?" Auntie Iyabo blares at me like a siren, lightly peppering in Nigerian English. She pulls my face down and looks at me. I avert her eyes and she doesn't say anything else about it, even though I know she knows what I've done.

"Hi. I'm Mindii," Mindii says. "I love the colors for your headwrap," she says. Auntie Iyabo clears her throat as she studies us both. The colors are bright purple and different shades of green, a galaxy of geometric shapes. A couple other aunties—not related to Ngozi—walk over to where we are, a beautiful array of colors and large hats. Ngozi's mom and some more aunties huddle around.

"Ankara is what we Nigerians call it," Auntie Iyabo says.

"We call it so many things," one of the other aunties adds. "Swahili people in Tanzania and Zambia call it kanga and kitenge. But these are all a little different. Different materials sometimes."

Ngozi is gliding toward us on her roller skates.

"We call it kente in my country. Ghana," Ngozi's mom says. "Good to see you, Sunny."

Mindii gives Ngozi a hug like they haven't seen each other in years. Ngozi looks at me quizzically. I half smile as I realize I've surprised her with my fucking rashness. I quickly stop smiling to give her the impression this is just who I am. Sunny No-Smile Full-of-Surprises Gill.

"Your Dafydd is fire," she whispers, and involuntarily I light up.

"Ghanaians were making hand-printed Bogolanfini thousands of years before anyone showed up," Ngozi's mom adds. "We had the largest empire in all of—"

"No, Mali had the largest empire," another auntie interrupts.

"Well, Uganda created barkcloth, the first clothing of humans everywhere," another auntie says. "All from the Mutaba tree."

"I mean it's all Africa," they concede.

"But," Auntie Iyabo says. "All this batik-batik comes from us Yoruba people before anyone was calling it batik or whatever."

"I thought it came from Indonesia," I whisper to Ngozi.

"I don't know," Ngozi whispers back. "You get into it."

"Yoruba people," the auntie continues. "Adire. That's the origin of all this tie-dye nonsense. Now it is kampala wax resist this and kampala wax resist that."

Ngozi senses a slight pause and takes the opportunity to lead us away from the Auntie Squad.

"Make sure you eat and vote," Auntie Iyabo says. "There's Nigerian jollof rice and a lot of other not-as-good jollof rice. Your choice." Ngozi's mom and the other women chime in immediately and in the midst of it, Ngozi says, "Okay, I'll show them where it is," which nobody is listening to anyway. She quickly leads us away.

In the middle of the roller rink there is a booth with a big colorful banner. DJ Lord Spit Fire. Balloons and streamers with the colors of the pan-African flag—green, yellow, and black—are fluttering away.

"Another cousin," Ngozi says, casually pointing at the DJ with her lips. "He's not very good, but he's cheap and my aunties think the Lord part means he's religious and not just into himself.

"I'm gonna get to the rink. Eat some jollof and vote or it's my head. Don't eat too much, though. The dance is starting in like ten minutes. The skates are over there." She points near the other end of the rink. She glides off.

There are four tables holding an endless spread of foil-covered baking dishes. Fragrant moin-moin, goat meat stew, fried plantain, salad with four bottles of ranch next to it, the unmistakable aroma of Peppa soup, and the stars of the show: different types of jollof rice with a score card underneath and five kids manning the booth presumably to make sure no corruption takes place.

Enormous black trash bags dangle off the side of each table. From experience I know they're filled with ice, sodas, waters, and beer. I found that out the embarrassing way a couple years ago when I threw a dirty plate into one. I know, throwing trash into a trash bag? Why would I do that?

I am about to put some of the goat meat into a bowl and it's snatched by one of the kids. She looks like she's about ten. "You trying to get us killed?" she says. The other kids are lined up behind the table.

"A war was fought because of jollof rice. Those aunties back there," a boy around the same age says, quickly glancing behind us, "will make moi-moi out of us if they think there is any shady business happening with the votes."

Each of them measures out a small portion of the reddish-orange competition-ready jollof rice into bowls, before placing them in front of us. They watch us as we take a bite into each. Good jollof rice is supposed to be able to stand on its own. We whisper our answer to the kids in absolute secrecy, then we fill up our bowls moderately and sit down at a table.

"Nigerian jollof rice all the way. It has kind of a smoky flavor. Maybe it's just the way this one was cooked. Rice tastes like long-grain, so the flavors really seep through." Mindii blows on a spoonful and takes a big bite.

"They're b-both delicious," I say. "Keep this on the DL, but I kinda p-p-prefer the Gh-Gh-Ghanaian jollof rice because they use basmati and it's more stew-like. The basmati is kinda the deciding factor for me. Half of Ngozi's family would disown me if that information was revealed," I say.

"I can see how an actual war could be fought over this," she says.

We lap up the moi-moi and fried plantains, resisting the urge to get seconds, so we can go make fools of ourselves on the skating rink. Mindii better not be some Olympic level roller skater. We walk over to the counter to get our skates and sit at a bench to unlace. Mindii takes off her combat boots easily. With great difficulty I take off my gigantic black low-heeled boots, which me and Ngozi worked on broguing up with all kinds of leather uppers and serration. After lacing up, I stand up, and instantly lose my balance. I grab the railing and manage to stay upright. This is a great fucking start.

Mindii's still sitting. "It's easy. Just stand tall, bend your knees a little, and keep your feet like fifteen point six inches apart. That's the average length for shoulder-width."

"I don't have an inchie-tape to measure my foot distance!"

"A what?"

"An inchie-tape. You know, to measure fabric and things."

"A measuring tape?"

"Inchie-tape," I say defiantly.

Mindii tries to conceal her laughter at the word and my activities involving it.

"Why aren't you demonstrating?" I ask, petulant.

"Because I only skate when it's time to destroy my enemies. Not to offer tutorials on standing. Now close your eyes. Imagine standing in place."

"Well, I don't have to imagine it," I say, leaning on the banister. "I am standing in place."

"And someone," she says, "gives you a light push." She stands up and moves toward me, loses her balance, her hands grasp at my elbows, her skates tangle with mine, and we both topple, slamming into the wall and onto the carpeted floor in a pile of limbs. We claw our way back up.

"After they give you a light push, you move your feet to regain balance," she finishes, her breath lifting my hair.

"You don't know how to skate," I say, going from steaming mad to laughing hysterically. "Unbelievable."

"I understand the theory of it well. Like really well."

Perilously, we skate-walk-grab-objects-and-people until we get next to the DJ booth.

The couple, whose engagement party we're crashing—Ngozi's cousin, Nneka, and her fiancé—are standing next to each other laughing as confetti is being thrown over them by the DJ. Nneka is wearing a bright pink feathery dress, a dazzling green circular fan-tied gele, a white sash with the words *IFE MI* in bold colors. I'm guessing it means "fiancée" since nobody else is wearing one. There are a lot of couples and singles and a mix of people. Some of the kids around our age look like they may potentially also have plans for the Snollygoster Soiree. They're in cosplay that could be from the world of Petrichor, but then again, they could be some Middle Earth elf or cosplaying as one of the Knights of the Round Table. Some are definitely dressed for other parties, though.

Ngozi wheels herself expertly to where we are precariously parked near the wall. There is some catchy Afrobeats music playing by Burna Boy. DJ Lord Spit Fire abruptly cuts the music and calls everyone participating in the final trivia hour to the floor. He goes over the rules and riles everyone up by playing a few seconds of a song by someone named Sister Deborah where she sings about the superiority of Ghanaian jollof rice. Ngozi laughs.

"The rules are easy," he says, pausing dramatically, maintaining eye contact with someone for a solid three seconds before loudly saying, "First of all, do not fall, or you will be disqualified. Only two people to a team." He breathes. "Second of all, there will be three rounds. The first you will hear a song played backwards and will have five seconds to name the tune, the second will be jollof rice, and the third you will sing. Ehhn? Is it clear?" He looks around the room like a very disappointed teacher.

Everyone nods. I look over at Ngozi and Mindii and we all share a conspiratorial moment. Ngozi goes off with a girl standing next to her. The instructions were not very thorough, but we're handed a marker and a whiteboard to write our team name.

"So what's our team name?" Mindii asks.

"I'm just trying not to die, man," I say, still holding the railing in a death grip. "The Cool Wizards? You choose. I can't be punny and maintain my balance at the same time."

"Cool Wizards? Nope. Not doing magical patriarchy tonight." She scribbles something on the board and places the placard's string over my head. Then she almost knocks me over again—and puts on her own placard.

I look down at the whiteboard and groan. If I wipe out tonight, it will be with *My Heffalumps Bring All the Boys to the Yard* scrawled across my chest.

Ngozi is blazing across the rink. Her team name blurs past us. "It's Bramble Time!" Clever. The lights dim, a loud siren goes off, and DJ Lord Spit Fire lays down some fiery beats over a familiar Afrobeats tune with the

relaxing yet fast rhythms of heavy percussion and auto-
tune. I recognize it immediately because it was Ngozi's
jam every single day for like two weeks when it came out
a few years ago. "Maradona" by Niniola. But just 'cos I
know it, doesn't mean I can sing it, or even pronounce
it. It's super fast and heavy on Nigerian English. Me and
Mindii start skating.

We are mumbling along incoherently to the Nigerian
slang. The music cuts off and everyone scrambles to get
to the wall, which we are thankfully close to anyway. Each
group starts singing and it gets to us and the only lyrics
I can think of are the hook. "O, Maradona!" I sing, and
Mindii follows my lead, totally off-key, but damn what
commitment. Ngozi belly laughs from across the rink. We
keep going, really belting out "Oo, Maradona, Maradona
mi," until the DJ takes pity on us and gets to the next
group, who fumble the lyrics and are sent out of the rink.
Round two, the jollof rice challenge begins. He plays the
same jollof rice song from the beginning, which gets everyone in the fighting spirit.

The first question: "What were the repercussions to
Nigeria's information minister, Lai Mohammed, when he
accidentally called Senegal's jollof rice the best?" Everyone
starts booing and stomping their skates on the floor. We
join in the booing. A sea of incorrect answers follows. Our
response is that he had to apologize. Ngozi's cousin and

her fiancé have the correct answer: "He was forced to resign because Nigerians were PISSED." Everyone belly laughs.

More skating with one of Ngozi's favorite Afrobeats songs because she has a crush on the singer—Simi. The song "Joromi" plays, all about a girl who is friend-zoned and does everything she can to get this dude named Joromi to notice her. I squeal as we hear it and desperately want to tell Mindii that the friend zone is fucking REAL, but opt to wave my hands like a fool at Ngozi, who waves back like an even bigger fool. The DJ reads the next question. "When was the only time Ghanaians and Nigerians came together on the topic of jollof rice?"

"F-fuck! I know the answer!" I scream as everyone else is perplexed and murmurs of "This must be a trick question" are heard. I quickly write down the answer and DJ Lord Spit Fire squints to read my whiteboard.

"Go ahead. Read it," he says to me, and brings the microphone to us.

My forehead is sweaty from blanking out. The microphone is inches from my mouth. I can feel a stutter storm rising. "You can read it," I say to Mindii.

"No," she says, gently touching my hand. "You're fine."

I take a breath.

"The D-Demon Ch-Chef Jamie Oliver!" I say.

"Two points to Team My Heffalumps Bring All the Boys to the Yard!" DJ Lord Spit Fire says.

Everyone roars with laughter and anger swells again as they remember the ingredients he used.

I look at Ngozi quizzically. She didn't write down the answer? She vented for an entire three weeks about him using exactly one deseeded Scotch bonnet pepper, and cherry tomatoes still on the vine, wrote countless posts with the hashtag #jollofgate. I was so stressed I was going to accidentally use a word like parsley or lemon wedge and she was going to destroy me.

Ngozi laughs.

Me and Mindii yell triumphantly as the scoreboard goes to two points; we're still screaming and falling over each other, whooping and hollering as we make our way toward the safety of carpeted grounds. We realize everyone is staring at us, not quite in the way crowds stare when someone wins a championship. We literally just answered one question correctly. The game is still going on and we definitely lost. But I don't care. I look at Mindii and she is glowing and sweaty, just like me.

When the competition is actually over ten minutes or so later, Ngozi rolls over to us.

"Wow," she says, smiling. "I've never seen you completely off your trolley like this, Sunny. I like it!"

I beam.

"What are we doing next?" Mindii says.

"I have to help tidy up and do evening prayers. And

saying goodbye to everyone takes longer than the actual party."

We both suck our teeth at the situation and smile. "Hey, do you have my guitar for the gig at Snollygoster Soiree?"

Ngozi turns to me. "Yeah, of course. It's in the usual place."

The Bramble Van.

Ngozi and Mindii are laughing when I find them after returning our skates.

"Fiery wit and the strength of a thousand elephant-toads? Arr, that's me yerr talking about arrite," I say, channeling Dafydd.

"You sound like a fucking pirate," Ngozi says.

"Arrr do not," I say. Sounding very much like a pirate.

"You better not put on that ridiculous Dafydd accent during our show."

She laughs, and it's like a small miracle. It's been a while since Ngozi and I have shared a normal moment, one not weighed by the threat of our friendship getting all weird after she leaves for college.

It's good to have my friend back. Even if it's just for now.

CHAPTER 10

A VERY FRENCH BAKERY

We arrive in North Fresno, which is usually my favorite part of the city because there aren't any surprises. It's a series of strip malls with all the chain stores, the Cineplex, fast-food joints, and hella parking, so no need to parallel park or find change for the meter. Best of all, Blackstone Avenue doesn't suddenly turn into a one-way street like it does downtown.

We are standing outside the darkened window of a locked storefront in the middle of a nondescript strip mall. There's a fancy script-y font etched into the window, but it's too dark to see what it says.

"Shall I find a brick to smash through the window?" I'm only half joking. Is this where my rash decisions take an illegal turn and I end up in jail?

"I would be very impressed if you were able to find a loose brick around here," Mindii says. "And my parents might be a little pissed if you smashed our windows." She takes out a key and opens the door to the place we're casing.

Her store.

She turns on the lights and hits a few buttons to switch off the alarm. It smells of bread. It's a beautifully decorated interior strung with fairy lights, chalkboard signs serving as the menu, and five small wrought-iron tables. But the centerpiece is a glass cabinet filled with brightly colored pastel pastries. There is a gigantic coffee machine behind the counter and a row of porcelain cups with gold handles.

"You're the first boy I've brought here."

I try to control myself to no avail. My face erupts in a large gleeful grin. I wonder what this face looks like with an enormous grin. It probably looks terrible, like a wrinkly foot in the bath, all my blemishes magnified. I blow air onto my blond streak to move it out of my eyes.

"You're also the first boy I've ever known who doesn't know what a macaron or a macaroon is," she says.

I try to think of a rebuttal, but I'm distracted by all the vibrant colors in the glass cabinets.

"What do you want?" she says, sliding behind the counter, pulling a frilly apron over her brambleberry dress. She waves her arms over the cabinet like one of those spokesmodels from *The Price Is Right,* which Biji watches every day, even though she doesn't really understand English. "I mean, what may I get you?"

"I'll have one of those little b-burger-pastry things."

Mindii lets out a mock sigh of exasperation.

"Is that a buffalo . . . m-macaron?" I say.

"A sky bison," Mindii says.

"Of course. A-a-appa."

"Yep, they're macarons," she says. I peer closer and recognize the blended *Last Airbender* animals. She stops and moves to a different part of the glass cabinet to take out a blob of a cookie topped with what looks like shredded coconut. "And this," she says, enunciating dramatically, "is a macaroon." Mindii places it on the counter and turns it so I can examine its golden brown crunchiness.

It doesn't look dangerous. I take a bite. "This is very dense," I say as I sink my teeth into a sweet crusted cluster of coconut, and place it back down into the tiny plate.

"It's fine. Not my favorite either," Mindii says.

She moves back to the burger pastries. "Macaroons don't take as much effort as macarons. The usual ingredients: vanilla extract, salt, almond extract, one egg white, unsweetened coconut. Triangle, great big dollop, dip it in chocolate. Done. Whatever."

She slides the cabinet door. "Macarons"—she gestures at the whole pastry case while looking straight at me—"much prettier and they need to be shaped and gotta be even. They're basically meringue-style French cookies." Mindii lays a pink catgator macaron onto a napkin on the counter.

It looks like the frou-frou version of cream-filled sandwich cookies. She lays out a few more, shaped like animals from the TV series: a dragon-moose, aardvark-sloth, Flopsie the goat-gorilla.

The designs are so completely her. I can see Mindii's personality coming alive through these hybrid animals from *Last Airbender*.

"These. Are. Fire," I say, peering closely at the animal macarons.

Mindii grins wide. She grabs my hand and makes me run my fingers across the top and bottom of the pink cat-gator one. "So smooth," I say.

"Goddamn right it is." Mindii slowly lets go of my hand to gesture wildly with both of her hands. "Like the top of Aang's head. See this?" She points at the ruffled edges just below the top. "They are called macaron feet. What flavor you want?"

I peer closely at the rainbow of choices she's laid out. Nothing is labeled.

"What flavor is Appa?"

"He's a complex sky bison. Rhubarb, banana, hint of matcha.

"Olive oil and lemon. Licorice. Yogurt and jasmine," she says, following my face from the other side of the glass.

"Do you have any normal flavors. Like chocolate?"

"We don't do that here."

I'm a little overwhelmed. I go with my instincts and look at an octopus-like macaron.

"Purple looks . . ." Don't say it. "C-cool."

"Taro it is. You picked my favorite. The pentapus."

"This is so artistic," I say, genuinely impressed at the level of detail. It has five eyes and five tentacles that evenly match on the other side with a thick filling in between. I don't know this creature, but it looks very . . . uh . . . pentapus-like.

"It's filled with lavender-taro-bacon ganache."

"Bacon? Nope." I back away from the counter, like this macaron might bite me. Which is entirely possible. Bacon and eggs sounds logical. Bacon with sugar? "Give me a moment to mentally prepare," I say, thoroughly flustered.

Mindii stands firm, holding out the tiny tentacled macaron, her tone strict but soothing, like she's trying to convince a toddler to eat broccoli. "Listen to me, Shamsher 'Sunny' Gill. You are going to try this lavender-taro-bacon ganache macaron."

I step back again. "I will not," I say, like an indignant white lady. "Where's the manager?"

"I am the manager, Karen." Mindii peers at me from behind the counter. "Also, you're not paying, so technically you're not a customer. You are, however, a costumer." She laughs at her incredibly terrible joke, and I start laughing too, involuntarily.

"Okay, let's do this." I run in place like I'm about to enter a grueling and much celebrated athletic competition involving a ball.

"The best macaron in the joint. See any cracks?" She smiles and plates it for me. "No! You motherfucking don't, because this is perfection."

She removes the apron and comes round to the same side I'm on. We both lean on the counter.

Mindii steps in close. She lifts the purple macaron to my mouth. I'm feeling a very peculiar kind of way about it. I'm being fed by a girl. Is this romantic? Ngozi wouldn't do this. Not to me. Another girl? Maybe. I take an awkward bite, crack through the top of the shell and the chewy, intensely rich, soft sugary interior hits all the taste buds. I giggle for the second time tonight as she takes the second bite, our cheeks almost touching. If I abruptly turned my head our lips would graze each other. My head remains steadfastly focused on the wall.

"This is delicious," I say, still staring at the wall.

"Doesn't the pentapus live in the sewers?" I say.

She smiles. "The sewers of Omashu."

I abruptly turn to look at her. Our lips don't graze, but damn are they close to each other. I suck in a breath and pause to finish chewing a tentacle.

"So," I say, my voice high-pitched. "What's the deal with the French bakery?"

She laughs and wipes the crumbs off her face. "That's the most creative way of asking where I'm from-from. My mom grew up in France, where she fell in love with baking. Mom's a Green Hmong, Dad's a White Hmong. Which makes me . . ."

"A light green Hmong?"

She laughs.

"I don't see color," I say. "Kinda racist you noticed your parents are white and green."

She laughs again.

The macaron is all finished. I slowly shuffle my feet and we stand up straight. She throws the paper plate away.

"So," I say. "What's happening tomorrow?"

"There would have been a time for such a word," Mindii says, a little ominously.

"What?" I say, more confused than usual.

"Tomorrow, and tomorrow, and tomorrow." Mindii's voice trembles with each utterance of the word. She's quoting something.

"Is that from *Last Airbender*?" I say.

"*Macbeth*, fool."

She smiles, her eyes distant.

"Tomorrow, the stall dies," she says matter-of-factly.

"The one you ran with your grandma?"

"Yeah. It's for an exciting reason," Mindii says, not sounding excited at all. "I'm leaving for ECB end of August."

"Ah. UCB," I say pretending to be whatevs about it. "Seems like everyone I know is going there." By everyone I mean Ngozi. And now, Mindii. It's not like I didn't know Ngozi was applying. After tenth grade, we barely had any classes together because she was taking gifted classes and AP this and AP that, all kinds of extracurriculars, while I was taking basic-ass classes and getting basic-ass grades. But we'd still hang out during lunch, or endlessly text each other about our ideas for the next song, or fanfiction we were writing, and spend hours on social discussing any and all things about the Jamie Snollygoster series.

My parents were so busy trying to figure out what the fuck to do with Goldy and the video store that they didn't have time to map out my life. Maybe they didn't know how to map out my life. So yeah, no. I didn't apply to any UC. Not even State. My only option is community college at this point and I haven't even applied for that yet. Of course Mindii is leaving. Of. Friggin'. Course.

"Not UCB," Mindii says. "ECB. Ecole de Boulangerie et de Patisserie de Paris."

My eyes widen at the way the French is rolling off her tongue, like it's been hiding there this whole time. I don't even know what it means.

"It's a baking and pastry school in Paris." Her tone sounds more resigned than excited.

"That's really . . . uh," I say, trying to come up with a

word that is the opposite of what I am feeling. "A ... uh ... a ... dream," I say like an amateur greeting card writer. "What happened to the bakery stall?"

"My siblings help out sometimes. And my parents got it on lock. But my niam tais's stall, nobody's got on lock. I've been running that for three years. And now it's just . . ." She trails off.

I'm about to say something, when Mindii perks up. "New rule," she says. "Let's not talk about tomorrow. It's so . . ."

"Boring?" I offer.

"Yeah. That," she says.

I nod, thankful she isn't going to make me talk about my stupid-ass plans to do nothing. ECB you say? Oh you mean Le ECB. I'm going to Le FCC. Oh you haven't heard? Le Fresno City Community College, only the most exclusive place ever.

"Wanna see a real paj ntaub?" Mindii says, grabbing my hand, not waiting for a response. My stomach flips, this weird energy works its way up through my hands and fingers. Familiar. Strange. "Step this way," she says, leading me toward a door on the other side of the counter. "For you and I must go on a journey if you wish to find out about this knowledge."

"*Alice in Wonderland?*" I say.

"Dante," she says.

"Wait. From the *Inferno*? As in a journey to hell? No thanks. I could just google *paj ntaub*," I say.

"Too fucking late. You've already begun seeking."

I raise an eyebrow. If she were a murderer, this would be a great place to dispose of a body. Her hand is still wrapped around mine.

We walk through the door that leads to another set of doors. "That's the kitchen," she says, pointing to an open room on the left with two enormous human-sized ovens. "Pantry," she says as we walk past another door that's locked. "This room," Mindii says, "is where I do my homework and stuff."

There is a brass knocker with a buzzer in the middle and the words *press for giggles* written on it. I press it and hear the muffled sounds of an old woman laughing.

"Love that sound," Mindii says. "It's Niam Tais from a recording I found of her during a family party."

"Such a joyous laugh," I say.

She presses it again. "The best."

We step inside the room. It's not as huge as the kitchen, but about the size of a small bedroom. It's cozy, decorated with lights, flower petals, a tiny window, and a shelf with extra pantry supplies. My eyes widen in mock terror as I see her doll collection on a small plastic table. It's a Hmong doll collection, but still. Yikes!

Mindii lifts up one of the dolls to show me.

"Did you make these?"

"I wish," Mindii says. "Neither did my niam tais. I buy a couple every year at Hmong New Year. Aren't they so cute?"

My eyes hover over the collection. *Cute* is not the word I would use. "This appliqué work on the placket is so detailed," I say. The dolls are six inches tall, with individualized Hmong outfits for men and women, impressively embroidered, adorned with various accessories like sashes and jewelry, the men with vests. Mindii snorts at my appropriate use of the word *placket*.

"Placket," she repeats.

"What's the difference between Green and White Hmong?" I say, looking at the medley of colors.

"It's complicated. Part of it is clothing. Green Hmong skirts are traditionally very colorful and White Hmong skirts are, well, white. But I don't really know because I've grown up with both cultures," Mindii says. "Some of it is also pronunciation. A lot of the clothing is provincial too." She picks up a doll. "This White Hmong dress from Sayaboury Province in Laos is a little different from this one." She picks up another doll. "This is also White Hmong, but from Xieng Khouang Province."

"So this placket." I pick up a doll with the placket on the upper left side. She snorts again. "What do you call it?" I say, irritated.

"Colorful flappy thing on left side of clothes."

"That's what you call it? Okay, so this flappy thing is on the side because of the region or Green Hmong or White Hmong?"

"Who knows? Maybe it's a Striped Hmong thing," she says. "Mostly we wear what looks good unless we're performing for Hmong New Year or something. At the end of the day, we're all Hmong."

"So, like pronunciation is different too?" I say.

"A little. Like the White Hmong pronunciation of grandmother is Niam Tais, which is what I use, but the Green Hmong pronunciation is Nam Tais. Not a huge difference, but there are other words that are like totally different."

"It sounds kinda like how some people pronounce *sneeze* 'chik' in one region of Punjab and 'nich' in another."

"Hmm." She considers. "We should do a TED Talk on linguistics."

"It'd be great," I say.

"My eyes hone in on a large tapestry on the wall, the reason we came to the back in the first place.

We put the dolls back and walk toward the story cloth.

"I was helping my niam tais to make this paj ntaub. It's incomplete," Mindii says. I get closer and see the beautiful colors of different embroidery thread to show landscape and people and a river I'm assuming is the Mekong. I could stand here for hours looking at all the details. "It shows her first husband and her in the fields planting, helping the Americans during the Secret War, then her husband's death, fleeing to Thailand, getting remarried. That's where it stops. I don't know how to finish it," Mindii says. "I don't know the details to finish the rest of the story, or how to embroider the rest."

"What is th-th-the Secret W-W-War? I've heard of it in passing from some Hmong friends, but . . . wait." I pause as a thought comes to me. "So is this what you sell at the stall?"

"Are you out of your mind?" Mindii says.

"Didn't you say Hmong started making these story cloths at the refugee camps?"

"Not these ones. Like shittier ones for white people to put up in their house and tell their dinner guests they got an authentic Hmong story cloth. Can you imagine some white missionary having such a private family history in their house?"

"Word," I say, taking it in. "So what's the Secret War?"

"I could talk your ear off for hours about this. You can google it."

"Can you give me the quick version?"

Mindii looks at me. "Okay. Typical American CIA bullshit. They're in the shit with the Vietnam War, so what do they do? They sneak around to Laos and use Hmong farmers and villagers with the help of General Vang Pao to fight for them against North Vietnam even though Laos is supposed to be neutral. There are still like eighty million unexploded mines in Laos thanks to America. They don't tell nobody nothing, media doesn't even know, it's kept that quiet, so when the Vietnam War ends, the CIA and Americans get out and leave the Pathet Lao to massacre Hmong by the thousands. And they keep the war a secret, which means we get no aid, no media coverage, and are just sitting ducks. Most Americans don't even know who the Hmong are let alone that we are part of American history. So eventually people like my niam tais risked everything to get to the refugee camps in Thailand, then risked everything again and started over in California and Minnesota. And like it's an oral tradition, so our stories are literally art, and once somebody is gone, that part of our culture is . . ." Mindii stops talking. I reach out my hand. She squeezes it and we let go.

"I can't imagine what it must be like for people to come from so far away, never being able to return home, and being like, this is it. This is where we'll start again," I say.

Our hands graze across the cloth. I'm in love with the intricate designs, the vibrant colors, the images of people making their way across a river. There's a ragged edge on one side.

"I kind of like it being unfinished," Mindii says.

I look at her intently.

I don't say anything, my eyes taking in all the details of the story cloth Mindii is working on, trying to unravel it, to understand.

I watch her hands running along the tapestry again. "This is different from other patterns I've seen," I say.

I can almost see Mindii and her grandma sitting in here together, weaving, sharing stories, laughing.

She takes out a mug from a small cabinet. It's wrapped in yarn, a familiar wavy pink-and-green pattern. I freak. "THAT'S MY TEA COZY!"

She smiles. "I thought it was cute."

"Okay. Cool. Cool. Cool."

I take out my phone and quickly look through her Instagram feed again, then look at my Loom the Fandom Instagram messages. Nothing.

"I didn't have a question. I just bought it directly on Etsy. I'm the VangsterWrapper. "

"You have an Etsy store?" I quickly scroll on down. And add her name to my favorites.

Her store has little poems.

"This is s–so cool. You sell poetry?"

"It was supposed to be me and Niam Tais. Some are her song poems. Some are on jewelry. I don't even know why I haven't closed it."

I'm not sure how to process this and try to mentally connect all the dots.

"You know, I remember you from Comic-Con too," I say. "I mean, I didn't recognize you at the time as Mindii Vang, the g-girl from my school. But I remember your cosplay."

"Yeah, my Sailor Moon cosplay took a while to make because of the bow," she says.

"N-nice try. I remember the conversation we had. I thought you were cosplaying the Borg from Star Trek because of all the cracks on your face and you let me have it."

Mindii chortles slightly. For the first time tonight, she is clearly taken aback.

"You don't remember who I was cosplaying, do you?" Mindii says.

"Puppet Zelda," I say triumphantly. "Your boyfriend was supposed to be Gandalf?"

"Ganondorf," Mindii says quietly.

"I just r-remember you were having a bad cosplay day and feeling sad and snappy that your armor was falling apart. And all it would t-take for me to help you was a needle, thread, scissors, and some spirit gum. I had all of it in m-my cosplay doctor kit. Wasn't even mad when you didn't say thanks and just took off. I'm a professional. It was t-t-totally fine."

"You weren't even a little mad?"

"I was fucking pissed. Used my good thread too. And half my spirit gum fixing your poorly joined together armor. You know spirit gum is like gold to a cosplayer? I'll send you an invoice."

She laughs. "Forgot about the boyfriend. He was a jerk. Or maybe I was the jerk, I don't know," Mindii says.

She pauses and clears her throat.

"Oh," I say. "Yeah, that motherfucker is the jerk."

It feels strange hearing Mindii use the word *boyfriend*. Hearing myself use the word. Boyfriend. It doesn't compute with the Mindii I've been getting to know.

"Everyone thought I was this terrible granddaughter, daughter, sister, auntie. Anything I was to anyone, they thought I was a terrible version of it. It was a couple days after Niam Tais had passed. I just didn't want to be at home with everyone expecting me to perform. Like be sad. I just wanted to get away, out of my body, out of my head."

I want to tell her I know what it's like, but can't find the words.

I nod my head.

"Can you say the line again?" she says. "The cosplay doctor one."

"Don't worry. I am a cosplay doctor."

"I know what I'm doing," she finishes.

I'm breathless.

I want to kiss her.

Just do it.

Do it.

Lean in.

I turn to face her.

CHAPTER 11

CURSE OF THE RED-BEAN DONUT

I can't believe I didn't kiss her. Her face was right there. The glow from the sign for Dhaliwal Gas is bright enough for me to write the couple rash decisions I've made so far. I lean on one of the pillars and angle my pen, a joyless impulse purchase from the dollar store. I wince as I look at Mindii's ruthless edits on the list of my first rash-ish decisions and quickly turn the page, the tip of the pen staining a fresh sheet of paper. I lift the pen back up. "Went to the makhi mandi and ate sausage," seems very reductive. So does "Then went roller skating."

I wish I understood this notebook. There's a pencil sketch of this thin dude wearing a plaid shirt and jeans. It's not a great sketch. I mean, it's a nice enough sketch with shadows and shit. I just don't understand it. There's a small smudge or something under his eye. In neat handwriting next to it, Goldy has written a poem. Another thing I didn't know about him. In romanized Punjabi, which is the most annoying thing to do to someone who knows

how to read the Gurmukhi Punjabi script because no matter how many times I read it, it still takes me five minutes
to slog through and connect the romanized sounds to the
actual sounds of Punjabi. I can't ask Mama or Papa or anyone to decode the poetry. Why can't I understand this? I
was breaking down sonnets written in iambic pentameter
when I was in third grade. I could recite the first stanza of
Heer by the time I was in sixth grade. I'm bigger than this
shit. All I've been able to decipher is it's something about
a bird who tries to fly and gets attracted by something
shiny on the floor. Then it dies. The fucking end. Profound
poetry by Goldy the Friggin' Poet.

Mindii is standing by the gas pump filling up. She looks
like the kind of person who would say "I'm hungry" while
driving around, then pull up to a random restaurant on
the side of the road to chow down. No hesitation. No
overanalyzing. No looking up endless incentivized reviews
for six hours, like I do just to say "Fuck this shit, I'm gonna
get a thousand-year-old hot dog from 7-Eleven for a dollar
ninety-nine."

I loudly and angrily close the book and put it back in
my pouch. I need to figure out how to write this and just
can't do it right now. Is there like a rash-decision-making
gene that I don't have? When I think about all the rash
decisions Goldy made it's mind-boggling. I don't know
when he began drinking or the moment he became an

alcoholic. There must have been a moment though, right? It can't be all of a sudden you take a drink and then that's it, you're an alcoholic. Even his death feels like a rash decision. He was sober for months before. There should just be one way to be an alcoholic. Then you can fix it. Punjabi songs always show alcoholics as being such happy drunks. Not like Goldy, drinking whiskey straight from the bottle in his bed, alone. My eyes start to water and I blink real hard to stop.

I can't even write these puny rash decisions by comparison: Had Hmong sausage. Went roller-skating. Why does it have to be perfect? If I feel I'm gonna stutter I can't just own it and say yep this is me, deal with it. Either I don't say anything at all and people think I'm quiet or shy or something, or I end up replacing words and become that weird dude. I wish I could be like Goldy and not give a flying pakora what people think.

An uncle comes outside to throw a couple small bags of trash into the dumpster. Every Punjabi dude around Papa's age who is not related to me is my "uncle," out of respect or whatever. It's hard to find a gas station or liquor store in Fresno that isn't Punjabi-owned. I'm trying to blend into the shadows and not make eye contact with this uncle, but it's inevitable.

He turns to look at me and I freeze. He freezes too. I realize I've probably confused him with my cosplay. I'm not sure how to unlock the gaze. Just turn my armored body and chain mail helmeted face away from him?

Mindii clasps her hands together and does a little bow.

"Sat Sri Akal," she yells, with pretty clear pronunciation. The uncle sees her and smiles. I clasp my hands and do the same thing. Not exactly the same. Maybe a little better, not that it's a contest. I get no smile, no love from this dude at all. He just glares at me, then walks back. I think he preferred it when he didn't have confirmation that I am Punjabi and Sikh enough to know SSA.

I bet he's going to be looking for the Punjabi-looking Dafydd who said hello to him in the gas station parking lot every time he goes anywhere with Punjabis, and will be looking for this figment at the gurdwara from now on. Maybe this moment will become the great enigma of his life. Like that book about the white dude and his incredibly boring search for a whale. "How do y-you know Sat Sri Akal?" I say to Mindii.

"Was it supposed to be a secret? I saw it in this really fun British soccer movie, *Bend It Like Beckham*. Super cute, starring Keira Knightley and Parminder Nagra before they blew up."

"Yeah," I say. "I know the movie. My parents own a video store."

"What does *Sat Sri Akal* mean?" she asks. "I'm guessing it's not just *Hi there*."

Without even pausing I say, "The full phrase is *Jo Bole So Nihaal, Sat Sri Akal*," and let out a laugh. This is not hardwired information. I only know it because my brother loved researching everything too. Like when we'd recite prayers, he needed to look up the etymology of a word in one of the fifteen Sikhi apps on his phone, like Shabad Khosh, or in an actual book he had special ordered online. Then he'd need to explain it to me. It would make daily recitations take forever. One time he looked up *Sat Sri Akal* when I attempted to argue it was pronounced Sas-rikaaaal, like it was one word instead of three, and said, "Okay, smart guy, what does it mean then?" He knew I was wrong, but it annoyed him that he was stumped and couldn't articulate the meaning.

"It's a jakara—a battle cry—and the whole phrase roughly means awesomeness. Like, I guess, h-happiness and stuff will be . . . uh . . . b-b-be-bequeathed." I pause, relishing my use of the word *bequeathed*. "To the person who yells out 'The Timeless Eternal Being is the Truth.'"

"So. Not *Hi there*, then?" Mindii says. She looks at me for a moment, not smiling. Just looking. I wonder if she thinks I'm smart. I look up at the sky as the nozzle pumps a last few gushes of unleaded plus into the bike.

She climbs on, and hits the kickstand. I have no rash decision and I didn't write any of the ones I've done. I have accomplished nothing.

I am standing next to the bike, tightening my buttocks in anticipation as she is about to start the engine. It's mostly dark, there are some trees and a field behind the gas station. No inspiration here. I could bluff and be magnanimous by letting her make an extra rash decision. No. Not doing that. I look on the floor. A torn black-and-white flyer illuminated by the lights from inside the gas station. The words *All-inclusive open mic. Characters of all identities welcome. Eat donuts.* I look back across the street and see the place mentioned in the flyer, a sign for Madam M's Marvelous Donuts. "So where to, Twinkle Toes?" Mindii says, revving the engine with glee.

Another *Airbender* reference.

"To, uh, the d-donut place?" I say, still standing, an eyebrow raised in an attempt to gauge how into this idea she is. "We could walk there for an added layer of . . ." I pause. "Danger!" I yell, using both hands to signify the level of irresponsible rashness I'm proposing.

"The open-mic donut place?" Mindii says. "The cosplay stuff doesn't start till way later. Prolly dead inside. I should write metal. 'Probably Dead Inside' would make a great song."

She chuckles and paddles the bike with her feet near a barbed wire fence next to a closed RV lot. I watch her in awe. Zero hesitation.

We cross the street—careful, even though there's not

much traffic now—and are in the tiny parking lot of the donut shop, sandwiched between some boring, box-like buildings. The parking lot isn't packed, but there are a respectable number of cars here. She takes out her phone to look at the time. Nine forty-two. We walk around to the back of the building. She takes confident familiar steps until we are directly in front of an enormous window with a metal door next to it. She's been here before. A secret entrance? Through a window, we see a middle-aged man in the kitchen, using a pair of long wooden sticks to turn donuts in the fryer. He looks at Mindii and his face lights up.

Of course she knows the guy. Of course she's been here. Of course she knows this random donut place.

"This is The Hangout," Mindii says. "I used to be in a poetry group, but haven't come here in a minute. Their donuts are so good."

She opens the door and we start walking through the kitchen. I take a strong whiff of all the donuts. "What kind of poetry were you doing?" I say, hustling in my armor to keep up.

"Slam. Fresh donuts and poetry. Can you think of a more perfect combination?" Mindii says.

"I love the smell of donuts. Sl-slam poetry sounds, wow." I'm at a loss for words.

"Why are they making them now? Don't they make

these in the morning?" I say as we stop to watch all the activity in the kitchen.

"No stale-ass morning donuts here. Cambodians make them throughout the day in small batches. Learned that from Uncle Ted, the reason this gem of a place exists in the first place, instead of Dunkin', Krispy Kreme, or Winchins."

"That's pretty smart. So they're always super fresh. What's Winchins?"

"Exactly," Mindii says. "Ted Ngoy is the reason none of these huge chains could break into the breakfast scene in California. One Cambodian refugee changed the entire industry. Hi, Uncle Channthy!" Mindii waves at the old man. He gleefully smiles at her, but continues deep-frying the donuts. "Just wait till you see the flavors," she adds.

"Are there a lot of Cambodians that own donut shops?"

Uncle Channthy turns to look at my face, then back to the hot oil. "Yeah dude. Read a book. Watch a documentary. They have both here in the main room. Bunch of people going around eating glazed donuts in bright pink boxes and don't even know who Ted Ngoy is."

"Word," I say. I have no idea who Ted Ngoy is.

We get to the main room, where there's a small space for a stage, wires everywhere for speakers and mics. The front of the shop is all large windows, a long bench, but my nose leads me straight to the beauteous glass cases filled with donuts. There are the usuals: plain, glazed, drizzled, bear claws, cinnamon rolls, long johns, jelly filled. There are also red-bean-filled donuts, matcha, and a variety of what look and sound like Cambodian-style donuts, noum kong.

"What's red-bean filling?" I ask.

"I don't know, guy who makes rash decisions. Why don't you tell me?" She is goading me.

A girl comes to the counter and smiles at Mindii.

"Haven't seen you in a while. Performing tonight?"

"Maybe," Mindii says.

It's the first time I've seen Mindii be noncommittal. Before I have a chance to ask her what she's performing or what she used to perform, Mindii is ordering.

"A matcha cream filled," Mindii says. "And a large boba. Thai."

"I will have a noum kong and a red-bean donut," I say confidently, then immediately second-guess myself. But I say nothing.

We take our donuts and sit down at a table by a large glass window. She watches me ogling the spread before us. She gestures with her hand to commence, since she's already started digging in. I bite into my red-bean donut and am surprised that I kinda like it on first bite—slightly sweet. Then it tastes mealy, a little strange. The actual red bean, which tastes just like you'd think red beans would taste. Despite my best efforts, my face contorts as I continue chewing. Mushed-up beans sprinkled with sugar. "Who," I say around a vigorous bite, "thought this was a good idea?"

"A lot of people like it," Mindii says, her mouth full of donut. "I don't. But this matcha is so good." She offers me a bite. It is delicious, warm, and soft.

I finish the red-bean donut despite still being unsure whether I like it, even after I take the last bite. Next, I sink my teeth into the noum kong.

"Wow." It's super chewy with a caramel glaze. "This is exquisite."

"It's deep-fried Khmer donut."

"Coconut milk?"

"Yep. And palm sugar."

We sit quietly for a few minutes, eating and sharing her bubble tea.

"I'm guessing that's Ted Ngoy?" I say, wiping my mouth and pointing to a documentary playing on the television in the corner. There are also photos on the wall of a serious-looking man posing with donuts, some black-and-white, some in color.

"Yeah," Mindii says. "Fantastic documentary. *The Donut King*, by Alice Gu. Plays on a loop here so at least people can get a bit of a history lesson. Ted Bun Tek Ngoy escapes genocide in Cambodia, learns about the donut business, buys a ton of donut stores across California, and sponsors hundreds of families who now do the same thing. And it wasn't even to get rich, it was literally just to survive in a country that creates all these messes in other countries, then is all, 'Why are all these brown people here?'"

She passes the boba to me and I take a sip. The documentary flashes snapshots of a new generation of Cambodians taking over their parents' donut stores.

"Spoiler alert," I say playfully. "Th-thanks for ruining the documentary," I say.

"Oh, I didn't spoil it yet. He loses it all gambling. Spoiler alert."

I smile.

"Such a strange niche." I watch more images scroll on the screen. "It's like those rags-to-riches stories of the first Punjabi immigrants who came to the US in the early 1900s. They worked on railroads and lumber mills and as farm laborers, and had to deal with so many openly racist laws made just so Asians couldn't make it. And still they took their shot, buying up things through white people they hoped they could trust."

I'll be glad to be out of school. Tired of reading about liberty and reciting the pledge when they can't even use the words *white supremacy* or teach Californian history properly in school. Adults are the ones teaching us their bad takes on politics and lack of critical thinking skills."

"Yeah. Like how is the Alien Land Law not taught in

history classes. Or the fact the Ghadar Party—the revolutionary movement to end colonial rule in British India was started by steel and lumber mill workers in Astoria, Oregon, in 1913. Not a mention of any of those things, and not a peep about the Secret War," I say, my voice getting indignant.

"Exactly!" Mindii says. "It's American history. Yet we got all the time in the world to talk about the greatness of the Founding Fathers, glossing right over them being enslavers."

"Like that whole-ass musical they made about enslavers," I say. "Took them five minutes to rebrand George W. Bush as a painter instead of war criminal. Watch, they're gonna include Hitler in an art history class any day now, and kids are gonna have an even more skewed version of what counts as racism."

"Dude," she says in agreement.

"Oh shit," I say, looking back up at the TV screen. "This is a terrible twist."

I stare in disbelief, even though I knew this was coming since Mindii kinda gave away the spoiler. The Donut King started gambling, and gambled so much that he started selling off his stores to other Cambodians, eventually losing everything, his money, his reputation, his family.

I feel sad for him. And angry. He's clearly addicted, but he's also the one who ruined everyone's life. I'm reminded of how I love and miss Goldy so much, feel sad about his disease, and am so angry at him. All those emotions at once.

"Whenever I watch rags-to-riches movies, I'm always so bored at how singular the stories are. It's like a freaking cornucopia for Hollywood, not that they've noticed," Mindii says, sipping boba. "Cambodian refugees escaped genocide in the late '70s by coming here with nothing and bought independent donut joints like this just to survive in America. That's the reason their sons and daughters and grandkids run this shit. Because if they lose it, that's it. A part of their family history and Californian history is just gone."

"Yeah, it's like in places like Yuba-Sutter County, Punjabis own ninety-five percent of the peach farming industry because of previous generations putting in that work. If one of those grandkids is like, I wanna be a computer engineer, that legacy is done." She looks down at the donut and I know we're not talking about Ted Ngoy anymore. She's thinking about the stall, and I'm thinking about Goldy.

The door chimes and two Hmong girls walk in to pick up a couple of pink boxes filled with donuts. One of them has blue hair and really impressive makeup, like some kind of dragon, and the other girl has orange fur and a tail, like a fox spirit. They look over at Mindii and leap up in the air with excitement. Mindii stands up and they give each other hugs while I awkwardly sit between them all.

"Oh my God, I can't believe it. How long has it been?" the girl dressed like a dragon says.

"Too long," the fox spirit says.

Mindii nods. She turns to me. "This is Yia"—she points to the fox spirit—"and Hazel"—the dragon girl.

"Hey." They both wave. "We used to be Poj Laib. I mean, we're still Poj Laib, just not in a group." They all laugh. I laugh too even though I don't understand the joke. At. All.

"Our poetry slam name," Yia says.

"Fighting the idea that women are bad anything just because the patriarchy says so," Hazel adds.

"An ode to all the bad modern daughters, bad wives, bad mothers, bad sisters, basically Poj Laib all over the fandom," Yia says.

"That's what Poj Laib means?" I say.

"Not bad pronunciation. David, right? From the books?" they say, skipping over my question.

"Dafydd," I say. "It's Petrichorian."

Yia turns to Mindii and excitedly says, "We never did Katara, did we?"

"No. I don't think so." Hazel, the dragon spirit, places a palm on our table.

"She is the ultimate Poj Laib," she chuckles. "We better bounce. We're on our way to the *Airbender* party."

"It's an anime party," Yia corrects.

"Oh, is this like an all 'fandoms' welcome thing, but it's designed with only one in mind?" Mindii says.

We laugh.

"What's the deal with the open-mic poetry? It's in cosplay?" I ask.

"That's kinda it. That's the deal," Hazel says. "It's a lot of fun. It started as just a general South Asian poetry meet-up, but then everyone all descended and Uncle Channthy was super nice, made everyone welcome. So it's been around for a good couple years now."

They lean in and give Mindii another hug and start heading out. The two girls leave and Mindii smiles at me. But there's something off about the smile, an emptiness behind it. I realize what she's doing. Pretending.

Apparently this isn't just something my family does. I've forgotten how many times I believed Goldy no matter how many times he let me down. Just looking at his face, the desperation to be believed, and everyone's willingness to just let us believe he had everything under control. Then, poof, it's gone.

We're all great at pretending. Until we're not.

CHAPTER 12

THANKS A MOCHI

Someone cosplaying as a giant robot with red eyes opens the door. Inside, everyone is milling around the house, some kids sitting on the stairs, but mostly loitering in the living room and kitchen, probably in the backyard too. I don't see any other Snollygoster-heads, but there are plenty of people in anime-related cosplay.

"You know," the robot says solemnly. "I didn't ask to be this big."

Neither of us knows who he's cosplaying, but I'm impressed with the work.

"Geez, man. I'm friggin' Alphonse. Alphonse Elric!" The robot stamps his feet. "The brother who loses his whole body! You know, from the failed attempt at alchemy to bring their mother back?"

He takes his head off. It's Shaiyar, an anime- and Minecraft-obsessed Twitch streamer I know from school and online. He and his sister, Kavya, used to run a You-Tube channel together a few years ago until their brands kinda diverged and they went their separate online ways.

"Arrr, *Fullmetal Alchemist*," I say, vaguely recalling the show about the two Elric brothers.

He smiles and puts his head back on.

"Foam?" Mindii says.

"EVA foam," he says. "And contact cement."

"Can't knock me down," Mindii says, striking a low pose and staring intently at him.

"Katara! Noice!" Shaiyar says enthusiastically. His sister, Kavya, walks toward us, a golden lightning bolt sewn on her deep blue salwar kameez, glitter all over her face. Kamala Khan, the new incarnation of Ms. Marvel. She hands him a plastic cup filled with some kind of blue punch. "Next time, can you just hot glue a straw to your helmet so you don't have to keep breaking character to take a drink," she says to him.

"A big fat plastic straw running from the top of my helmet to my face IS breaking character!" Shaiyar says with irritation as she starts walking back to the party. She pauses to look at me. "What is that, some kinda crepe wool?"

I nod.

"Cool." She continues walking away, as Shaiyar awkwardly maneuvers holding his helmet and drinking punch simultaneously, #cosplayproblems.

We mosey on through. It takes me a minute, but I recognize the music playing in the living room. The original

Cowboy Bebop theme song in all its glory: purely instrumental, 1970s pulp sounds. Fitting for an anime about nihilistic bounty hunters in space.

I can almost see the visuals. Big poofy Afros, sunglasses, sleek spaceships, that constant sense of being broke and hungry. Just as the music crescendos into a fast-paced trumpet-like balloon squeal, the two girls from the donut shop—the fox and the dragon, Yia and Hazel—jump into the only clear space in the house, a makeshift stage between the sofa and TV. They start spitting rhymes, thick hip-hop lyrics in mostly English punctuated with Hmong and Khmer. Not that I'm an expert in either language, I just know what they sound like.

The girls are really revving up the dramatic arcs of *Cowboy Bebop* like lyrical gangsters.

They finish and find me and Mindii.

"That was straight fire," I say.

"Thanks!" Yia in her fox cosplay replies.

"I gotta ask," I say.

"Vulpix," Yia explains, apparently not dressed as a nine-tailed demon fox from *Naruto,* as I thought.

"Ah," I say. "From Pokémon."

"You could say that. It's from Nintendo and Game Freak."

"Ah," I say again.

"Dafydd is so cute," Yia says to Mindii.

Mindii blushes and my face becomes a great big question mark.

"Hi. I'm Tohru. In case anyone wants to know," Hazel says pointedly. "From Kobayashi Tōru. I'm a dragon-maid. A hungry dragon-maid. Snacks?" she says in a tone I recognize as wanting girl-talk time. I stay put as Mindii and the girls disappear into the crowd.

I head to my favorite section of any party: the bookshelf. I comb through the coffee-table-sized special-edition hardcovers of classic manga—*Attack of Titans, Bleach, Deathnote, Black Butler, Cowboy Bebop*. A lot of them are written in Japanese, which I recognize because of the cover art.

Goldy used to be obsessed with all these depressing-ass post-apocalyptic manga and anime. Every time he'd come back from rehab, or from attempting to "resolve the situation," like alcoholism is a hostage situation to blast through, he'd be really into all these philosophical concepts, acting like he was suddenly some deep thinker. I watched some of his shows with him, like *Cowboy Bebop*. But I didn't understand the existential themes of loneliness and whatever the fuck ennui is, or Goldy going on and on about how the characters can never return to the past. *Avatar: The Last Airbender* was a TV series I actually really liked because the ideas were much easier to understand, even with some really complex themes happening and the characters still forming their ideas and identities. I wish he had just been obsessed with the Kardashians. His life would be so much easier to piece together.

Some dude dressed as Zuko is attaching a large white bedsheet to the patio doors. Then a portable projector starts displaying quick-paced images from an anime with a super-catchy title: *Sakunosuke Bungo Stray Dogs*.

Ah. Fight scenes. The area clears out a little and a group of people walk toward the newly created space, carrying electric guitars, which they plug in to the amps. One of them is wearing something that looks like a toga, a large hat with a fluffy maroon rectangular prism on top, a necklace of flowers. Next to him is a dude with a regular mustache and beard, a yellow gardening hat with a pink flower on the side, a white kimono with pink sashes and a large strip of pink across his belly. There's also another guy just wearing a purple kung fu outfit.

Suddenly it clicks. "The Cave of Two Lovers"? The episode where Katara and the gang get stuck in the cave when they attempt to take a shortcut to get to Omashu. This is the hippy band from the episode. It's been years since I watched it, but the thing about *Last Airbender* or rereading sections from Jamie Snollygoster is I may not remember the words, but I remember the way it makes me feel. On edge, queasy, excited, nervous, happy, sad, devastated, destroyed. Yes, there is a huge difference in the last three words. I bet this is where that whole Destination Fever line she used on me earlier this evening is from. I'm about to say something clever to her when the guy with facial hair points his guitar at me.

"Sunny G! The man who can make metal magic!"

This is definitely a rare occurrence. I hardly ever—I mean, pretty much never—get recognized for my guitar skills outside of the Snollygoster crowd. And even that's only if Ngozi is standing right next to me. Are THESE my people? I quickly hand Mindii my phone.

"Take photos. And video," I say as someone hands me an electric guitar.

"I'll take one photo," Mindii says. "I want to enjoy the performance."

I don't have time to argue, so I give her a look to indicate, fine, just fucking fine, do it, then. But it looks more like I'm bubble-facing—pouting with a full face of air.

The guitar is more or less in tune. The background image on the bedsheet changes to show the original band from the "Cave of Two Lovers" episode. The band starts playing and Zuko moves the mic stand near me. Do they expect me to sing? I don't know the words. Or this crowd. I love doing low heavy metal guttural screams as much as the next metal head, but they may actually want to hear the lyrics. *Shit.* Sweat pools under my Dafydd robes.

Then they start singing. "Secret tunnel, secret, secret, secret . . ."

Okay. Now I remember the song. Looks like lyrics are actually not that important.

I stretch out my fingers, pressing them into the chords. I start strumming the guitar strings, slowly at first, then with more anger as I send out a small metal growl. The crowd starts singing along. The image on the bedsheet changes again—a fight scene from *Sailor Moon*—and we start playing a familiar moon rock tune on the spot. The next song we play is from a fight scene from *Deathnote*, and it's already pretty metal. So I make it more metal with super-fast chord switches. The crowd roars as the music pulses through me, fast and furious.

The image shifts back to *Last Airbender* and a scene I remember from Goldy's notebook. It's Uncle Iroh, the reformed warmonger turned tea-drinking pacifist, putting flowers on his son's grave. I study Uncle Iroh's face, remembering the way Papa looked at the cremation in his large wrinkled turban, wrinkled face, a hollowness in his eyes that scared me. Like there was something that was just gone forever. Maybe that's why we never talk about Goldy. Like, actually talk. Because for Mama and Papa, it's over. He's just gone. In Sikh theology, death just *is*. It's part of the natural cycle, but I don't know if that applies here because there's nothing natural about the way Goldy died. A disease. That's what got him. Like how Ted Ngoy got so addicted to the rush of gambling he chose the rush over everything, everyone. What feeling was Goldy chasing? Whatever it was, that's what consumed him and made him choose it over everyone. Over me.

At first, I follow their lead plucking the strings meditatively. Then I feel this strange angry and sad energy pulsing through my body, forcing my fingers into overdrive as rage fills my voice. Not the usual, low notes I usually aim for, but a piercing, high-decibel metal scream. "Leaves from the vine falling so slow!" I roar as I think of Papa and Mama and Biji and their deafeningly silent grief. Or am I thinking about myself?

The song winds down and I'm drenched in sweat as I finally look into the crowd. They're all clapping and cheering. Except for Mindii, who's standing there, a little bit shocked, clutching my phone in her hand and staring at me.

I hand the guitar back to the band. "Rad, man," one of them says as they fist-bump me. "I have never heard a rendition like that." In the midst of huffing and puffing, I smile brightly at Mindii as she makes her way toward me.

"Just when I think I kind of have you figured out," Mindii says. "You manage to surprise me." She hands back my phone. "Let's get you a drink," she says.

We walk over to the snack table, where there are several bowls filled with four different colors of punch. Water. Earth. Fire. Air. Mindii lines up four glasses of the punch. I'm so thirsty, I chug down all four glasses one after the other, careful to angle my beard to avoid spillage, taking in the sudden hit of wetness and sugar and chemicals making my mouth immediately sticky. Now that I've caught my breath, we take a second to look at each other.

"Actual water?" Mindii says. I nod vigorously.

I scroll through the photos on my phone.

"You took seven pictures. And a video. Holy shit! And made a GIF?" My grin's so wide, my fake beard's lopsided.

"I was feeling generous," Mindii says, but she's smiling too. "You want some mochi?"

"Assuming it's a type of food, I'm going to pass. I had enough adventurous food for now."

Mindii laughs. "There's nothing adventurous about mochi. It's a delicious Japanese dessert."

"What's inside it?"

"Traditionally, red-bean paste."

I grimace. "What is it with South Asians and red bean?"

"Japan is not in South Asia," Mindii quips. "So that, sir, is racist."

"Fine, get me a fucking red-bean-filled mochi. Things I do to show my antiracist activism," I say.

Mindii disappears to get the mochi.

I take a closer look at the photos and see this person

168

I kind of recognize, but don't think is me. Is this what an out-of-body experience feels like? Mindii didn't take a single photo from when I posed pretty for the camera. All of these are of me and my intense face. Like she sees right through me. Posting any of these feels too intimate for any of my socials.

Shaiyar and Kavya are standing around the punch bowl, stuffing their faces with snacks.

"It was fine," Shaiyar says unprompted.

"You made some bold choices," Kavya says, and makes some kind of face that I think indicates approval.

"And most importantly, it was still canon," Shaiyar adds.

"Uncle Iroh is cool," I say. "I wish they added that to the film. The vignettes were really nice."

They stop what they're doing.

"The film?" Shaiyar says like he's unaware it exists.

"What is happening?" Kavya says, completely pausing her snacking.

"No, I mean. The m-movie was bad. Like the whitewashing and stuff. I just meant . . ." I'm sweating more than I was on stage.

"There is no movie," Shaiyar says matter-of-factly.

Kavya's eyes narrow to support her brother's claim.

Goldy was distraught after we watched the movie adaptation. At home that night he joylessly ate muttar paneer—his favorite—and when I asked if everything was okay, he said, "I just can't believe it. They couldn't pronounce Aang's name right and even took out the *Avatar* part of the title. That's how clueless or callous this motherfucker is." Like genuinely traumatized.

I'm kind of dreading the movie adaptation they're finally making with the Snollygoster series. It's surprising it took so long considering there are no characters coded as anything other than white and heterosexual, so Hollywood can oh-so-magnanimously do their bit for diversity with one Asian or Black side character who's just there to nod at whatever Jamie Snollygoster is saying.

They're not responding, so of course I keep talking. I don't even know what I'm saying, but I'm still talking about the film. I can feel myself rambling. I feel myself speaking in slow motion as I turn my head and see Mindii barrel toward me, her arm outstretched, holding a giant green ball. Is that a mochi? I realize she's speaking. Yelling maybe? Before I know it, she's shoved the mochi into my mouth. It feels like a lazily inflated miniature balloon.

If I could speak, I would probably be all, "What. The. Hell?" I can't even taste anything. Just a great big squishy thing making it difficult to breathe. Ice cream fills my mouth. Mint and thankfully not red bean.

I don't have time to enjoy the flavor. I look over and hear an unmistakable *kerplunk* sound. My hands go light, my heart becomes heavy.

It's the *glug, glug, glug* of my phone. Drowning. My eyes slowly move toward my now empty hands and then to the punchbowl. Of course it's in Fire Nation waters. Of friggin' course.

Mindii immediately fishes it out while I gape at the punchbowl in suspended horror.

"You big dodo bird," she says, trying to dry it off as I stand there, blinking hella-wide, hella-fast.

"Oh my God," I say, my voice shaking. "This is what people on those documentaries on Netflix are talking about when they say their life flashes before their eyes."

"Uhh . . ." She's being annoyingly dismissive. She slides the wet phone across the table to me and I'm breathing rapidly. The screen is dark. I don't think I've ever seen it like this, so blank, so lifeless. I feel my way around to its side and press the power button, willing it back to life. She slaps my hand.

"You're gonna kill it dead. You gotta take the battery out, then put it in a bag of uncooked rice to let it dry for forty-eight hours."

"F-FORTY-EIGHT HOURS? WE'LL ALL BE DEAD BY THEN!!" I scream, disoriented. "Where the hell am I gonna get a bag of rice? I should've taken some jollof from the roller-skating party!"

I angrily chew the mochi. I don't let Mindii see I'm enjoying it, though, and lower my eyebrows and pucker my lips for the proper effect. I swallow the rest of the mochi, and become instantly enraged.

"M. Night Shyamalan. M. Night Shyamalan!" I scream the director's name at Kavya and Shaiyar, who clutch their invisible pearls and let out a gasp. I glare at Mindii, then take manic, clompy steps out of the house, closing the door behind me. I don't even bother to look back at the destruction I'm leaving in my wake.

My phone is dead. I gasp. Did I back everything up on the cloud? Did anyone upload photos or videos of me playing? Maybe they're lost forever. Is Mindii going to come outside?

The door opens. It's Mindii. She looks sternly at me, then bursts out laughing.

"That was the most spectacular display of self-sabotage I have ever seen. Truly spec-fucking-tacular," she says. "If anyone else had done that, I would be so mad.

"You should totally add a cute little dumpster truck on fire in your journal," she says, shuffling her combat boots on the ground. "Maybe you can crochet it."

"I'm going to make you the driver," I say.

She stops cold. "How is this my doing?"

"You came barreling at me with your mouth open like you were trying to . . ."

We speak at the same time:

"Kiss you?" Mindii says.

"Eat me," I say, awkwardly finishing my sentence.

We look at each other suspiciously, neither of us saying a word. I savor this odd moment, sweet and salty and unfamiliar, wondering what to do next.

Then my brain spirals again, thinking about my phone and everything in it, about where to get this uncooked rice. It's like ten o'clock. What's even open?

I focus on Mindii's face. Her lips. I didn't know lips could be that pink.

She catches me staring. I freeze, looking away.

"Stop thinking," Mindii says, and I look at her. She looks at me. I lean in.

"What are you doing?" she asks.

"I . . . um," I say.

"I'm just messing with you." She leans forward, our faces inches apart. She smells of lilac perfume, dust, and punch.

"You look like you have one eye," I say as she stands on tiptoes, my face in her palms.

"Like Hesiod's highly skilled blacksmith Cyclopes?" she says, a little breathless.

"You're so smart," I say dreamily.

She breathes on me, blowing warm air onto my face filtered through the beard. She slowly places a hand over my chin and lifts the beard up.

Our lips touch. She tastes like punch. My beard rises up,

blurring my vision with the added pressure of her face on mine. What to do with my hands? Should I rest them on her shoulders? Too awkward. On her hips? A definite no.

I stop overthinking, my hands move toward the small of her back.

We. Are. Kissing.

I close my eyes and start humming a tune from one of my many favorite scenes in *Dilwale Dulhania Le Jayenge*. I abruptly stop as I realize I'm humming into her mouth mid-kiss. She sucks in air and starts beat-boxing. I burst out laughing, she giggles.

Slowly the memory of my gurgling phone clinging to life reemerges.

"Except this is opposite day," Mindii says. "In *DDLJ* Raj and Simran spent that entire song rejecting each other. Your move. Let's go!" She punches me hard in the shoulder as she leaps back onto the bike, leaving me completely dumbfounded. Again.

My heart pounding, lips still tingling.

I know exactly where we need to go.

CHAPTER 13

BUT FIRST WE DRINK CHA

My body is still bursting with energy from the anime party. The kiss. The performance. The kiss. And my phone. My chest tightens as I remember the sound of it drowning, the nothingness of its unlit face. I'm glad we're back on the road, because I don't even know what to do with my fingers right now. Or whether we should further discuss the implications of The Kiss.

It's not just a phone that died. It's my life. And I don't mean that in an overly dramatic way. All my memories, all my notes, my countless drafts of my carefully curated online life, boring messages to Goldy, everything is on there. And yeah, Siri. For a stutterer it's nice being able to talk to someone who won't judge too much. Who will let me have that stutter storm, and try the sentence again and again and again. I'm pretty sure it all adds up to way more than my iCloud backup data plan can hold. So cue panic mode.

Mindii's driving as rationally as you can on a motorcycle in the middle of farm country. There are just a few more exits before we get lost in the darkness of farming towns scattered across the Central Valley. I nudge Mindii to exit and we drive along the old Highway 41, a mile away from the peacock gurdwara we used to go to before Goldy's reputation made things really awkward. We pull up to Filmy Chaat, the video store my family owns, because that's the only place I can think of at this time that has uncooked rice. It's marked by the statue of an upside-down plane on the top of the building.

"I recognize this place," Mindii says as she gets off the bike. "We used to drive up and down the highway to go visit family in Kerman on Saturdays after the flea market. And then hit every tiny-ass town 'in the vicinity' to say hi to some random Hmong uncle or auntie."

"My parents would always drag us to some random person's house to get supplies for the store. Every weekend, sometimes during the week. D-D-Delano, Firebaugh, Selma . . ."

"Hanford, Kerman," Mindii finishes.

"And way too often, we'd slog down Highway 99 for two hours to go to Delhi, pronounced 'del-high.' I don't think Papa even liked the uncle who lived there. He just liked seeing the sign that says *Delhi,* so he could crack the same joke he's been making for years."

Mindii waits, tapping a foot. "Well, what's the joke?"

I tighten my fists around the handlebars to emulate

driving a car. "I must have taken a wrong turn," I say loudly, in an exaggerated attempt to copy Papa's mannerisms. I pause, then gleefully pretend to see the Delhi sign. "We're back in India!" I say with much jubilation, then climb carefully off the bike.

Mindii laughs. "That's a solid dad joke. What's the deal with the plane?"

"A World War II fighter jet crashed nose down into the roof," I say, grinning. "That's what we tell everyone who comes into our store anyway."

"I like it. A piece of American history literally crash-landing into your family store."

"Want to know the actual story?"

She squints up at the sign: *Filmy Chaat*.

"Nah," she says. "The truth ruins everything."

I nod because those are facts. I take out a small set of keys from my pouch and unlock the door, entering the code to disarm the security system. Not that anyone is trying to break in. What are they going to steal—a bunch of samosas and a suitcase full of incense holders Mama and Papa decided would be a great investment?

Initially they received two gigantic suitcases filled with incense holders in exchange for cash from some dude with a tax-free hookup. I don't even want to know how much they spent. This was a couple years ago. We sold a bunch, and are now down to one suitcase. The place is bizarre.

I've grown up knowing it and have learned to accept it. Mindii assesses the treasure trove of absolute junk: Punjabi suits in a portable closet on wheels next to an aisle with a whole section of Haldiram's Indian snacks, along with masalas and quick-cook meals from Gits, a wedding sword behind the counter, gaudy religious products that light up, stacks of Punjabi newspapers and magazines. Seventy-five percent of the space is full of the weirdest assortment of things: lamps, lightbulbs, chapati flour, basmati rice, spices, musical instruments, carrom boards, hair oils, skin-lightening creams, coffee grinders.

Oh, and the entire back wall behind the counter next to the cha and chaat station is devoted to old-school Punjabi and Hindi audio cassettes and VHS tapes. Yes. Tapes.

Mindii examines a series of posters on the wall. There are a couple with Punjabi singers like Diljit, a big-ass poster of an old-school Punjabi film, Maula Jatt with him wearing his classic loongi and carrying a sharp gandasa to cut down wheat and anyone who crosses his path. Lots of Bollywood posters from across the decades. Mindii is looking at baby-faced Ranveer Singh in a red-and-black plaid shirt with a tiny bit of stubble, flashing his signature mischievous grin before he got super famous. Next to it is a more recent poster of him with the requisite waxed chest, designer beard, and chiseled Bollywood abs. There are black-and-white throwbacks of Shammi Kapoor,

Madhubala, a coal-stained Amitabh from decades ago, Madhuri Dixit, Sridevi, Anil Kapoor. Anywhere there's any space, you'll find a poster, a flyer, a business card taped to the wall, jewelry advertisements with close-ups of brown women decked out in gold.

"You know what I find so powerful about Hindi films?" Mindii says, and I really hope she doesn't say some white feminist shit: such power in their resilience, beauty in poverty, the vibrant culture, spirituality.

"How no matter how fucked things get, Ranveer Singh taking off his shirt will fix everything."

I look right at her and laugh, like straight up laugh with abandon.

"Yeah, Ranveer Singh is so dreamy," I say, mock swooning.

"Shirtless Ranveer is the best Ranveer," Mindii says. I laugh again. "And his comments on Deepika's posts are so adorable," she adds.

I look at her quizzically.

"I follow them on social."

I take a moment to absorb the fact that this is not a person with a passing interest in Bollywood films. Was she joking when she said she's been to the store before? I remember my phone and the whole reason we're here, but my feet are planted and I don't want to move them to go get the basmati.

"What does the name mean?" Mindii says.

"Whose name?" I say, confused.

"Filmy Chaat."

"Oh. Yeah. My mom loves the word *filmy*. She uses it all the time. "It means being 'extra.' Like when I gave her this impassioned speech when I was eleven that I didn't want her packing me delicious sabji for my lunch anymore because the other kids made fun of me. She's all, 'Stop being so filmy. Want me to pack you bread and a lump of butter?' Then Papa chimed in with, 'Cold pasta made from maida?'"

"I'm digging it," Mindii says. "What about the chaat?" she asks, extending the vowels in *chaat* very disconcertingly.

"Chaat are d-delicious roadside snacks you find all over the subcontinent. It literally means to lick, like finger-licking good. M-mostly they're made with crispy fried dough and chunks of potato, fried bread, sour chili and tamarind and coriander chutney, seasoned with tons of spices, like cumin and kala namak. There are a million varieties. My favorite is papri chaat drizzled with yogurt. There's also fruit chaat, samosa chaat . . ."

"Stop talking," she says. "Go make me some papri chaat. Also some tea would be . . ." She makes a loud kissy sound and points to the empty cha and chaat station.

"Now?"

"As the great philosopher Dafydd Brambleberry probably said, yes, fucking now."

I suck my teeth at her and go past the cash register and

the wall of audio and video tapes to the chaat station. I smash up the masala and add water to a small saucepan on a portable burner, then start on the chaat. I take out a knife and quickly start chopping an onion. I don't get it. I should be panicking about my phone, focused on finding that bag of rice. Instead, I pull out the deep-fried papri crisps, dousing them with yogurt and chutney and an extra dash of laal mirch. I check on the cha, and add the milk, then wait for it to ubbul, so I can put in the Lipton yellow-label tea bags, sugar, and a few spoonfuls of loose tea for color.

The silence in the store is odd. There's always the chatter of people talking, of Papa restocking items and singing poems, of Mama arranging the VHS tapes and spices. Even when it's not busy, the television and VHS player are playing and dubbing, the sounds of Bollywood or Bhangra floating through.

This one time when I was like twelve, Mama and Papa left me to handle the store because Goldy had gotten drunk. I started watching *Devdas,* the one with Shah Rukh Khan, and was caught off guard by how catchy the song "Chalak Chalak" is. It's about two dudes drinking like lunatics, smashing bottles, having a great time, right before Devdas's long, drawn-out death. There's a much older version of the same movie where instead of the song, there's a scene where Devdas starts drinking again after he's been sober for a while, and he feels like shit at first, and then likes the comfort the alcohol provides. Every time I think about that scene, I get real sad. Sometimes I cry because I feel like I understand Goldy a little better.

I replay Goldy's last moments. The words from the report echo on repeat: *He voluntarily consumed alcohol.* I remember Goldy saying he didn't want to die. Me stuttering. I wanted to scream at the doctor, "Then why the fuck did he do this?" I didn't want to think about words like *addiction* or *illness*. My brother is gone.

Mindii squeals with delight and pulls me back into the present. Usually whenever someone sees the wall of VHS, I get very defensive, preemptively informing them that there was a shipment mishap and we're waiting to replace the tapes with spices or something. But I feel no urge to do anything like that today.

"I watch the movies mostly with subtitles now, which is not as fun as the dubbed ones I watched with my niam tais back in the day. She used to insist on stopping here." She looks around, her eyes lost, wistful.

I layer the papri and don't say anything, but I have a gigantic question mark on my face. Although, to be fair, that's been my face for this whole night.

Mindii has been to Filmy Chaat. The store. My store. She wasn't joking.

"So, uh. So, you and your grandma . . . uh, used to watch dubbed Hindi films?"

"In White Hmong, yep."

"Sure," I say. "Makes total sense."

I shouldn't be that surprised. We used to carry a lot more Hmong-dubbed movies, but still have a good amount.

She picks up a VHS tape with a cover of Shah Rukh Khan in a dorky black hat, fake leather jacket, and jeans, carrying Kajol, dressed in bridal orange, the letters *DDLJ* scrawled in ballpoint pen. It's Goldy's handwriting. *Dilwale Dulhania Le Jayenge.*

I really hope she doesn't ask me to translate it.

"What does it mean in English?"

Of. Friggin'. Course.

"Big . . . uh . . . hearted dude will take the b-bride."

"What does that even mean?" Mindii says.

"Obviously it's about this dude, right. And he is big-hearted. So he takes . . . you know."

"The bride?" Mindii says, then laughs.

"Yep."

"This was Niam Tais's favorite. We watched it like a thousand times. Even though we already knew the part was coming where the dad says 'Go, Toubee, live your life,' we'd cry every time."

"Okay," I say. "I feel like we've watched the same film in parallel universes. Who is Toubee?" I say.

"The main girl."

"Simran? The girl played by Kajol."

"Correction. Toubee, the girl played by Kajol," Mindii says. "What does the Hindi version mean in English? Is it like really poetic?"

"Jaa, Simran, jaa. It means . . . uh. Well. It means Go, Simran, go."

"Hmm," Mindii says.

"You know who the best Hmong dubbers were?" she muses.

"Sy Lee and Lee Vang," I say, not even looking up.

She is silent, surprised I know who they are.

"How?" she says. "Wait, did you use your phone?"

"Yes, I used my time machine to go back in time before you killed my phone, then transported four seconds into the future, so I knew you were going to ask me that question, then I looked up the answer on my phone before traveling back to the present, just so I could see that stupid look on your face. So worth it."

She sticks her tongue out at me.

"My mom," I say. "Even though VHS has been obsolete forever, a few years ago she bought a box full of what she thought were Hindi VHS tapes from the flea market and refused to throw them away when we found out they were Hmong-dubbed because we don't throw anything away. A lot of them were really bad, but this dubbing team were fire. The dubbed songs were pretty catchy too. So yeah. I know who Sy Lee and Lee Vang are."

Mindii dabs at her eyes. "This is one of the only places my niam tais would make an effort to come to just to pay a dollar to rent a VHS tape. I'd bring her here sometimes, sit in my car outside, and she would walk in here with her dollar for the VHS rental and her limited English and walk out so happy."

I look outside, imagining Mindii waiting in a parked car.

"Maybe I met your niam tais. I would have liked her."

"I think so too," Mindii says.

"So tell me about these dubbers," I say. "All I know are their names."

"Sy Lee and Lee Vang were one of the best teams because they could dub the songs, not just the dialogue. I had a weird mix of Hindi, Thai, and Chinese movies on tape. So no one ever got my pop culture references. Niam Tais and these dubbers made my childhood weirdly specific. It's why I never understood why the other Asian girls at school were so obsessed with looking like Disney princesses. Or the white characters in all the books they gave us to read. I was all, 'Why would you want to look like a ghost or a demon?' They didn't know what I was talking about. Then I got to middle school and was like, 'Ah. White supremacy. Got it. As you were.'"

I strain and pour the cha into the disposable handleless kulhar clay cups that Mama insisted on using instead of the way cheaper foam ones. I quickly wash the dishes.

The chaat is ready. I hand Mindii the kulhar vali cha and a bowl of chaat. She looks delighted.

"I just take a bite?"

"No. You spread it over your face like a skin exfoliator. Then you crush and snort the papari," I say. "Yes, you just take a bite."

I laugh as she digs in, truly inhaling.

"I feel like this should be a competition."

"Of course. Why eat in peace when there can only be one true champion?" Mindii says, laughing.

"Yeah, okay. What are the rules?" I say.

But she's already eaten half her bowl. I don't stand a chance. She finishes first and declares herself the winner of this totally rigged game.

I take my defeat in stride. She smiles, taking her sweet time wiping the saunth off her face.

"Next time I'll make you gol guppa. That's a real competition," I find myself saying. Next time.

"Now for the cha," Mindii says, her tone lowering and rising. Do they use the same word for it in Hmong too? "Let's not do a competition for this one."

"Never," I say, actually shocked at the suggestion.

"We'd get these from street vendors at train stations in India," I say, holding the kulhar carefully. I take a tiny nibble of the earthen cup and loudly slurp.

"This tastes terrible," Mindii says, immediately spitting

it out into a napkin. "Are you gonna tell me that's the cul-turally correct way to drink it?"

I laugh. "It's more of a Goldy and Biji thing. Goldy used to bite into the kulhar for 'the earthy aroma,' so I started doing the same thing, and Biji enjoys the soorka, the slurping. She thinks that's where the fun of drinking cha comes from."

Mindii takes a moment to appreciate the aroma, taking a loud slurp.

"This is definitely more fun," she says. "Like bringing your face down to the bowl to slurp pho."

One of my favorite memories of India is when I was about ten and all my cousins were either ignoring me, making fun of the way I spoke Punjabi, or making big-time fun when I was stuttering in Punjabi and not pronouncing things properly. Like, I triple fucked up. Goldy saw how upset I was and cursed them out, then took me down the street to get Panj-Pani vale gol guppe. Just me and him. And boy did he get yelled at by everyone afterward, despite my protests, because even at thirteen—no matter how on point his Punjabi sounded or how big and bulky and hairy he was—Goldy was still seen as an American kid. They were worried we'd get sick from eating outside food, from drinking unfiltered gol guppa pani. Or that we'd get kid-napped, robbed. The usual.

But it was worth it. I still dream about being with totally sober Goldy, who stood up for me against the extended family as we enjoyed the forbidden taste of dunking crispy, crunchy puris into minty-cool spicy water that burst in your mouth. And the intense pressure to stay ahead of the gol guppa guy, who was quick as lightning, impatiently waiting to hand us the next one.

Mindii walks behind the counter, closer to me.

She scrunches her nose. It's adorable. "Hey," she says. "You reek of onion."

"So do you."

"Perfect! As long as we don't talk to anyone else, we'll be all good."

I grab our plates and throw them in the trash. Then I walk over to one of the aisles and grab a bag of rice.

"What now?" I say.

"I imagine you open the bag up and put the phone in. What were you planning on doing with it? Making a nice basmati iPhone biryani?"

I laugh even though my phone just may be dead forever. I pour enough of the uncooked rice into the pouch and place my phone inside. It weighs a ton. The clock above the door says 10:31 p.m. and I'm in no rush to leave.

"But first," I say. "You want some more cha?"

She nods, looking at me like I'm the center of the universe.

CHAPTER 14

A JOY MOST METAL

We're standing in the final parking lot of the night, the series of rash decisions almost over.

In all the years me and Ngozi have been coming here, I'm usually the first one to point out all the minor and major inconsistencies with the Snollygoster-inspired designs and cosplay. Ngozi claims "It's not canon!" is my go-to catchphrase whenever I see people taking a little too much liberty with the world of Jamie Snollygoster.

But tonight is different.

For one thing, I'm phoneless. The added weight of uncooked basmati is making this pouch feel like an albatross around my . . . uh, belt. I look over at Mindii. She picks up a twig that landed on the bike seat. She turns to look at me, stern. "Forged in the fiery waters of Noddy's Fjord, the sorcery is strong with this one"—repeating a line Safia Brambleberry says just before her enchanted stick breaks in half and she has to scramble to find a new one. Her face glimmers in the moonlight. She looks down for a second, then back up at me. I take a breath. Is she looking at me the same way I'm looking at her?

"Could pass for stone wood," I say.

"Really?"

"No. You know how rare stone wood is? And the ceremony to secure the sorcery needs to be performed by a fox-orca at sunrise. It's a nice twig, though. I like it. Looks functional."

She laughs. "Go on, say it."

"It's not canon," I say. "But also who cares? As the old saying goes, it's supposed to be cos-play, not cos-boring."

Mindii snorts at me, then starts heading toward the warehouse for the Snollygoster Soiree. I take the opportunity to quickly raise one bicep to my face and covertly sniff my armpit to assess the damage of the Fresno heat, combined with running around all night in my crocheted faux moleskin summer vest. I smell kinda pungent. But I am wearing my extra-strong, special-order cinnamon deodorant, so maybe I'm giving off a nice woody, cinnamon-y vibe.

I race to catch up, then freeze when I see Goldy's ice cream truck near the entrance. Of course Raj is here. There's a lot of ice cream sales to be made tonight.

"Isn't that . . . ?" Mindii turns back to look at me.

"Yup," I say, and power-walk past the long line of people in cosplay waiting to order. Mindii stops in front of the large Illuminated Book—the fight-y-defend-y enchanted book protector of all the ancient stories and legends of the realm. This one happens to be tied to a tree. "And the sword wielding large snails dangling from the branch. Nice touch," she adds. I lean in and see little ceramic colored snails dangling from the tree.

The line is snaking all the way around the building.

This probably took at least three days to make, a thing that most people will just walk past so they can get inside. Neither Alejandra or Rosa, the two trans women who organize Snollygoster Soiree every year, would let mediocre decorations slide. But they are a little more relaxed about cosplay. Perhaps too relaxed sometimes.

My eyes hone in on one dude who has the audacity to show up with a Band-Aid on his nose in the laziest homage to Jamie Snollygoster. I don't even like the character, but there's still more depth to him than that. I mean, I could have just glued cotton balls to my face and worn a plastic bag as armor. I wish I were the type of person to exact revenge for misuse of cosplay. I'd find out who this fucker is and methodically destroy his life over the course of ten to twenty years, then show up when he's lost everything to be like, "Remember that time you wore a Band-Aid to Snollygoster Soiree in Fresno? Well. This is what you get, man."

I smile as I picture his demise. Mindii grins at me, even though she has no idea what's happening in my head.

A red velvet rope lines the sides of a door for the performers/media/crew entrance. The bouncer is a large, tank-like Punjabi dude. I recognize him immediately because of his ridiculous neck tattoo: a dagger and the word *Respect*. He's one of Goldy's crew. His real name is Gaganpreet, but he goes by G-Dawg because like a lot of Goldy's desi crew, he thinks he's an up-and-coming rapper.

G-Dawg ushers us to the front of the line.

"Oyyyy, Dafflee Burger-vala. Kidaan, Sunny?" He slaps the back of my shoulder and I bristle at his touch. He's the bouncer every year I've been coming here with Ngozi. And cracks the same joke every single time he sees me. Doesn't even make sense. *Dafflee* means friggin' tambourine and in his head, *Burger-vala* probably sounds like *Snollygoster*. Which is NOT even Dafydd's last name. That's it. That's the fucking joke.

Kidaan is a little too slang-y for my taste, but easy enough to respond to in Punjabi.

Instead, I say "Hello," in my whitest, unfriendliest voice, which he doesn't seem to notice. Most of Goldy's crew don't realize when I'm being intentionally curt by responding to things in English. They probably just think I don't speak Punjabi.

Mindii holds up her phone and G-Dawg scans her ticket. Dammit. I realize my ticket is on my phone that's nestled between the basmati. "My phone is dead. It has my e-ticket," I say in Punjabi.

G-Dawg is taken aback. "Oh snap. I didn't know you could speak Punjabi all rat-a-tat-tat. It's all good. Lang ja." G-Dawg is a few years older than Goldy. I don't know that much about him or the rest of the desi crew, except that every time Goldy has been in trouble, this clown has always been there. Not in a supportive Safia Brambleberry I'll-rescue-you-kind of way. In a more sinister Jamie Snollygoster I'll-unleash-demon-frogs-and-fuck-up-your-day-kind-of-way, where Goldy goes to a house party, then ends up in jail or the emergency room, and G-Dawg gets no repercussions. He's never been there when Goldy needed a ride to or from rehab, or when he was passed out on the floor. What really gets me angry is that all of his friends drink like they're in one of these magical Punjabi music videos where people drink bottles and bottles of whiskey and never once vomit or shit or die.

Fuck this guy.

"I'll hook you up," he says, like he's actually hooking us up with anything. In a flash he hands us two green wrist-bands with *Over 21* scrawled on them in bright white letters.

Mindii gives him a cordial smile and I glare at him, which I'm not sure is as intimidating as I think with my crocheted beard.

Mindii leads me through the crowd, holding my hand, gently, to let me know there is more to this grip than survival. Our hands are sweaty but neither of us seems particularly bothered by it. Or I mean, like, I'm trying not to be.

There is a loud but lovely breeze inside. I crane my neck upwards and see the multi-headed hound-dragon— Baloo, one of the fearsome protectors of the Malmesbury Academy grounds. Her heads are papier-mâché and spray-painted with black-light-reflected color. Each of the heads is secured to scaffolding just in front of the industrial fan, so it looks like it's jumping out as soon as you enter. Sheer curtains hang from the walls, and fairy lights adorn what would otherwise be pretty ugly wooden beams. The tables are decorated with lanterns, and there are designated areas with house colors for all the major fiefdoms.

The music is loud, nervous energy exuding from the acoustic guitar. Music here is always live. Right now there's a two-person band playing with one acoustic guitar between them. They look younger than when me, Ngozi, Shirin, and the Georges formed our first sorcery metal band.

Mindii's mouth is moving. I get closer to see if she's flirting with me and how best to respond. "Will you move your ass?" Mindii says as I abruptly awake from the dream. She's still holding my hand as we elbow our way through the crowd. There's a blank wooden sign for the unnamed inn Dafydd and Safia Brambleberry run. "I'm so thirsty," Mindii yells over the music as we get to the counter.

We order two plastic pewter glasses of essentially water, although it's called Thandajal from the one scene it's mentioned in the third book. The bartender pours the pewter. Barkeep? Tapster? No, too modern.

We make our way through to the center of the warehouse, next to a large foam rock designed to look like we're hundreds of miles underground. We laugh because neither of us wants to say out loud that we just spent almost eleven dollars each on water.

Thandajal. Tastes fine. And I must admit, it does taste better in a pewter.

We lean against a wall with hologrammed portraits designed to look like The Great Spirits who guard the fjords and the wilds beyond the school grounds.

Stefan comes shuffling his feet, like he got told there are no more free food samples at the mall. He's carrying a plastic cup with the word *MINOR* written in glow-in-the-dark Sharpie.

I take a gulp of Thandajal.

He points at me and bursts out laughing. If this Thandajal weren't so damn expensive I would throw some in his face, ruin his fancy imported suit. I can't even fantasize about doing it because it's so wasteful.

"You know," Stefan says, "we spent all evening trying to hunt down tickets to this party because of your, uh . . ."

"Shenanigans?" I offer.

"Can you believe how closely they're checking these wristbands? Hold up," Stefan says. "How did you both get the green band? Trade with me."

"Can't, man," I say. "I love alcohol. I'm drinking some right now and going back for more. To get faded."

"More faded," Mindii adds.

"So faded," I needlessly add to her add.

"Very drunk," she needlessly adds to my needless add to her original add.

"You two are so weird. I got a hookup anyway," Stefan says. He frowns at our lack of awe and accolades. I realize he is not used to being alone, without his crew to back him up, and almost feel sorry for him. Then he says, "If I ever went down to that magic school I wouldn't bother with—"

"Sorcery. Not m-magic," I say, gleefully interrupting him. Stefan is a little flummoxed, but he gets his train of thought back in a few seconds.

"Okay. Uh. Yeah," he says. "Well. Anyway. I'd go straight to the cool caste and learn war magic. That other one doesn't seem worth it."

"Plentyns?" Mindii says. "You need to be born a Plentyn. You don't learn sorcery as a plentyn. You hone it."

"W-war sorcery is c-completely different," I say, taking

196

a sip of my overpriced Thandajal. "You know what really gets my goat?" That's something I never thought I would be saying to Stefan.

"Self-placers," Mindii says.

"Yeah. You can't just place yourself wherever you want, you daft bastard," Ngozi says, sidling into the conversation along with Shirin.

"You're born into a Misl. Short of a revolution, that is fucking that," Shirin says.

Stefan squirms, unsure of what to say. He clears his throat. "What?" he yells, pretending to respond to someone calling him away from the crowd. He's about to awkwardly walk away when the music comes to a halt, the lights dim, and all eyes are on the stage.

The two organizers, Alejandra and Rosa, excitedly welcome everyone to the sorcery metal lineup. Sorcery metal is the general term for any kind of music in the Snollygoster series. A little bit of Jamie Snollygoster country music, experimental Fjord Bhangra, hip-hop. Basically everything.

Alejandra begins with, "We are very pleased to be bringing you yet another year of some insanely talented musicians! You might even say it's going to be . . ."

"Sorcerific!" Rosa says as someone does a jazzy *womp womp* sound from a guitar.

I love the corniness.

After the opening speech, the first band starts setting up. The Georges are near the stage wearing their crazy-ass metal bird cosplay. Shirin is wearing small, glow-in-the-dark studded earrings, a chain mail skirt to emulate the armor of Jamie Snollygoster, black-light-reflective leggings, and multicolored sunglasses. Ngozi is wearing the same outfit she was wearing earlier as Chur, with a much more dramatic presence.

Our set will be starting soon.

Our final set.

Oof.

I've always loved how smart Ngozi is, even if it does get incredibly annoying sometimes.

"That was fun making Stefan fuck off," I say.

"Yeah, that was fun," Ngozi says. "Let's make sure we save some of our rage for the stage."

"Uh. Yeah," I say.

"Uh. Yeah, izzit?" Ngozi says.

"I mean. Yeahhh! Let's do it! Woo!"

"Fucking better. Let's gather the fam."

This is it. I'm so not ready.

I head to the stage with the Bramble-core crew.

We're almost at the stage and I'm feeling all kinds of things rising up. I want to lean in and hug her, but I just can't do it without crying. If I stay rooted, though, I'll be fine. I usually am.

Immediately an announcement comes on for the next three bands to line up. That's us. I find a quiet corner to settle my nerves. I take the pouch in my hands and pull out Goldy's notebook. My hand trembles, filled with all kinds of energy and thoughts and feelings I don't know how to express or deal with. A lanky Sikh dude walks up to me. I stop what I'm doing and pause to look at him. He's wearing a bright-ass Thor outfit, except instead of blond hair, he's wearing a red dastaar. In the middle of Snollygoster Soiree. Yeah, he definitely stands out. But there's something familiar about this guy. He approaches me as my finger absentmindedly traces over random artwork in the notebook.

"Hey," he says. "So this is a cool party." His accent is slightly Indian.

"Yeah," I say. "I–it's cool."

I see Mindii approaching and I look up, ignoring Sikh Thor. Not like we were having some deep conversation, anyway.

"Take your beard off," Mindii says.

"I'm not that kind of boy," I say, fake-offended. "Is it crooked?"

"Just do it."

I reach my hands behind me to unhook the beard.

We're standing side by side, my hand brushing hers.

I feel I should compliment her. "You . . . have a nice face."

"Oh Jesus Falafel Christ," Ngozi says.

"Give me a friggin' moment!"

The Thor guy, whoever he is, is gone.

Mindii's hand clasps the back of my neck, the world pauses for a few seconds. We kiss. Then we kiss some more.

Time slows. This entire place feels more magical. I feel a sudden burst of energy. I want to sing a love song. "Good luck," Mindii whispers, her breath nuzzling my ear.

My crocheted beard is dangling on one side.

"I feel like doing an upbeat musical theater guitar solo now."

"Oh no," Mindii says, laughing. "I take it back. Rewind!"

"Not on yer life."

I get on stage, then yell at Mindii. "Just to confirm. Was that just a good luck kiss or another thing?"

"Another thing, fool," she says.

I pick up my guitar. Ready to rock.

CHAPTER 15

A VERY METAL DEATH

The familiar feeling of performing live settles in, the rush, the joy, the terror, the fear. I love it. I examine the blond strand in my hair and move it out of my eyes for the millionth time today, then reach up under my crocheted beard to touch my face. I am getting kind of used to this. It's still not me, but I'm closer to knowing what "me" even looks like. I think.

I look over at our crowd, a sea of brown and black, with a few specks of white. They are all clapping and cheering, excited to see us, listen to us, watch us.

I turn to look at Ngozi. She's beaming and already screaming into the mic, even though we haven't gotten into formation and Cambodian George is still tuning her harp.

In ninth grade, me, Ngozi, the two Georges, and Shirin were some of the only kids in our whole class who had read Jamie Snollygoster. When our history teacher talked about fascism like it was a thing of the past, or segregation or McCarthyism, we knew the deal. We'd lived through the Great Misl War in the third book and understood fascism was more about good people doing nothing than bad people doing predictable bad-people shit. We get into formation. Japanese George is on drums, Cambodian George has finished fine-tuning her harp. Shirin is on bass, Ngozi at the mic stand. My guitar—the Epiphone Flying V—makes that familiar crackle as I plug it into the amp. I run my fingers over the special-order strings for Ultimate Death Metal Shredding.

I watch Ngozi adjust the mic stand and am grateful she went to the trouble of recruiting Mindii and bringing all my shit.

I sometimes wish we could go back to ninth grade, when everything was new and exciting, like we had all the time in the world. Like we had forever. Actually on second thought, ninth grade was shit. But at least I get tonight.

The lights dim. The audience starts yelling louder. I scan the crowd and spot Mindii toward the front.

"We're Unkempt," Ngozi growls into the mic, over the applause.

We start playing our first song, all about how Safia hates brushing her hair. I feel energized and full of joy, watching Mindii watching me. I walk up to the mic Ngozi is using and very politely scream into it.

It's a joyous scream, which transitions seamlessly into

a metal-rage scream. Like we're still who we used to be. At least for now.

We're all drenched in sweat. Ngozi turns my way and gives me a subtle wink to start the shredding. The strobe lights flash and all the instrumentalists give each other space to take the spotlight—Japanese George is going to town on the drums, Cambodian George is violently strumming her harp, Shirin decided to abandon her instrument and is headbanging across the stage. Then it's my turn again, and I really go for it, slashing chords on the eight-string like this is my last night left on this Earth.

The crowd erupts as we walk off the stage for a dramatic exit, and immediately come back on to do our skit. On cue, I walk up to the mic, and in my super-authentic-above-average Dafydd accent, say: "I-I-I'm Dafydd." I pause a really long time as my eyes watch the Sikh Thor wade through the crowd toward the doors.

Suddenly I recognize him. Not from the gurdwara or around town.

From Goldy's notebook. I know the exact page number. There's a sketch of a boy that looks just like this Thor without the cosplay. I've always thought it was a smudge under his eye. It looks like a birthmark or a scar or something. What's the deal with this weird Punjabi poem Goldy wrote? What is going on?

Ngozi lightly elbows me in the ribs, prodding me to set

the joke up. I touch my pouch and feel my dead phone, the rice, but where is the notebook?

Everything is in slow motion. My lips are moving, panic rising in my voice. Sniggers in the crowd. Some people probably think I'm nervous, others know I'm stuttering live on stage. As usual. Some might think it's part of the joke.

"Ach a Fil!" Ngozi says, with amplified offense. The crowd roars with laughter at the inside joke; even people who didn't properly get the joke are joining in. But my mind is elsewhere.

Did Thor just steal my notebook?

What. The. Hell. Why? I storm off the stage as everyone looks on quizzically. Ngozi ends the set the same way we usually do. "Unkempt out," she growls into the mic.

With a fizzle, our last performance is over.

I can see nothing except bodies for miles as I attempt to barrel through to find this thieving Thor. I don't see Mindii or anyone familiar as I push through. I'm getting shoved, my shoes stomped on, but my elbows are out as I force my way to the door.

I pause to breathe in the parking lot. The ice cream truck has moved to the other side, but there is no line now. And there's Thor! He's talking to G-Dawg in the distance.

Who is this guy? Why'd he steal the notebook? How does he know G-Dawg?

You are a dead man, I consider screaming. I walk a little

closer to them. *You are both dead men,* I think is a better line. Or maybe a more direct, *Give me back my fucking notebook, or you gonna die tonight.*

But I'm still way too far away for them to hear me anyway. Sweat trickles down my neck as I just stand there in the middle of the parking lot.

I could theoretically punch him. Or G-Dawg. I bet I could land one solid punch. Maybe not on both of them, but one of them. G-Dawg would never see it coming. The downside to his humongousness is that it would take him at least twenty seconds to block my fist. Kapow, and the mass of muscles is on the ground.

One punch is all I need. Straight to the nose, or the throat. Or the balls. That's it! A punch straight to the pakoray. Then I could take back the notebook. Find Mindii and Ngozi.

Goldy may have been a selfish alcoholic, but his notebook is all I have left.

A couple years ago, Goldy came out to me while eating samosa and watching an old Shammi Kapoor movie. "I am a gay," he'd said mid-bite, eyes still on the screen.

I wasn't sure if he was joking or serious. But saying "I'm a gay" all deadpan is not funny. And not Goldy's kind of humor anyway. Two minutes passed in near silence while Goldy crunched his samosa and my brain went into overdrive.

After deciding this was definitely Goldy coming out, I dove toward him and attempted to hug him. He was finishing a bite of samosa, pouring some Sweet and Spicy Maggi onto his plate, and grinning as he watched Shammi be extra camp. My arm knocked the plate over and spilled sauce all over his pants. He looked at me, startled, and gave me a half-hearted hug back.

"Thanks for the support, uloo da pattha," he said, peeling me off him. "You're cleaning all this mess and doing my laundry. Now go buy me another bottle of Sweet and Spicy Maggi, khote da khur."

That was kind of it. He didn't tell me about anyone he was dating, but would sometimes comment on shirtless men of Bollywood. But to be fair, so would I.

That notebook is all I have. To decode him. To understand him. I need to get that notebook back now.

And then I see it. Hear it.

The screech of wheels peeling out. Thor and G-Dawg are gone.

All that practice making rash decisions, I lament. And I still haven't written a word down. I can make a rash decision to eat friggin' red bean, but can't make the rash decision to confront Norway's brownest, skinniest Thor, who apparently made it into my big brother's dumbass journal. Couldn't I have just started with "Hello," and gone

206

from there? Did I have to make it so damn complicated? Too little, too late: the Sunny G Story.

I ponder heading back into the warehouse to find Ngozi or Mindii. Neither of whom have bothered to come looking for me. But before I can make a move, I see the bright flashing lights behind me and realize why everyone left in such a hurry. It's the po-po. The Five-O. Or as the British say, bobbies on the beat. Even though Ngozi insists nobody in England calls it that. The internet wouldn't lie to me.

I watch a gaggle of bodies in their black-and-blue uniforms hustle past us. The party is getting shut down.

I see Stefan, who is attempting some kind of swagger. Or maybe he's just drunk. It's always idiots like him that shut down parties like this. But then again, we didn't actually need to have alcohol at the party. As my mind goes back and forth between blaming drunk guys like Stefan and the actual alcohol, I finally spot Ngozi and Mindii.

Ngozi and Mindii come marching toward me. I'm expecting Ngozi to be furious, but she just looks at me and says, "Might as well tell me. You have that face."

"I do not," I say.

"You bloody well do."

I need a moment to compose the words.

"Goldy's notebook," I mumble. "It's gone."

They both let out a gasp. Before either of them can say or do anything, a loud voice tells those of us outside to have a seat on the ground. A couple kids start running and get full-on slammed wrestling style, tackled to the ground by grown-ass men in blue.

Drunk Stefan thinks it's hilarious.

I've never seen drunk Stefan and I'll be honest, I kinda assumed he would be a nicer drunk. Like when Goldy would start drinking, he would start telling me he loved me, said sorry about all kinds of shit, even things that weren't his fault. Like the electoral college and Common Core.

I feel a pang in my stomach. The kind you get when it's four p.m. and you realize all you've had that day are chips and a soda and your body is furious at you. I bite my lip as I think about being rash. If I'd made a rash decision and just gone up to Sikh Thor and G-Dawg, maybe I'd still be sitting here, but at least I would have the notebook.

Goldy's notebook is gone. My notebook is gone.

I stifle a sob as my words settle in.

CHAPTER 16

A VERY DARING HEIST

Police officers are frantically pacing around the lot. There are three cars and about six cops. They've handcuffed a few kids, but mostly they're just barking orders and posing rhetorical questions. *Sit down. Stand up. Don't move. Move. Wanna go to jail?* I definitely do not want to be here right now.

I'm sitting next to Mindii and Ngozi.

"Gonna do it," I say out loud to psych myself up. "Just... gonna be rash and ..."

"Do what?" Ngozi says. "Run past the cops through the car park like a dozy pillock?

"Wot've you done to Sunny? Thinks he's Jackie Chan," Ngozi whisper-yells to Mindii. Mindii shrugs. Ngozi's eye catches a girl with beautiful brown skin, a yellow Afro, and a nose ring sitting across from us. She's got squiggles carved onto a silver square on her headband, and a bright orange jumpsuit. She could be cosplaying anyone. A prisoner?

"Which Hokage are you?" Ngozi says to the girl, referencing the coveted title of Naruto, who this girl is apparently cosplaying.

The girl smiles brightly. "I am the Seventh Hokage. You are?"

"Chur."

Yellow Afro has no idea who that even is.

"By the way, where's the accent from?" she says.

"Issss g-global, innit," I answer for Ngozi with a smirk.

Ngozi glares at me.

"Don't make me look like a tit in front of Hot Naruto," she whispers.

"I'm from Crawley, a town in West Sussex. On a street called Fitchet Close. It's where Gatwick airport is," Ngozi overshares with the girl.

"Ah. England," the girl muses.

They both nod at each other like bobbleheads.

Unbelievable. I'm in the middle of a crisis and Ngozi is flirting. I've seen her flirt since ninth grade and it usually ends in absolute disaster. Her game has not improved one fucking bit. Now she thinks she's some kinda expert.

"Ngozi," she says, introducing herself.

"Aisha," the girl says.

"H-h-hanji. Hello. I'm Sunny. A Virgo. My favorite food—" I say, interrupting their little bubble.

"Is red bean," Mindii interrupts my interrupt. "So what's the plan?" she says.

I scan the parking lot.

There's got to be some way to make our great escape.

Bingo.

Raj is sitting at the end of the sidewalk. Past him is the ice cream truck, parked there in all its glory. I bet the spare keys are right where Goldy used to leave them. Under the mudflap.

I look at Mindii and nod toward the truck. She follows my eyes and knows exactly what I'm saying.

"Let's do it," she says, squeezing my hand. I'm so thankful she's here.

"Not you too," says Ngozi. "Tell this daft bastard he can't just go clomping across the car park undetected."

"Well. This is not something to make a rash decision about," Mindii concedes. "But, if we strategize, we could totally go clomping." Our fingers touch, and I clasp Mindii's hand.

"Fine," Ngozi says. "Both of you have completely lost the plot. With my help and Mindii's help we might be able to pull it off. You just need a distraction."

"No," Aisha says. "You need a distraction who is non-threatening to the police." The three of us look over at Stefan.

"Perfect," Ngozi says.

211

"I kinda wanna get outta here too," Aisha says.

Ngozi softens. "We could. You know. Leave together. Me and you."

"Lit." Aisha and Ngozi stop speaking to look at each other's faces.

I roll my eyes so hard, I'm surprised my eyeballs are still attached to my face. Before I know it, Mindii and Ngozi wave him over. The cops barely bat an eye.

"That cop," Mindii says to Stefan, "said you seem a little drunk."

"I AM NOT DRUNK," Stefan slurs as he stumbles over to the cops closest to us indignantly.

Oh man, this might actually work.

He's getting closer and closer to the two police officers and getting more and more animated. The cops stare at him, totally confused, totally distracted. Not sure whether to quietly arrest him or make him a soothing cup of chamomile tea.

I make eye contact with Mindii. She tosses Ngozi the keys to her bike and points in the direction of where she parked. Ngozi covers her mouth with excitement as we stand up. There's still a moment where we can sit back down, act like we were just stretching our legs. Stefan is slurring about white privilege not being real. His voice fades into the background as me and Mindii break out into a sprint, still holding hands.

We make it to Goldy's truck.

I fumble around and find the keys under the mudflap just where he used to leave them. Sure enough, they're here. I unlock the truck and start up the engine. The sound of ice cream music remixed with bhangra blares.

Shit.

I quickly lower the volume and look over at the two cops. And they're looking back at the truck, one of them frozen in butt-scratching position, both of them slowly realizing what's happening.

Raj is standing up now, waving his hands slowly yet angrily in my direction. Everyone starts scrambling to their feet, looking at us. I see Ngozi and Aisha strolling on down toward the bike as we pull out of the lot, onto the streets.

And we're out of there.

It's almost one in the morning and I am wide-awake, adrenaline pumping through my veins. Or maybe it's the two cups of cha from a few hours ago? I have no clue where to even start looking for this Thor guy. I don't even know where to look for G-Dawg. Someone must know.

Even though I've turned the volume all the way down I can't escape its sound.

"This music is kind of catchy," Mindii says.

"You hear it too? Good. It's not just in my head."

She laughs.

"Interesting seat belt."

"Oh yeah. You gotta hold it," I say.

"Yep," she says, already holding on to the loose strap.

I bite my lip trying to figure out what to do. Should I exit, turn around, park on the side, and just run away?

The streets are suddenly filled with cars pulling out. The inside of Goldy's ice cream truck is lit up with black lights, the freezer is making that familiar buzzing sound. "I sometimes think he's still here," I say. "During h-his sober b-bouts, me and Goldy used to sit back there and eat ice cream and listen to music."

There's a long silence.

"The ice cream truck music?" she says.

I look back at her and burst out laughing. I pull off to the side of the road, then start crying. Then laugh again. She lets go of the seat belt and holds me close.

"You must think I should be in a room with padded walls right now, huh?"

"I don't think anyone should be in a room like that. Sometimes, everyone just needs a hug."

I don't feel awkward about saying any of these things to her, or acting like a fool. It's a weird feeling, not feeling weird because I'm not being judged for it. Not even the silence feels awkward.

I start the truck back up and we get on the road. I look over at her and feel a little calmer. We come to a red light and I turn my head to see the glow of the Paradise Liquor sign, like a beacon in choppy waters, the only thing that's lit on the entire block.

I don't know who runs the place, but odds are it's Punjabi-owned because that's just how it is in Fresno. As long as it's not some old-ass forty-year-old uncle working tonight, someone may know what party G-Dawg and Thor will be at. And as much as I don't want to think about it, odds are Goldy has been here and bought the garbage that sent him right back to rehab, or that ended things completely.

It's worth a shot. It's the only thing I can think to do.

I take the U-turn and pull into the lot and park right in front of the store.

"So what's the plan?" Mindii says.

"No fucking clue. Gonna throw some bottles, set some things on fire," I say, getting out of the truck.

"Great," Mindii says. "Glad I'm wearing the right earrings then."

We open the door and walk inside. It's bright with fluorescent lights. Bhangra beats are playing loudly, and the TV is on with the anime *Afro Samurai* playing. A Punjabi dude wearing a gold necklace and a "Thug Life" T-shirt rests his elbows on the counter. He has a sketch pad in front of him, fine-tip Sakura pens, colored pencils, and markers scattered on the flat surface next to the cash register. He's a young kid around my age, with a heavy muscular build that makes him look older than he actually is. He doesn't go to our school, but I know his face. Preet. He blinks real hard at me and scrambles to step back.

"We're closing! We got cameras, man. The money is already out," he announces forcefully. "And I'm armed. There's a gang of people in the back. Oyyyyy, Chacha! Mamu!" he screams.

He is still scrambling behind the counter and unsheathes a flimsy-looking katana, aiming its blade at us both from ten feet away. We move behind a stack of chips and corn nuts.

"I–I'm just looking for Sunny," I say. "I mean, I'm Sunny. I'm looking for a notebook."

"What?" he says as the blade of the katana shakes.

"We're not robbing you, dude," Mindii says.

"Then why are you dressed like that?"

"What are you talking about?" I say, perplexed for a moment. Then I remember. I'm the weird one in this context. The fake beard. The boots. The Dafydd.

"Anyway, we don't sell notebooks. Go write on your hand or something." He is still aiming the katana at us.

Two guys emerge from the back, near the sodas and beers. I immediately recognize Jagpal Saini. He is technically an uncle, but he's too much in denial of his age for anyone to ever call him Uncle Saini with a straight face. Looks like he's forty, thinks he's twenty-five, a bald spot on the top of his head, a few gray hairs in his stubble. Randeep is slowly walking behind him. He's wearing a large football jersey, a small white turban, and an untrained beard that looks like it's having way too much fun on his face. He's only slightly older than us, around Goldy's age. I know all of them from various parties I've been forced to attend over the years. Under normal circumstances, they would probably recognize me. Randeep used to hang with Goldy at these events back in the day.

"Man, put your dumbass sword away, Preet," Jagpal says.

"Is it Halloween?" Randeep says. "Are y'all gonna duel? You look like a Punjabi leprechaun."

"Yo, that's it! Is that a knitted beard? Where's yer pot o' gold?" Jagpal says, doing a very ungraceful and inaccurate jig. This is why nobody calls him Uncle.

"It's crocheted," I say icily.

"I don't doubt you think there's a difference," Jagpal says.

I sigh heavily. "Of course there's a motherfucking difference!" I shriek. "Knitting involves two pointy needles and if you drop a stitch that's it, your life is fucked because the entire thing will unravel. Crochet is more forgiving and done with a single crochet hook. And that's just the basic difference."

Jagpal and Randeep look at each other. Then keel over with laughter.

"On second thought, you ain't no leprechaun. You're like that one dude who's all, 'Thou shalt not pass,'" Randeep says in a deep voice.

"Nah, son, it's like this." Jagpal clears his throat. "Thou SHALT not pass!"

"I'm not Gandalf from Lord of the Bhenchod Rings," I say in exasperation.

I grit my teeth. "I'm Dafydd."

They all stare blankly at me.

"I'm cosplaying." I sigh. "I'm dressed up as a character named Dafydd."

"Anyway, that's not the line," Mindii says.

"That's not the line? Of course it's the line. You know how many times I've seen the movie? That's Gandalf's most famous line," Randeep scoffs.

"Well. I've read all the books and watched the movies," Mindii says.

"You've read the books?" Randeep says incredulously.

"The big fat books? Like *The Hobbit* and shit?" Jagpal adds.

"Two nerd bros want to question my nerd status. What a surprise," Mindii says, leaving them at a loss for words momentarily. "Yes, motherfucker. I have. And 'Thou shalt not pass' is not the line. Not in the book. Not in the movie."

"What's the line then?" Randeep says.

Preet lets out a snigger while putting the finishing

touches on his preliminary sketch, a lone Sikh with robes and a mechanical eye, holding a spinning circular blade.

"In the book, it's 'You cannot pass!'" she intones, placing a bag of corn nuts and a bag of chips above her head to emulate Gandalf's one-handed sword and staff. Her voice sounds like it's coming from the pit of her stomach. "And in the movie, it's 'You shall not pass!'" she says even more dramatically.

"I don't know. Is that right?" Jagpal says, turning to Randeep, then irritatedly at Preet as he continues sketching.

"Let me try it again. Thou shalt not pass!" Randeep booms, using two Oreo packets near him as props.

"That sounds right," Jagpal says, and halfheartedly adds, "You cannot pass."

"Oyyy meditating bandar!" Jagpal yells at Preet. "You're constantly barking in my ear from morning to night. Now I'm getting my ass handed to me and you're quiet like a digestive biscuit. Say something, fool!"

Preet closes up his sketch pad and starts putting his art supplies away. "You're not enunciating, that's why it don't sound right. It's from *The Fellowship of the Ring*."

"Damn," Randeep says.

"Oh ho ho. I'm not enunciating? Go on, Sir Ian McKellen. Let's hear your enunciation skills, professional actor," Jagpal mocks.

Preet steps away from the cash register, grabs some

chips, and smashes them together in the air violently. "Go back to the Shadow!" Preet says super loudly. It's almost comical how serious he's taking these lines.

"You cannot pass!" they all say in unison.

I look at Mindii, Preet, Jagpal, and Randeep behaving less like professional enunciating actors, and more like professional bandar. Dafydd doesn't look anything like a leprechaun or a wizard.

Mindii opens up the bag of chips she was holding and makes slow crunching sounds as she eats.

I exhale. "Well, so glad you find all this funny." I change my tone from awkwardly conversational to a tone most fight-y.

I clear my throat. "I am looking for my brother's notebook. It's super important and was stolen like half an hour ago. G-G-Gaganpreet. Goldy. Gill."

"Yeah," Mindii chimes in, her mouth full of chips.

It feels so strange saying the name on his birth certificate like that. I don't think I've ever heard him called Gaganpreet, not even when my parents were extra pissed at him.

A hush falls over them all and the only sound is Mindii crunching the last of her chips.

"Goldy was a good dude," Jagpal says.

"Yeah. He was cool."

"That dude knew how to party," Randeep says ruefully, like this is a compliment. "I remember this one party.

Four beers and I was buzzed. Goldy downs a full bottle of Johnny Walker. Are you hearing me? He just straight chugged it. The most baller thing I've ever seen."

"No soda. No water. Solid Punjab da puttar," Jagpal says.

"Well. He's dead now. But glad he entertained you with his party tricks," I say sharply.

They're silent.

"You're his little bro," Jagpal says.

"That shit was tragic, man," Randeep adds.

"Which fool's party are you talking about?" I say, ignoring the bullshit sympathetic tone of his voice.

Don't say Chotu. Don't say Chotu. Don't say Chotu.

"Chotu," Randeep says.

Foibles. Foibles. Motherfucking. Foibles.

"That boy's an alcoholic, man," Jagpal says. "Ayy, Preet, that's the party you're going to, right?"

"Word," Preet says.

"Goldy was an alcoholic too," I say.

"An alcoholic? Goldy? Nah, man. I know alcoholics. Goldy was only like that at parties. That's just being Punjabi. Like what's it called. Drinking socially and shit," Jagpal says.

"Social drinker," Randeep says.

"Chotu's definitely not a social drinker," Preet clarifies. "Unless by social drinker, you mean a complete alcoholic, falling over and shit."

I'm about to smite this pajama and his whole store, Punjabi genes and all. Before I have a chance to react, Mindii bulldozes past everyone and grabs another bag of salt and vinegar chips and two orange sodas, putting them down on the counter.

She looks at them.

"I'm not paying for this shit. Give me a bag though. Where can we find a big chesty guy named G–Dawg?" Mindii says.

"And a Sikh guy dressed as Thor? He's the one who stole Goldy's notebook," I say.

"Wait. Thor? Isn't that the guy Goldy was going out with a while back?" Randeep says as Preet puts the chips and orange sodas into a large paper bag.

Preet shrugs his shoulders.

"When you. When you . . ." I sputter. "Say going out? Do you? Goldy . . ."

It takes them a minute to understand what I'm saying.

"Sometimes people are gay," Preet says.

"I know that!" I explode. "Why do you nobodies know that."

"I'm gonna let that slide because you're upset," Jagpal says.

"We are not nobodies. We are somebodies," Randeep says.

"But you're being kind of a dick," Preet says, taking a pencil and tucking some stray hair back into his turban.

"And possibly homophobic. I can't fully tell based on the context, but it's leaning that way," Randeep says.

I am genuinely disturbed, shocked, a little nauseated, and feeling kinda light-headed. Of course I knew he was gay. I'm his brother. When he came out to me I thought it was a special moment. But. What the hell? He told these bird brains? Does everyone know? Did he tell Mama and Papa?

"It's kinda common knowledge. Some people are dicks. Some people are like supportive and stuff. And some just don't care." Randeep looks over at me.

"Who else knows?" I say.

"I don't have a guest list. There wasn't like a coming-out party." He shrugs.

"He wasn't advertising or nothing, but not like hiding either," Jagpal says.

I really thought I was the only one who knew.

"Chotu's throwing this gamer party. G-Dawg will be there," Preet says. "Maybe this Thor guy will be with him if they just left."

"These kids with their terminology," Jagpal says. "Gamer party? It's called video games. I'm telling you, you're addicted to that screen. At least my generation had to wait for our modem to make that *khhhhhh* sound to connect to the internet."

"How many TikToks did you make today?" Preet barks.

"That's different!" Jagpal retorts.

"You going to the party now?" Mindii says.

"I've been ready for an hour," Preet says, looking right at Jagpal and Randeep.

Preet rolls his eyes.

"Just go with these nice people. I'm going to sleep," Jagpal says. "You're gonna get wasted and spend all night there anyway."

I look at Mindii and she has that expressionless face.

"Can't believe this shit," Preet says as they usher us outside and start locking up. He grabs one end of a duffel bag and points at the other. I reluctantly pick it up. Damn, that shit is heavy.

"I guess we're continuing the rash decisions," I say to Mindii.

"Who would have thought," she says. "Stefan and his caucacity were the key to keeping this night of rash decisions going."

CHAPTER 17

YAAR, WHERE'S THE DESI PARTY?

The duffel bag is making all kinds of clanging sounds as it shifts around.

Dammit. This thing is full of liquor. Of course.

I look Preet right in the eye. "You know my brother died because of this shit?"

"That sucks for your brother, but what do you want me to do? Not bring this liquor? Close our business? You wanna go to this party? I'm doing you a favor."

His gold chain jingles as I help hoist the bag of poison into the back of the ice cream truck.

Once we're inside, Preet adjusts his light-up belt buckle so it's more centered. The buckle has a gaudy flashing dragon on it, like an insect slowly devouring itself.

It reminds me of the light-up framed religious pictures Goldy still has hanging in his room that he insisted on buying on our last visit to Punjab.

Preet looks like an idiot.

"You even know how to drive this thing? Give me the

keys. I can get us there without my beard endangering all of our lives."

I bite my tongue.

Preet's beard looks like what my beard used to look like. His turban is definitely not what mine looked like, though. "There's no way I'm giving you the keys to my ice cream truck."

I have a right to it. It's Goldy's, and Raj didn't exactly pay top dollar for it. He paid nothing. Mom and Dad just gave it to him. For nothing! I mean fine, I didn't want it, but still we could have sold it.

"Nope," I say, gritting my teeth. I start up the truck and my hands go everywhere trying to contain the black lights, the ice cream truck music, the bhangra beats. On cue, the broken windshield wipers decide to go off right now too. Mindii presses a couple buttons and most of the panic-inducing sounds are over.

I put it in drive.

"Yo, sick beats, man. You remix that?"

"Kinda. It's my brother's."

"So, not kinda. Like at all," Preet says. Man, this guy is irritating.

"Well, it could be kinda. You don't know. I could have inspired him. Laid down a beat. A track."

"Nah," Preet says, not even entertaining the possibility that I could be the type of person to lay down beats.

I don't even need this dumbass for directions. I know where Chotu lives. We haven't been to his house in years. I don't know even if this Thor guy will be there.

"First off," Preet says, "when did this girl call shotgun?"

"This girl's got a name, Dollar Store Texas Ranger," Mindii says. "Couldn't get a brighter fucking belt buckle? You gonna wrangle up some . . . what are those things called?"

"C-cows?" I say.

"Yeah. Those? I'm Mindii. Call me by my name if you like your kneecaps."

"Yeah, f-fool," I add, like she needs my help with anything.

Preet gets quiet. If his skin were lighter, it would have turned bright red.

"Not even a cushion back here," he says. He's taken out his phone. "What's that hashtag when you get your gaand handed to you by a girl?"

"Besti complete?" I say.

It was one of Goldy's favorite hashtags. He'd sit there for hours coming up with funny besti complete situations, often involving me. I smile as I remember the time I had just bought this really expensive button-down from Express and Goldy warned me not to wear it while I ate Mama's spicy tari vala chicken because she uses a lot of turmeric. It immediately splashed my button-down and it looked awful. Goldy chased me around the house just so he could take a photo of me and use that hashtag.

"What is besti?" Mindii says.

"Humiliation. Besti complete means you can't do no more."

"Oh, I could do more," Mindii says. "Don't post that yet. Your besti hasn't even started. Always use a girl's name. And don't talk about me in the third person either. Or Mindii is gonna beat Preet's ass."

"Then it'll really be #BestiComplete," I say.

I consider telling Mindii and Preet about some of the things Goldy would post about me with that hashtag. But I want to keep those stories. They're mine.

Mindii opens up the bag of chips and offers him some. Preet takes a handful and crunches them loudly.

The only thing worse than sitting in the passenger's side of the ice cream truck is sitting in the driver's seat. I try and adjust my driving to account for the terrible suspension. The seat moves up and down, absorbing every single movement. I can hear the random ice cream bars shuffling around inside the freezer. Mindii's holding the seat belt.

I stop at a red light before getting on the highway and hope nobody pulls us over because I can't even put on the pretense of anything about this being legal. I'm kinda glad we're driving in the wild. No cops come out here this late unless they're called. Raj wouldn't call them. Would he?

We exit the highway and now we're driving in pretty much pitch-black. "Chotu's place is right past the walnut trees. See that ghetto-ass vineyard ahead with all those trash cans in front of it? Take a right and keep going down that road," Preet says.

I go over a bump in the road and hear him groan as he bounces in the air.

I take the right and the farmland starts to feel familiar. Sure enough, out of nowhere a ginormous gate appears. I can see silhouettes of the Sierra Nevada foothills behind the house. The ice cream truck starts gasping for air as soon as we hit the gravel driveway. There are cars and trucks parked outside the gate, but we pull right up to the intercom.

"Yo," a muffled voice comes through the machine.

"We're friends of Ch—" I say.

"Chad," Preet booms, leaning over my shoulder.

I turn to look at him.

"What? That's his name in mixed company."

There's a pause and the gates buzz open. We drive in and I maneuver around a fountain with a statue of a kid peeing. Some Roman art thing. Chotu used to be so embarrassed by it when we would come to his house back in the day.

I look at the cars and Hummers and hideous limo-Hummers lining the driveway. His parents are super-rich farmers. They bought the place off of super-rich Mexicans, who bought the place off super-rich white people. And every one of them thought this ugly-ass fountain connoted high class.

"Okay, the entrance looks like it's on the other side of this pedo fountain," Mindii says. I crack a smile because we are both thinking the same thing.

"It's Europeeing," Mindii says. We crack up.

Preet looks confused. "Well, the origins are probably the Renaissance, so yeah I guess that's accurate. I'd say fifteenth-century Italy." He strokes his beard with no hint of irony in his voice. He doesn't even register the highly intellectual pun. Europeeing. So good. "It's a replica of the Manneken Pis that's been in the Brussels City Museum since 1619. But sculpture of young male children has been around for—"

"Why are all these people crowding us?" I interrupt Preet's incredibly boring TED Talk, a little panicked. Then I remember I'm at a gamer party and we just drove into the compound in an ice cream truck. So we may not need the Scooby-Doo team to solve this mystery after all.

"Uh . . . what are we supposed to do with all these people?" I say.

Mindii shrugs her shoulders.

"Come on," she says after a beat. "Let's go sell this shit like capitalists."

"A real capitalist would buy a whole fleet of ice cream trucks and send his uninsured low-paid workers here," Preet says cheerfully.

I reluctantly turn off the ignition, duck my head to avoid hitting the roof, and walk past Preet as confidently as I can. Me and Mindii move toward the window. I open up the freezer and thankfully it's halfway full.

Raj has kept it pretty well stocked, but mostly with random unknown ice creams. I only recognize the choco-taco and the drumstick. Everything else looks complicated. And there's no price list anywhere.

"Yo," I whisper to Mindii. "Where's the price list?"

Preet looks over at us. I grit my teeth and smile.

There's an empty makhan da dubba—a container of butter that Raj is using to keep the cash like a professional.

"There's never makhan in it," Preet says. "Always in the fridge with some random sabji or leftover mystery masala."

I laugh.

Preet stays to sell some of the ice cream. "There ain't no price list because this is a shady business. We do the same thing at Paradise Liquor. You see a bunch of rich kids out to get drunk, charge 'em full price."

"See an alcoholic, give 'em a discount 'cause you know they'll be back, right?" I say. He looks sheepish.

"I'm okay with overcharging these people," Mindii says.

I look outside and see a bunch of fools standing in

video game cosplay they just bought from Party City and I shake my head. "Yeah. Fuck 'em," I say.

"Tourists," Preet says. And we all know who he's talking about. The ones in elaborate cosplay that make it difficult to sit down. "How are you gonna play video games if you got a five-foot foam axe embedded in your Viking helmet?" Preet says, annoyed.

I slide the window.

"Six dollars for the firecracker, eight for push-ups, sixteen for the SpongeBob," Preet announces. There's a slight murmur and then cash starts slipping on through. I can't tell if Preet wants a cut. I don't really care. He can keep the money. I'm anxious to be done with this. I can't imagine going from being at a university in Monterey to coming back home to doing this every day, every night.

After about two minutes, I boom, "A-all right guys, we're ou-ou—" I pause and take a breath. "Out of inventory," I lie as the line threatens to replenish itself. We're not here to make money. We're here to find whoever this Thor dude is.

Mindii takes a drumstick, Preet picks out a choco-taco. I ponder the choices, but grab a chocolate sandwich. Can't go wrong with that. Unless bits of paper get stuck to the ice cream or worse, the soft, chewy shell. Sigh. I've made my choice.

We help Preet unload all the alcohol near a brightly

decorated trailer. I wonder if this is how Goldy's alcohol- ism started. But it could have been at our house. Not like alcohol is so difficult to find there. Every weekend there was a poetry meeting where Papa and his friends would drink whiskey and club soda and spend hours singing and talking. It could easily have been there. It took Papa a really long time to figure out Goldy couldn't just have one drink or be around alcohol.

It was only after Goldy's third time at rehab that Papa finally eliminated all of the alcohol. Like all of it. That also meant his poetry meet-ups stopped happening because a lot of Papa's friends didn't want to do it without alcohol.

Chotu. I don't even know his actual name. Except for Chad, I guess. *Chotu* means little, and it's a nickname people give to kids that they outgrow, like Junior. And yet here this dude exists. In his twenties, probably another aspiring rapper.

I remember their senior year, Goldy got drunk with Chotu, and from what I gather, they were both in the car with a bunch of bottles of whatever it was they got drunk off. Doesn't really matter. Vodka. Whiskey. Whatever. They didn't crash the car. Nobody died. It would make the most boring movie in the world. But the cops got called. Chotu got dropped back home because everyone knows his parents. Goldy gets a record, spends a couple of hours in jail.

So yeah, I don't care how awesome this guy's party is,

or how great his rapping skills are. I hope Chotu gets his ass beat.

We watch three guys take off their shirts and run into the backyard where the pool is.

"Let's just go blend," Mindii says.

She laughs. Then I laugh. Everyone at this party looks absurd, with people in video game cosplay and designer loungewear. Even the ones in bathing suits are wearing brand-name shit that cost in the hundreds, maybe even thousands.

We join the small line outside the trailer, behind a kid in brightly colored makeup using an equally bright wheelchair with a little computer screen attached. It's totally tricked out. As soon as the bouncers see us with the alcohol, we're ushered straight inside.

The trailer looks super fancy. I'd definitely go camping with it. The outside is painted black with the words *Game Guru* in hideous yellow font emblazoned across it.

"It's been real," Preet says. He disappears toward the back.

The ambience feels very much like the interior of the ice cream truck. Like a wannabe DJ has just given up on life. Everything glows. There are several game controllers on a shelf, HD screens in cabinets. I spot G-Dawg. He's laying out a flat ramp and the girl with the bright makeup I saw outside rolls on up in her wheelchair. I spring into action.

"What're you doing here?" G-Dawg says, surprised to see me.

"Where is Thor?"

"Asgard?" G-Dawg says. "Back of the line if you ain't here to game."

"I'm just here to game," I say.

"Me too," Mindii says.

"Where is Thor?" I demand.

"I don't know where Resham is now. Probably trying to find Chotu so we can get paid before he passes out and we gotta wait weeks for the money."

"He's a Game Guru?"

"He's my business partner."

G-Dawg starts his spiel. "Welcome to Game Guru. Some of you know me. For those who do not, my name is MC G-Dawg. Feel free to play, but when the entertainment— that's me—begins, please pay attention to the music and all announcements"

Everyone grabs a controller and there is a big hoopla as they turn on game consoles. The room goes fully dark. A lava lamp is in the corner, and black lights, glow sticks, stuffed black-light-reflective toys are lit up. A long sofa is on one side of the room, the gaming systems on the other.

We're not going to find Thor in here.

"Inside the house?" Mindii says. "That's usually where the host would be."

"Sounds like a reasonable assumption," I say. "We find Chotu, hopefully we find this Thor Resham guy."

Resham. What a name for Goldy's . . . what do I even call him? Friend. Boyfriend. Significant Other. Lover?

We make our way over to the house and immediately see Chotu. He's wearing a red silk kurta pajama and he's drunk off his ass.

He staggers toward me. "Do you see this?" he whispers in the general vicinity of everyone on the sofa. He points at my crochet beard. "A shrubbery!" They all laugh and continue drinking.

There's a crowd milling around in the room. No sign of Thor though.

"And who is this beautiful young . . ." Chotu says, stumbling toward Mindii.

"Nope," Mindii says, jumping out of the way.

Is this what it was like for Goldy? Was drinking till blacking out an inevitable part of the night? My stomach tightens.

"You guys want?" Chotu says, pointing at the glasses like he's offering us cha and Nice biscuits. He downs a couple shots, then takes a big gulp of air like he's about to hurl.

"Do you know where Thor is?" I say.

"In New Mexico with that scientist, the astrophysicist Dr. Jane Foster?" Chotu laughs. He grabs my hand and I shudder. "I love you, man. You know that, right?" he says. I remember Goldy being like this. A good, friendly, non-aggressive drunk. Maybe that's why nobody said anything or did anything. He didn't break shit or beat people up. I guess that's a plus.

"Hey," Chotu gurgles. "You remember when we played that tabletop RPG, Monsterhearts," he slurs, "because the description said, 'the messy lives of teenage monsters' and then"—he pauses to guffaw—"it was about horny LGBTQ+ teenage monsters hooking up. And you were all, 'this is so gay,' but we played it for years anyways?" He takes a drink. "Good times, man."

Mindii and I look at him.

This saag for brains thinks I'm Goldy. Now I'm the one who wants to hurl.

"Where is Resham?" I say.

"Good idea! Let's sing." He starts singing the line "Resham ka lehenga mera, resham ka lehenga," a sexually charged Hindi song from the movie Khal Nayak about . . uh . . . silky outerwear.

"Seriously," I say sternly. Stop with the bund pangey. "Where's Thor? The guy dressed like Thor?"

"You know how corny you sound? Where is Thor?" he says. "WHERE'S THOR?" he repeats, even louder, for everyone in the room to hear.

"Rehab, man," he says, trailing off again. I let out a loud groan. "Don't do it. That's how they get you. They get you hating everything about yourself and then you don't know what's what. It's like a cult. No. It is a cult."

I slap a mosquito that just bit me on the face.

"Machhar," Chotu says, grabbing my hand and sitting down on the stairs. "Did you know mosquitoes breathe at different times, so all of them have the opportunity to drink blood and share equally? That's a community."

"Hey, didn't you have a beard?" Chotu says, grabbing my face. "Wait a second, you have a beard! So soft. Like resham ka lehenga." He gurgle-croons the Hindi song from the '90s.

"What is with those sketch-as-hell cult meetings at the library you were going to?"

"Wait, what cult meetings?"

"One a.m., two a.m. I'm going to the library. You invited me a couple times, but yaar. Why am I gonna leave my house," Chotu gurgles. "To go to the library at Fresno State? I wouldn't even go there in the daytime." He starts laughing hysterically. "I'm surprised you ain't at your cult meeting tonight."

He tries to stand up. Sits back down.

"Ain't it exhausting?" he says.

"What?"

"Just everything?"

"Yeah," I say, and give him a hug. As much as I want to hate Chotu, I can't. All I see is a lost dude. A dude in pain.

I see the door fling open. It's more of Chotu's "friends."

CHAPTER 18

A VERY RASH LIBRARY STAKEOUT

We turn onto Barton Avenue and I veer into the lot, recklessly taking up three faculty parking spaces in front of the library. Mindii grabs two choco-tacos from the freezer and tosses me one as she settles back into the passenger seat. I move my fake beard aside and take an irritated bite, ripping into the chewy exterior and chocolate topping with my teeth. The cold vanilla ice cream slides out of the shell much faster than anticipated and I have to contort my face to catch it. There is no way to eat this and keep my dignity. Meanwhile, Mindii is angling her entire body to avoid collateral ice cream dress damage. We take a moment to look at each other and appreciate the absurdity of the situation.

She moves a strand of blond hair away from my face. I take the last bite of choco-taco, giddy from the intimacy of the moment. I'm wide-awake. It's a quarter to two, but it might as well be noon.

We step out of the ice cream truck and onto the sidewalk where the campus begins. We both look at the ice cream truck taking up so many parking spaces. I'm stressed out looking at it. It just looks so . . . messy.

"Go ahead," Mindii says. I rush toward the truck to repark. It's still technically stolen and parked illegally, but it definitely looks neat. Several streetlamps light our path toward the multistory Henry Madden Library. It's weird being here this late. Early?

I still can't believe we came here solely based on the words of drunk-ass Chotu. I don't know which is less believable, a cult in the library or rehab in the library at close to two in the morning.

"I wouldn't be surprised if Goldy was in a cult," I say. "Sometimes it feels like I don't know my brother at all." We walk on in comfortable silence, our eyes looking out at the grass and trees on either side of us.

"I feel that way about my niam tais sometimes," Mindii says. "Not the cult thing," she clarifies. "Just so many puzzle pieces, man."

"Why do you feel that way about your grandma?"

"When I hear about the camps or see photos of her with people I don't recognize . . . it's like she had this whole other life and I only got to see a tiny little part of it. An incomplete part."

"Well, I'm an open book," I say.

Her deep brown eyes look into mine. "You're one of the most complex people I've ever met. Like a multivolume book series I have no chance of ever fully piecing together."

I gulp. "And you, uh . . ." I say. "Are like a-a-an onion. A nice-smelling onion."

She laughs and skips toward the grass. "Come on, let's frolic for a minute."

"Dafydd doesn't frolic," I say, taking slow steps.

She jogs back to me and grabs my hand. We break into a run, her arms moving up and down, emulating wings. "Fine, I'm about to frolic," I announce.

I hold on to my pouch and leap up in the air, clicking my heels together. Mindii does a wave motion with her arm as I jump on a bench and dance. If Goldy were here, he would have turned this into a competition to definitively establish himself as the BEST frolicker, just like he is BEST at yoga.

The sound of crickets is loud and staticky as we make our way toward the darkened entrance doors. Mindii gently pulls the door handle. Then tries again with immense force. A small whine escapes my lips. Of course the doors are locked. I'm annoyed at myself, like I'd expected a different outcome.

We stand next to each other and then start walking. The library was one of the few places me and Goldy used to go together that didn't involve running errands.

"Tell me something nice about your brother," Mindii says, like she can see into my head.

I look at her and think hard. "He was g-good at making sandwiches," I say.

"I said something nice, not basic human functionality."

I look down at Mindii's boots that are playfully zig-zagging across the concrete as we snake our way toward the entrance of the library. "I was around eleven and had a bathroom incident at my cousin's wedding reception."

Mindii stops cold. "You peed your pants? That is mortifying. But also a little cute."

"No," I protest. "I was wearing a really fancy and expensive white kurta pajama, and the naala was very difficult to tie and untie. As I said, there was an incident. I was so stressed that the other kids and adults were going to make fun of me. I mean, worse than what they did already because of my stutter. It was right before we were supposed to do a super-boring self-choreographed Bhangra routine to Jazzy B, one of like thirty performances by family members. Goldy didn't even hesitate. He poured a glass of bright red Rooh Afza all over his white kurta, then makes a big show about it and has this huge stain on all the family photos. Papa was so pissed. But Goldy saved me from humiliation that night."

She smiles. "That was really nice."

I try and savor this positive image, but inevitably I start

thinking about the times I thought I was helping by lying for him. "You tell me something nice now," I say.

"Sure." She thinks. "Her laugh was like a symphony. My favorite smell in the world is fresh jasmine flowers in the morning because my niam tais used to bring them just for me before anyone else woke up. After she died I used to gather my own and sing to them in Hmong to make me feel like she was there."

I turn to face her.

"Does it get easier?" I say.

"It gets different. Like she's further away. It hurts less."

"I can't believe I lost his notebook," I say, my voice cracking. I'm such a fool. Thor wasn't exactly incognito. He stuck out like a . . . well, like a Thor with a pag. And he made off with Goldy's notebook—stole my rash decision notebook in plain sight. How did I let this happen? What was I thinking?

"I remember a little of the poem he wrote in his notebook, though. With the sketch of Thor," I say.

Not because I found it to be so beautiful and meaningful or anything. I guess it's a poem. Looks like one. I just can't connect with the idea that these are my brother's words, thoughts, feelings. Metaphor, simile, allusion, those I get. But reading the poem feels like I'm reading a stranger's words. It's my brother I don't get.

Maybe Thor is the cult leader, sitting inside in the dark, hatching some kind of villainous plan.

"Poetry reveals all," Mindii says. "The poet can't hide shit with it. The listener can't hide shit. And it all comes tumbling together in a great big wave of emotion. That's why I love live performance."

I desperately want to hear a poem she wrote. I don't ask her to tell me one, maybe for the same reason she doesn't ask me to recite Goldy's poem. It's way too intimate. Like asking me to crochet in front of her.

We sit in silence. She raises an eyebrow at me. I furrow my brow. Then something moves in the window of the next building.

"You saw that, right?" Mindii says, standing up.

"I don't know. Kind of a light. A flashlight? Could be nothing."

"Yeah, but have you considered the other possibility?"

"It's security?"

She's already creeping around to the side. We push our faces against the window and see pitch-black. No lights, no flicker. But there's another door.

"Ah," I say. "It c-could be something. That was the other possibility."

I jiggle the doorknob. It turns. We are both taken by surprise. Mindii pushes the door open just a crack and we peer inside.

Black lights make the whole place look like a two-dimensional computer-generated program. Strangely familiar instrumental disco music plays in the background.

"Dude, this is super weird," I whisper.

Brightly glowing faces and bodies are seated around a large table.

"So far this is looking very cult-like," Mindii says.

"You know we can hear you," a voice says, and it scares the jalebi out of me.

Two bright lights—blue and red—emanate from the table. Lightsabers. "This is a Star Wars party?" I say out loud.

"This is a Star Wars–themed Dungeons and Dragons campaign."

Just as my eyes refocus to see what else is in the room, I hear the sound of footsteps and the door starts getting heavier. My feet lose their grounding as we start slipping back outside.

Are we in a portal?

Nope. Someone is pushing us out.

Mindii maintains a grip on the knob, refusing to let go, turning it one way, then the other, so it can't be locked.

"No," a muffled voice bellows from behind the door.

"What do you mean no?" I say, panting.

"No," the voice says. "Just you know. No."

This sounds highly suspicious.

"Wait," I say, my ears perking up. "I know this song. Goldy used to play it all the friggin' time. I got the record in my room. Rebel Blockade Runner.' From the album *Star Wars and Other Galactic Funk* by Meco."

The weight of the door feels lighter.

"This is some . . ." Mindii says, her voice rising. "BULLSHIT!" she screams, and we both charge full force. The door feels weightless and flings completely open as we tumble into the room. A large Chewbacca stands upright. He makes his classic growl, a synthesized blend of purring vocalizations.

Someone hits the switch and the ugly fluorescent lights turn on, making it look more like a room in the library again. Chewbacca closes the door and walks back to his seat at the table. Everyone sits awkwardly looking around.

"We're in the middle of a very pivotal moment in our campaign," says a girl with two large Afro-puffs on either side of her head and a terrifying black mask. She twirls her lightsaber.

"Ah. Darth Vader," I say.

"I'm actually Darth Mader," she says, taking off her mask. "I'm one of the librarians."

"What are you all doing here?" Mindii says.

"Well, tonight is special. But we usually meet here every week for our long-term D and D campaigns," an Ewok says.

"The Star Wars one we started eight hours ago," Darth Mader says.

"We were about to capture the Pirate Queen," the Ewok says with much irritation.

"Or at least unmask her," a Princess Leia cosplayer adds.

I look at Darth. "Apologies, Dungeon . . . uh . . . Mistress," I say. Wait, that doesn't sound right.

There is a pause.

"Mistress? This ain't S and M, it's D and D," she says, and the whole table roars with laughter, like it's the funniest thing ever. "It's Dungeon Master whether it's beast, goblin, Ewok, or sexy plant."

"We're looking for someone dressed as Thor?" Mindii says.

A hush settles over them. Deliberate. Annoying.

"We don't share things about our group with outsiders," Chewbacca explains, breaking the long silence.

"So he's part of this group?"

Everyone looks at Chewbacca.

"No," he says loudly. "No. I said we don't . . . that doesn't mean he's a part . . . I don't even know who Thor is. Ah! Nerf herder!" He makes his signature Chewbacca growl and takes a deep breath.

"That Nordic fucker stole my brother's notebook."

"Your brother?" Chewbacca says. His normal voice sounds weird coming from that cosplay.

"My brother. Goldy Gill. Do you know him?"

They all exchange a look.

"Have a chocolate-covered Klatooine paddy froggy bite. It'll make you feel better," the Ewok says, handing it to me. I eat it, though odds are this is still totally a cult.

I am so confused right now. I look around the table, trying not to judge, but these are not people Goldy would intentionally hang out with. They're dorkier than me. And that's saying a lot.

"So this is not a cult," I say. "What is this, then?"

"Goldy was safe here."

"We all met each other at . . . uh . . . camp," Chewbacca says. Now it all makes sense. They're rehab acquaintances. Friends?

"No shame in saying the word," Darth Mader says.

"Rehab. Not summer camp," Chewbacca says. "At first we'd meet up to talk about how things are difficult, play some cards, video games, and then it just became a regular thing."

"Especially on nights like tonight when there are so many parties happening," Darth Mader adds.

"We know how destructive it can be. We all do," the Ewok says. "To come back to reality where not every minute of the day is structured like at rehab. Plus a lot of people don't even think it's a medical problem. Not everyone is ready. And I mean not just the alcoholic, I'm talking their support system, their family, their friends."

"Like when an alcoholic acknowledges they have a

problem and tries to get better, other people don't want to acknowledge that the problem is there, and definitely not that it's a medical one. They think an alcoholic can figure out a way to just have a couple drinks and then call it a night. Our brains are wired different," Darth Mader says. She stops to cry for a moment, the Ewok patting her back supportively. "But he was trying. He would talk about you all the time."

I'm not ready to hear this.

"So this is what we do, man," the Ewok says. "We play long-term campaigns with elves and warlocks and stuff. And some nights when it's needed, we do short one-night campaigns."

"That we're interrupting," I say.

"Yeah," Chewbacca says, offering another chocolate frog.

I look over at the table and there's an extra chair.

"Goldy's. We miss him too. He was like family," Darth Mader says.

I look at a stack of books of the table.

"He loved this stuff," she says. "On long nights or nights when we were waiting for people to arrive, we'd all bring other things to do. He would bring these books. Would talk about them like he had written them himself or was getting a cut of the proceeds."

"Crime fiction," Darth Mader says.

"Yeah, Jo Nesbø. But why?" I say.

They shrug their shoulders. But I know why. Because Harry Holes is an alcoholic and never has to change. When it's time to solve crimes, he can put on his big-boy pants and get shit done. He is in control of "the situation," of his bowels. Never has to suffer the indignity of going to rehab, or lying in a pool of his own vomit. Not even once. I read his whole collection. He is essentially a cool alcoholic. That's fucking why.

First time Goldy went to rehab, nobody told him to do it. It was one of those ones where you come home at the end of the day after you take like coping and anger and art therapy classes or something. He decided to check himself in, started going to the meetings. I thought I had my brother back. No drinks for weeks, months. I thought he was cured. Hell, he probably thought he was cured.

And then there was a family party, where I covered for him when I saw Goldy with a beer and he'd said he had it under control now. I even covered the next time when I found a bunch of empty glasses under the bed on a random afternoon. And the next time, there was no covering up possible, and it ended with Mama crying and Papa yelling. Even with the slurring and the realization he had fucked up big time, Goldy could eloquently state his argument for binge drinking. "So I messed up. It happens. Not a big deal. Like I know the process to get better. I gotta restart the twelve-step program from the beginning any-way. Might as well enjoy tonight." It was never just one night. It was always at least three. Every time. He'd attend the meetings, get those sobriety chips. And now it's over. For him anyway. We're here picking up the pieces.

As I watch everyone, I think about how Goldy would be interacting with everyone here. Would he know what a daunting vigilance check is? How into this would he be? Which Star Wars character would he be dressed as tonight? Would he have strong opinions about Jar Jar Binks? Did he dress up as a regular thing? Put on dramatic voices? Get super pissed if his character got mugged by a fairy or some shit?

I close my eyes and try to remember the lines of poetry he had written. I don't remember any of it.

"Did Goldy ever write poetry?" I ask.

"Goldy? I don't think so," someone says. I think it's the Ewok.

"But the boyfriend does . . ." Chewbacca starts, and immediately covers his mouth.

Fucking Viking. Am I missing something about the poem and the drawing? Is there some deep metaphor that's eluding me or is this just the dumbest poem in the world? Couldn't he have just plagiarized a couple lines from the classic Punjabi tragic love story: *Heer Ranjha*. At least I could have found something online about understanding it, the musical tune it is sung to. "Now what?" I say. "We got nothing."

"We know where Thor'll be," Mindii says. "There's not a lot of places to do poetry at two in the morning."

"Assuming he performs Goldy's poem tonight. Could be tomorrow night. Or next month."

"Thor is performing tonight," Mindii says confidently.

She takes my hand and we exit just as Darth Mader puts her mask back on. The overheads are off again, the black lights illuminate everyone. They return to their game. Heavy breathing resumes. "You arrive at a forest with fresh moss, the two moons of Tatooine have risen. On the ground, you see a battle-ravaged lightsaber. Do you . . ."

We hear lightsaber sounds as we walk back out into the night and close the door.

CHAPTER 19

OPEN MIC AT THE DONUT SHOP

We return to the Cambodian donut joint we had gone to earlier hoping that Thor will be here to perform. It makes sense. It's open mic. It's poetry. He's definitely in cosplay. I am so perplexed about why he stole Goldy's notebook. My notebook. It's got a crocheted cover, for fuckssake.

Unlike a few hours ago, the parking lot is now absolutely packed. So is the parking lot across the street at Dhaliwal Gas. Because we're driving the ice cream truck, Mindii tells me to go past the twinkling sign for Madam M's Marvelous Donuts and we park near a large trash receptacle at the back of a nondescript beige office building. Perfect! We bypass the blaring horns. We walk on through the main entrance this time.

All of the tables from earlier have been put away. There are seats for the audience set up all around the small stage, making it a very intimate experience.

The place is bustling. Cosplayers from across so many

fandoms are sitting, standing, milling. I see Ngozi and her new pal Aisha cosplaying Naruto a couple rows back. I wave at Ngozi. She waves back.

But I'm really looking for Thor. I scan the room to no avail. There are way too many people here for me to be able to identify Resham.

"Just a heads-up," Mindii says. "Things may get weird." She takes out a nail file from her purse and starts filing.

"Uh . . ."

"Uncle Channthy!" Mindii yells out as he takes the stage to adjust the microphone and move the speakers. He pauses to wave.

Taped to a chair in front of the stage is a glowing neon sign that says *The Hangout.*

I'm mesmerized by the colorful cosplayers sitting, standing, leaning, squeezed in to narrow spaces. I don't even recognize the fandoms, but want to take a closer look at the material and design work. From this vantage point, it just looks like a blur of spandex, armor, and feathers.

"Can you believe," Mindii says, "that there was a time in your life you didn't even know what a red-bean donut tasted like?"

"It's a travesty," I say, grinning at her. Then I frown again. "You weren't kidding when you said this place was gonna get packed earlier."

"I don't joke about situations involving parking. Okay, do you see him anywhere?"

My stomach sinks. Thor the Destroyer and Stealer of Notebooks. I'm ready to confront him, to take back Goldy's notebook. But what I really want to do is find out what else he knows about Goldy. And what the hell is so great about the poem.

One of the things that nobody ever tells you about cosplay is that it isn't as simple as it sounds. It's not just dressing up. There are a lot of considerations that go into the art of costume play, and the most important is balancing character integrity with your own comfort. I wore long-sleeve moleskin one time to San Diego Comic-Con in August and vowed to never do that shit again. Hence the breathable Dafydd outfit I'm wearing now. Every time I've been a cosplay doctor, there's always someone who busts a heel or gets armor stuck, or tears part of the material in a most embarrassing way while attempting to use the bathroom.

A group of cosplayers make their way toward us. They're wearing easily recognizable Starfleet uniforms from *Star Trek: The Next Generation*. One has curly black hair, a purple dress, another has bright red hair, a long, flowing light blue cloak.

They talk to Mindii in Hmong for a minute as they're headed toward the stage, and she gets this weird look on her face. I may not understand what they're saying, but I am an expert in awkward and uncomfortable situations. One of them, a dude cosplaying Data, with gelled-back brown hair and android-white greasepaint on his face, is looking at Mindii with a keen interest.

My stomach churns. Is this *the* boyfriend? Who am I under the circumstances?

"Do you add a special powder to keep the f-fff-ffff?" I'm standing close, almost spitting in his face. "F-foundation from smearing," I say, exhausted from that stutter storm.

"Baby powder," he says, leaning back a lot, eyeing me with suspicion. I look at his triangular Starfleet point and immediately want to cover my sideburns with my fake beard.

"M-may the Force be with you," I say nervously. Data looks irritated. They all do. Shit. I know the Force is not Star Trek. I don't stutter when I'm nervous, but apparently I do get my fandoms mixed up. Sue me. At a Star Trek convention, this would probably get me killed. Cause of death: Mixing up the fandoms.

"Nope," I say, flustered. "Not that. May the Force not be with you is what I mean, but then why mention the Force at all," I muse aloud, "because it doesn't exist in Star Trek, although . . ." I gasp and take a huge breath. Let out a laugh. Data is pointedly not making eye contact with me. The girls in his group are chuckling. Instead of shutting the fuck up, I continue speaking. "Captain's Log. Stardate . . ."

The girls crack up. Mindii doesn't even try to stifle her laugh. It's beautiful and loud.

Mindii puts away the nail file and I see her inhale deeply. It's the first time I've seen her do that all night. Suddenly, I don't give a shit about who this guy is. She isn't looking at anybody the way she's looking at me.

She reaches over and takes my hand. In front of people. She looks at them and smiles, broadly. "This is Sunny," she says. I feel volts of energy coursing through me. Like the euphoria of waking up to the aroma of Mama's freshly brewed masala cha.

The lights dim, we take our seats, and the troupe of Trekkies take the stage.

Data takes a seat in the center of the stage, the other members taking their places around him. It's a poetry recital within a poetry recital. So meta. He starts by explaining the poem is in honor of his pit bull. "I call it . . ." He pauses. "An ode. To my pit bull, Sparky." We all laugh, and the comedy of the scene builds the more seriously Data takes the poem.

It's funny and poignant because of how Data doesn't get human emotion and can't read the room. This dude is fully committed to the character and the poem, while the other Star Trek cosplayers are hamming it up with how excruciating it is. He doesn't care how boring it is. It's hilarious. We snap our fingers with enthusiasm. It's kind of fun and not as pretentious as I envisioned. Over the next ten minutes a series of groups and individuals cosplaying and performing as Doctor Who to Sailor Moon take the stage and they're all fun, yet I have knots in my stomach. Where's Thor? I still don't see him.

It's not just about getting my notebook back anymore. I have questions. If I had my phone I would have started compiling them already. This may be a one-shot deal.

And then the crowd shifts and I see him walk on through. The red dastaar, the beard, the Viking clothing, the hammer. Isn't Thor supposed to be blond? What's with the red? He's making his way to the stage. There are a couple of other Sikhs with him. The two dudes don't look like they're in cosplay. They look like, well, turbaned Sikhs. The three women are also wearing turbans, but also odd maroon face coverings that are definitely not a part of Sikhi. And they're up next.

The first Sikh is wearing a purple collared achkan flowing down, his thick black beard resting comfortably on his face, his turban a tartan parna that's usually just worn around the house. I recognize the cosplay. Randu Singh. Super old-school. Friend of Jason Blood from a comic book from the '80s. I used to crave any kind of media: books, comics, movies, TV shows, literally anything that featured anyone who kind of looked like me. Randu Singh was constantly rescuing Jason Blood, who, I'll be honest, was the most boring character in the entire series.

The spotlight goes on Randu. And he starts his poem slam style.

"Ran-Do," he says to a hushed crowd.

"Ran-Don't," he says, extending the vowels, pausing for effect.

"Ran-Do. Ran-Don't. Run, D!" He puts both palms to his temples like Randu did in the comic book. It's that racist-ass orientalist mind control shit the white writers tasked him with.

He steps back. Fingers clicking.

Next is Sadhul Singh from the same series. My eyes glare at Thor standing on the side. Part of me wants to beat his ass, but a bigger part of me wants to hear him perform his shitty poem and have everyone laugh at it because of how terrible it is. All of a sudden the three women explode into a medley of hip-hop and spoken word, tearing up the floor.

"Mera naa Gun."

"Te menu kehnde Fist."

"Blade naal panga," the third says, followed by all of them rapping in unison, "will not be changa!" They stomp real loud to make it sound extra. Kind of. I guess you gotta use your imagination a little. It's really entertaining and catchy. Meanwhile Thor remains standing, stoic, his hammer shielding him. Then all eyes are on him. Doesn't even talk about being Thor. Or why his dastar is red. Opens up Goldy's notebook like he owns it. Recites two lines.

"Ik munda panchi vangu udd da." A boy soars through the sky like a bird.

"Thale lishqdi kach nu vekh ke." Distracted by a shiny glass on the ground . . .

It's not just a poem. There is no raag, there is no tune. There's only a beat. And Resham's voice. He's rapping. And as much as I hate to admit it, it sounds pretty good when you ignore the lousy lyrics and focus on the other elements: the beat, the tempo, the rapping skills. I hate that this isn't garbage.

I hold my breath. This is not how I imagined those lines would sound. At all. I'm in the middle of translating the poem in my head. Another poetry group goes on as Resham's group shuffles offstage and heads toward the exit.

I sit in my chair, stunned, watching Resham walk away.

I'm kinda tired of learning all this different shit about Goldy. Was he secretly a cosplaying Nordic rapper too? Sometimes you don't want to learn things about people.

Then I suck in a breath as a dark cloud moves over me. Why am I still sitting here letting the notebook escape again?

I exhale loudly and angrily, leaping out of the chair. I leave Mindii sitting there as I comb through the crowd, pushing past cosplayers and donut eaters. Is this Thor da bacha already outside?

I can't breathe. I need air.

I rush to get outside to the parking lot.

And there he is. Thor. Resham. He's holding a red cup in his hands, surrounded by a handful of people.

I don't move. My hands graze my face and I must look like I'm mauling myself, because I'm just not used to touching my face without my beard.

I march straight toward him, pushing past all the people surrounding him. Fans? Resentment raging like bile in my stomach, in my mouth. Other people notice me, but don't really pay attention, like I'm another fanboy, desperate to get in a word. Then Thor looks at me, curious, confused. He takes another sip from the cup.

I push my way through the circle and my hand rises up with one rage-filled slap, knocking the cup right out of his hands, sending the liquid flying out, splattering all over clothes and shoes and faces. It lands a few feet away with a less-than-satisfying *thunk*. It's what I wished I would have done to Goldy every single time he was "just keeping things social."

Is Thor an alcoholic? I don't fucking know. Could be. I don't know shit about Goldy. The "poem" in his own notebook isn't even his. Goldy is the damn panchi. The bird. The glass is what? The alcohol? Who came up with these basic-ass metaphors? If this madarchod gaslights me and tells me I'm reading too much into it, that it's literally about a bird, I'm going to . . . Who am I kidding. What the fuck am I gonna do. I'm too delicate to get into a fistfight. Thor crunches up his face, rotates his hand Punjabi style, fingers pointed upward in a "what the hell?" gesture, then vocalizes it. "What the deuce, man?" He doesn't seem even the least bit bothered that I'm here. He obviously recognizes me. He sought me out to steal my notebook.

Everything feels like it's in slow motion. The drink has splattered everywhere, on people's clothes. Then everyone starts yelling at once. The liquid is clear. It's odorless. Vodka?

"Give me my notebook." I may have stamped my foot like a toddler. Maybe.

"It's not your notebook." His voice is even, patient. He hasn't said no.

Everyone stands there awkwardly, then they start to disperse as they realize the drama is not worth their time. Thor walks over and picks up the cup, which still has some of the liquid in it. He brings it to me. "This," he says, annoyance seeping through, "is water."

"You're so . . ." I say, clenching my fists and biting my lip. But I can't get the words out.

"Give me back the notebook." I'm not crying. Yet.

"No," he says. "It's not yours. It's mine. Do you even know what it is?"

My rash decision notebook. My only connection to Goldy. The answer to everything.

"It's his art therapy journal," Thor says, his voice low, patience thin. "He started it in rehab. Before he met me. And then kept adding pages to it as a way to stay calm."

"You know what, keep the goddamn journal," I say, my voice breaking. "You're a terrible lyricist and rapper. You will never make any money as a poet. Couldn't even find a yellow dastaar? Thor is blond, you fool!" I say. This guy deserves nothing.

"Go read some Norse mythology," he says loudly. "Look, I know you think this is gonna bring you closure." He steps closer. "But this notebook is not it."

I flinch. "Why'd you write that dumbass poem in Goldy's journal?"

"I didn't," he says. "The night before Goldy left for recovery housing . . ."

"What?"

"The rehab in L.A. Where he stayed there . . ."

"Just say rehab," I bark.

"Okay, yeah. So before he left for the rehab, he wanted me to freestyle a love poem. So I did and he wanted to write it in his journal before he left. He drew a picture of me just because that's what people do. The poem is there to remind him to come back to me." His eyes are watery.

He laughs sadly.

I'm not sure what to do with this. "What other faltu poems you write?" I ask.

"He made me sugarless cha one day and I got really pissed. We got in a big fight. Then I felt bad about going off on him and wrote a poem in iambic pentameter, you know like Shakespeare, called 'toon cha banai bina khand ton.'"

"That literally means you made me sugarless tea. Fuck, man. Do you got another job?"

"I work in insurance," he says.

He looks down, like he's lost somewhere, in a moment long ago. "I mean, there's more to the poem than just cha. It's a—you know. What's that thing called?"

"Metaphor," I say quietly. I feel as though an incredibly heavy rock is on my chest. Goldy is gone again, but in a much more profound way. He's actually gone. Never coming back gone. I realize that, even if I wrestled this notebook away from the fucker, it isn't meant for me.

I don't know how to fix this. My eyes dart around as I realize what I've just done. Holy shit, I just left Mindii inside. I look at the entrance, which has cleared out, and I could easily walk through and just find her. Why am I not moving?

As if on cue, Raj pulls up in Goldy's ice cream truck. He gets out, leans against the wheel, arms folded, beard conveying some emotion I can't properly read. It's not jubilation, I can tell you that. If I were in his position, I would not simply be standing there with folded arms. I would have a plan. Perhaps this is Raj's plan. Maybe in his notes, he has written:

Step 1: Confront Sunny by looking menacing while leaning on ice cream truck.

Step 2: Beat his ass.

Step 3: Tell his mummy and papa.

I could just run in the opposite direction. Raj doesn't look like he's got the energy to catch up to me, not this late. But I don't have the fucking energy either. I grip my crocheted pouch tightly, my palm pressing into the contours of the phone in the basmati. I wish I could just turn it on.

I raise my hand in front of my face. "Siri, how do you outsmart an irritated, angry Sikh man standing next to an ice cream truck?"

Mindii's probably still stuck inside, wondering why I disappeared. Ngozi is outside, out of breath. Naruto isn't with her.

"You all right?" she says.

I want to tell her the truth. No. Instead I force my emotions down to the pit of my stomach, down to my knees, until they're all the way at the bottom of my feet and I can step on them, crumbling them to dust.

"Give me the keys to Mindii's bike. Quick. It's a matter of g-great urgency." I take quick breaths as I consider what I'm about to do. There's no going back from this. I'm about to leave Mindii. I'm ending the night. I feel a hollowness as I look back up at Ngozi.

Ngozi looks at me, incredulous. "Have you completely lost the plot? You don't even know how to drive a motorbike."

"I've been riding on the back of one all night long."

"You don't want to steal her bike."

"Are you trying to hypnotize me?"

"I know you, Sunny. And I know you're upset and hurt. I love you. I'm here."

This would be a beautiful, tender moment for us to hug. Instead I feel my face tightening up.

"Fucking typical!" I yell. "You don't get to dictate everything. Gordon Bennett!" I say, getting louder. Raj is patiently waiting through my outburst, just leaning on the tire. "You go enjoy the rest of your night!"

She says nothing. Me and Ngozi have been friends so long that she knows when I'm self-destructing.

I curl my hand into a fist and let out an aggravated scream.

She stops talking and leans in toward me, arms outstretched.

"I'm sure it'll be awesome leaving Fresno." I'm shouting now. Louder. "And going to your froo-froo faraway college. 'Ooooh. I'm Ngozi. I study neuroscience and the classics at Berkeley. I only tell jokes in Latin now!'" Then I pretentiously laugh just like I imagine her new laugh with her new friends in her new life will sound like.

"Hang about, am I laughing like a daft cow because of the hilarity of Latin jokes? Latin? Like the dead fucking language, Latin?"

"Yes! That was you A-AND your new crew ALL laughing like a motherfucking gaggle of daft cows!" I say.

"Well, none of these scenarios makes any sense," Ngozi says.

I see Mindii start walking out. She's looking for me.

"You don't even make sense!" I yell at Ngozi. I stomp loudly toward Raj.

I don't look back.

I don't need Ngozi.

Don't need Mindii.

I can tell Raj is about to say something, and I'm ready to beat his ass. How's that for a plot twist? He's about to say something slick and then kapow, I'll kick him right in the face. Knock him down. Then steal his ice cream truck. AGAIN.

Dammit. I'm tired. And before I do any of that, I need a nap. But Raj doesn't say anything to me. He opens up the ice cream truck, starts the engine. I slowly open the passenger side and sit down, holding the seat belt tight to my chest.

We drive in silence. No yelling or quietly telling me he's disappointed. No nothing.

I've done it. Ended the night. Ended things with Mindii. Whatever this thing even is. Was? Now what?

CHAPTER 20

THIS NEVER HAPPENED

Raj says nothing for a few minutes as we drive in darkness. I don't even know where we're going. I can't bring myself to care.

"How'd you know I wasn't going to call the cops?" he finally says, shattering the silence.

I shrug, not that he can see me. "I took a chance."

As annoying as Raj is, he's one of the few good dudes in Goldy's life. After he came back from rehab, he just completely shifted his lifestyle. Like no more partying, no more drinks, let his hair grow out, started wearing a dastaar. I get really resentful when I see Raj, though, because he was able to do what rehab is supposed to get you to do. Rehabilitate. Say *not today, alcohol.*

While he's generally a good dude, he does let himself get talked into taking shady capitalist shortcuts. A black-market ice cream supplier, a sketchy deal on a freezer. So odds are low that the paperwork for this ice cream truck transfer is completely legit. Also, he knows Mama and Biji and Papa would have beat his ass if I'd gotten a record for stealing my own brother's ice cream truck. So yeah, I took a chance.

"Don't drop me home," I say. I can't face the quiet or the chaos.

"You are such a padh," Raj says. His eyes are red. Ready for sleep. He doesn't swear and when he needs to say something mean, it's in Punjabi and always sounds funny. And the best he comes up with is padh. Fart.

I would laugh, but it's almost four in the morning and I have used up all the fucks I have. "Do you know how long I've been looking for you? All night long! I haven't stayed up this late since I used to . . ."

"Be an alcoholic?" I say.

Raj gets quiet.

"You do know that I'm still an alcoholic, right? I was gonna say, since I worked the night shift at my chacha's store."

"That was not cool," I say. "I'm sorry." I surprise myself with just how easy it is to apologize.

"I'll always be an addict, man. It's an illness, plain and simple."

"Why couldn't Goldy do it?" I say, on the verge of tears.

"I don't know, little man. Everyone is different." He reaches out a hand and squeezes my palm as he continues driving around aimlessly. "But you gotta remember, Goldy was sick. It ain't just willpower. It's environment, genetics, habits, and there's the whole Punjabi and general dude culture that makes you feel like you're a punk if you admit you got a problem. They just want to throw you off the cliff like they'd do in Sparta. There's something in our brains that makes us alcoholics. We literally cannot drink two glasses and then be like all right, peace out."

I stare at the dashboard listening to every word coming out of Raj's mouth. I've never thought about how hard it must have been for him to admit he's got a problem. "You know who gave me my first drink?" Raj says. "My pops. You've met him. He's not a bad guy and I don't blame him—anymore. I used to blame everybody. Most of all, I blamed myself because I thought I just wasn't trying hard enough. I hated that people had seen me in such embarrassing situations. But it never stopped me. That's what this kachra does to you. Makes you shameless and forget that you are a child of God. But Goldy wasn't just my friend, he was my brother."

"Word," I say.

When Goldy confided in me and told me he was an alcoholic, my reaction was to tell him to be a man, that nobody else in our entire family is an alcoholic. Which I don't know how accurate that is because there's so much we do in secret. Carry all this pain. The only times my stutter is acknowledged is when someone has a kooky plan to fix me with yoga or very sketchy homeopathy involving pastes made from things in the masala tin and the garden. For years I just thought I was broken. No actual therapy because Punjabis don't do that, just stumbling around on the internet trying to figure shit out. Trying to figure me out.

I wonder if Goldy ever tried doing what I used to do to fix my stutter: looking up videos with advice, thinking it would actually work. Breathing techniques. One article by a therapist who clearly didn't actually stutter suggested replacing words you stutter on with different words. Meanwhile I'm like, I don't know if I'm going to stutter on those words because I haven't used them yet. I wish I'd had a conversation with Goldy about my stuttering. Obviously he knew—hell, everyone does. Just wish I'd said it out loud and my brother heard it. I close my eyes as I think about Goldy in that hospital room. How I couldn't have just given him a hug when he told me he was an alcoholic the same way I did when he told me he was gay. Nobody ever says alcohol poisoning out loud. It's dehydration, jaundice, heart problems, liver problems. Any kind of problem except what it actually is. "Drop me at the peacock gurdwara," I say.

Raj snorts. "You know, you can start becoming more spiritual tomorrow."

We keep driving. I doze off for a few minutes. The

truck rolls to a stop, and now we're here. The grand stone gates looming, the sound of birds honking like trucks in the background. The peacock gurdwara. He could have just dropped me home so he could get some sleep. But he knows I need this. It's what I like about him.

The night is over. How do I face Ngozi? Mindii? I just tried to steal her bike. What was I thinking? I shake my head as I think of how badly I behaved. But maybe abrupt endings is how I should leave things. Preemptive measures.

Most of the gurdwaras across the Valley have long-winded names that nobody ever remembers. They're usually referred to by the geographic area. If it's a small area like Caruthers, boom, Caruthers vala gurdwara. If it's by Highway 99 in Fresno, 99 vala gurdwara. The peacock gurdwara is the only one in Fresno that people know because of the peacock that roams around here and not because of its location. One time, Papa and I were getting gas at Costco and this Sikh truck driver asked me in Punjabi where the Guru Nanak Dev Center of the Central Valley is. And I immediately was like, "No idea. Not in this city." Papa jumped in and told the dude to follow us to the morni vala gurdwara. The gurdwara with the peacock. It's a sprawling white building with that familiar dome, and a tall flagpole with the Nishaan Sahib fluttering in the air.

"You can bounce. I'll walk back," I say to Raj as I start climbing out of the truck.

"You're gonna walk three miles?" He's leaning toward the passenger side, frowning down at me. "In the dark?"

"I'll figure it out," I say.

"Well, I'll be here. You already wasted my night. Might as well wait till it's completely ruined. What are you planning to do here anyway?"

I shrug. "I don't know."

"This ain't Harmandir Sahib back home where it's lively all the time with kirtan going twenty-four-seven. And you can't go in the divan hall dressed like one of King Arthur's rejected knights of the kiddie table." He gestures to my cosplay.

"I know," I say. I'm not going to wake the Granthi or go inside. I get out of the truck, and walk out toward the area me and Goldy used to call the forest.

It's really dark. Kind of eerie, like moonlight and mist have descended or something. Straight out of a horror movie. I almost turn back. But something drew me here tonight. So I walk a little farther into the darkness, stumbling as I go.

All of a sudden, I see Goldy's face appear. He's wearing his sharp Kenyan-style pag with a big starched flap. It matches his bright blue button-down. Familiar. I almost reach out to touch it.

I know I'm hallucinating. Maybe he is too. Because he's

273

taken aback when he sees me. Then he grins. He walks along the far end of the gurdwara grounds, where the fairy lights glitter like diamonds. So I follow him.

"Remember we got yelled at when we tried climbing those almond trees," he says. The trees are much taller now, towering, bearing fruit. Or nuts? Yeah, nuts.

"You're not real," I say.

"So what? You remember it or not?"

"Those are walnut trees, actually," I say definitively, just to take a counterposition, and be nonsensically argumentative. The way I always was.

Goldy walks up next to me. His phone is out. Do ghosts have phones? "There." He looks at me all smug. "I liked your post."

I can't tell if he's goading me or thinks that's the kind of person I am. Cheered up by the glittery fakeness of a social media like.

Obviously, I am that guy. I love the glitter.

Except I don't even look at my phone. I can't. It's dead. "Dead." I laugh.

But there I am on his. Pictures from a lifetime ago. Earlier today. Prom.

"It's all a big ruse anyway," I say. One second I got my arm around someone, all smiles; another I'm making corny-ass selfie poses; and the very next second I'm alone, as usual.

But Mindii didn't give a shit about the fake me. Ngozi isn't about that faux life either.

Am I not that guy? Do I not love glitter?

I don't even know who the real Sunny is, the one Mindii thinks she knows. Dude with this clean-shaven baby face wearing a fake beard? Dude from two days ago with a small but real beard?

Goldy starts walking again, and I race behind, afraid to lose him. He heads closer to the gate where the actual gurdwara is. It is unlocked, and he walks right through, so I follow. The Nishaan Sahib—the triangular saffron flag of the Sikh nation or panth—flutters peacefully above our heads. "Why do they even have a peacock here?" He's grinning, his teeth crooked and white in the dark, like a messed-up fence. "Like how did that conversation come about?"

"You ever see the peacock?"

"No," Goldy says.

"I found your notebook," I say.

He laughs. Something he would never do if he were real.

"My art therapy notebook?"

"Is that what that piece of shit was?"

He laughs again.

"You know the worst thing about art therapy was answering the therapist's questions because they would get all up in my grill and ask things like, how has your addiction affected other people? And I'd always be like, this shit is for my recovery. MINE. It's my addiction. It ain't affecting nobody. Let everyone else do their own damn rehab. It took a lot longer than it should have for me to stop being so full of myself. I thought about you. About Mama. Papa. I'm so sorry. Listen, Sunny," Goldy says as he steps closer towards me, my lips quivering. "I'm an alcohol—" I leap into his arms before he has a chance to finish. "—ic," he says, gasping for air and returning my hug.

"Thanks for n-not making me feel bad about my stutter," I say.

"There are so many other things to make you feel bad about," Goldy says with a smile.

I start crying. He cries too as we eventually disentangle ourselves from each other. "I put way too much energy and so much significance into your notebook. You must have been entertained watching me run around town like a fool," I say.

"If I knew how to switch on your channel, yeah, prolly would have found it entertaining."

"How come you didn't just leave me something? Anything?" I say.

Goldy shrugs his shoulders. "I didn't plan on dying."

"Then why'd you . . ."

"There was this experiment they did in like the 1950s on rats. There was this button or lever or something that would stimulate the pleasure center of the brain. And some of the rats would choose it instead of food, instead of water, instead of taking care of their own kids. That's how insidious this disease is. I'm that rat. I just can't stop myself." Goldy looks at me. "So basically, I don't know."

I meet his gaze.

"Your boyfriend's Thor, huh?"

"We don't like labels." He grins. "But yeah, he's totally my boyfriend."

He laughs. I laugh. It feels good to laugh together, familiar and well-worn, like a rediscovered favorite T-shirt that Mama washed a million times, soft and comfortable.

We start walking. He doesn't want to say goodbye. I don't want to say goodbye. He's stalling. I'm stalling.

"You ever heard the taus?" Goldy says.

"No. What is it?"

"It's the predecessor to the dilruba. You know its name in Farsi means a stealer of hearts because the music is that beautiful. The taus is much heavier. Still got the metal frets, strings are plucked like a sitar, and played with a bow, but it's shaped like a peacock! It sounds incredible. I could sit for hours listening to bani played with the taus, full of soul. The beauty of traditional Sikh instruments before the British forced the foreign sounds of the harmonium on us. Here, I'll play you a few notes . . ." Goldy purses his lips together.

Nothing.

I hear nothing.

"*Taus,*" Goldy says, then pauses for dramatic effect, "means peacock."

"So we're here to find the peacock?"

"I mean, that would be pretty cool."

"Okay. So is there a late-night kirtan with the taus happening here?"

"Not exactly. Nobody plays the taus at this gurdwara. Or like at any gurdwara here in the Valley. At San Jose there's one Kaur, who learned it from the UK. Anyway. Not the point."

"What's the point then?"

"Don't be in such a hurry to get to the point," Goldy says.

I let out a huge laugh.

"Destination Fever," I say.

Goldy lights up. "Exactly!"

"Remember when Mama was really tired one morning and had to walk us to school and I was so urgent to be on time because I didn't want to explain why I was late to the teacher?" I say.

"I remember. You were like six or seven. Mama had had it with you and was all, 'Are you a doctor? Is someone on fire? No?'"

"*Then shattap your face!*" we say in unison, and crack up.

Goldy walks a little farther.

"You know, when I told them I was gay, Mama brought me here to try and find the peacock that roams around here. It symbolizes love or something."

He ignores all of my interruptions, but I am—as Ngozi would put it—gobsmacked. This is a hallucination though, so maybe it didn't really happen in reality?

"So when I told them I was gay, it wasn't as big of a deal as I thought it would be. Thought Papa would swear at me like he would every time I got drunk. He didn't hug me or nothing, but prescribed some poems and we ended up drinking cha and singing for hours. But when I told them I was an alcoholic, there was no prescription of poems. Just an hour of fittey-mooh-kutte-da-putt-haramzada and various conjugations of that.

"Mama and Papa started watching *Queer Eye* after I told them I was gay because that was them trying."

I laugh. "I always thought they started watching that to figure out their other weird son."

Goldy laughs. "We're both pretty weird. And awesome. So we were all in the garden and Mama and Papa came to where I was weeding or something, and they said, 'Je tu fabulous banna, fabulous ban.'"

If you want to be fabulous, be fabulous.

"Dude!" I say. "They said that to me too. That same line."

"That's shady, man. Double dipping. I was stunned. It was so hilarious, I wanted to die laughing, but all I could do was blink."

I smile at the thought of Mama and Papa sitting and watching *Queer Eye*, trying to support, to understand.

"Why do you think Mama brought you here?"

"She latched on to the word *fabulous*, which was kinda cute, to be honest. And she would tell me all about the brown dude on the show."

"Tan France," I say.

Goldy looks at me, his eyes glittering. "Yeah. Tanveer Wasim Safdar. What a zabardast name. Then she started talking about the white peacock, who loves flaunting his feathers. She probably thought I was gonna start dressing better all of a sudden, and start using more vibrant colors. Maybe decorate the house more. Be more responsible. Not become all . . . you know . . ." His voice goes quiet again, far away.

Goldy is looking at me, half familiar, sort of a stranger.

"I feel like a fraud," I say, touching my face. Still startled. And a bit disappointed. "But that's not why I did this. To my face. I did it to not be me anymore. I don't know if I actually like me?"

Goldy pulls me close, his arm a heavy weight, but comforting, familiar.

"Don't worry so much about your face, how sharp

the folds of your dastaar are, or how dark your beard is." The weight of his arm. The weight of his words. He feels real. "Sometimes you need to feel anger and sadness. Go through a whole process. Not just come up with an answer." He steps away a bit. "See this tattoo?" he says, tilting his neck.

"Rahao," I say.

Pause. Reflect. It's in key sections of some shabads in the Guru Granth Sahib. "It's not about how many pauris you got memorized or how well you tie your pag. It's about taking the time to understand."

I nod and look around.

"I love you," I say, and feel Goldy's eyes looking at me. Neither of us steps closer.

"I love you too," Goldy says.

"Think I'm putting too much significance into this note-book?" I say as we stand there in the silence. "Like that keedi story you were telling me that one time?"

"Keedi story? Like an insect?"

"That one with the aliens. And the ants."

"Unbelievable," Goldy says, laughing. "The Strugatskii brothers? Two of the world's greatest science fiction writers? 'The Roadside Picnic' is one of the greatest science fiction stories—and you reduced it to 'that keedi story.'"

Goldy laughs. And I hear it. The honk of the peacock.

His eyes light up as he thwaks my shoulder, excited.

"You hear that?" he says, stepping away, ready to chase shadows. "You coming?"

I shake my head, gesturing off into the distance. "Nah. I got someone to find."

I wake to the unsettling sound of nature. Crickets chirping super loudly, the cool air rushing out of the open window, cooling as morning looms. I smack my forearm in a futile attempt to thwart a mosquito bite.

"You were out cold. Did you know you snore?" Raj says, turning briefly to look back at me as we fly down the street. I must have dozed off, my head absorbing the roar of the wind.

I look around, confused, as the ice cream truck rumbles down my block.

CHAPTER 21

AND SO IT ENDS

W e're pulling up to my house and nothing makes sense. Weren't we just at the gurdwara? Was I asleep?

"Dude," I say. "I don't snore." Raj looks at me like I'm the weirdo.

"You one hundred percent do. Go take a shower. Put on some non-wizard clothes."

"I'm a sorcerer. A warrior sorcerer. Not a wizard," I clarify.

We sit in the ice cream truck awkwardly until we fist-bump and Raj drives off. I keep walking, opening up the front door and quietly going inside.

I walk up the stairs and go into Goldy's room. I jump back for a moment as I recognize Papa sleeping on Goldy's mattress. Glasses on top of his house pag, arms folded like he's ready to quickly read a poem if a burglar wakes him up in the wee hours of the night. I look at his face and see the man who used to sing us lullabies, tell us dramatic renderings of old Punjabi folktales, try and keep up with the world of Pokémon and dinosaurs. The man who would let me sit on his lap as he drove the tractor, the power and joy of it thrilling in our veins like some ancient bloodline. He was the man who would reduce entire rooms of people to tears with a poem. But would tell us to behave like men when we'd cry because we scraped a knee, especially in front of company.

Ever since I can remember, there has always been poetry in the house. When people would come over and complain about all kinds of things, both Mama and Papa would prescribe poems. Open-verse kavitas, couplets, verses, sher, all kinds. Goldy had his first drink at one of those parties. Everyone thought it was really cute and funny. Meanwhile I couldn't stand the taste and they said I needed to learn from Goldy. Fast-forward several years. Goldy is drunk at so-and-so's wedding, at so-and-so's birthday and is getting yelled at while he's drunk. I feel like I got robbed of memories of my brother. I just don't know who the robber is.

I hear footsteps. It's Mama. She opens the door, surprised to see me. And I can't help it. I burst into tears and she quickly puts down the two teacups she'd brought for Papa and her and holds me. She runs her fingers through my hair like she used to when I was a kid. Papa wakes up, doesn't tell me to stop being a pajama, or to stop crying. Instead he holds me close. All three of us lie down on the bed.

"I don't know why I did this to my face," I say. Papa looks at me.

"Don't be in such a hurry to understand everything," Mama says.

"There is time," Papa says.

"Do you play the taus?" I ask Mama. "You know, the musical instrument?"

"I know what it is. No, I don't play," Mama says.

Papa rolls up his sleeve. There's a small tattoo I've seen hundreds of times, but never paid much attention to. "I have a tattoo of a peacock, though. This tattoo is what decided our marriage," Papa says.

Mama laughs. "It's true," she says. "I liked the peacock tattoo."

Papa turns to me. "Do you remember when you and Goldy were so little and you wanted to prescribe poems like me and Mama?"

"I remember," I say. "I thought it could actually cure things."

"Often times it can. Poetry gets into your veins and in your mind. It heals you from the inside. Slowly. Slowly."

Mama gets up. I stand up as well. She takes my head in her palms and lifts my head up. Papa stands up as well. "I am tired," Mama says. "I don't have words anymore."

Papa runs his hands over my chain mail. He laughs. "What can you prescribe us today?"

I think about it.

"I would prescribe a poem to laugh," I say.

"Good. Let's hear it."

Mama and Papa sit on the floor in a small circle drinking their cha to emulate a darbar.

"B-b-banyan lehn ja-jaande o," I begin Anwar Masood's rhythmic poetic nazm about the existential struggles of buying various undershirts that either don't fit, or fit so snugly, you can't take them off again. I still have it memorized and recite as much of the poem as I remember, stuttering be damned. Then Mama chimes in, then Papa, and toward the end all of us are cackling. We're laughing hard and then as if there's some secret symbol, we stop and let the collective sadness in.

"He was our light," Mama says. Papa says nothing, but I hear him make a sound I've never heard before. He is crying. We hug each other. Mama hums an old Punjabi song.

Within a few minutes they are back in the bed, asleep, breathing lightly. I should sleep too, but I have something important to do.

Maybe there is no meaningful notebook. But I know my brother better than I think I do.

Biji has already started her morning prayer, which is

meant to calm the mind. Mama jokes that the only person whose mind is calmed is Biji's because she doesn't use a hearing aid, so she can't gauge the sound of her own voice. Not even at four forty in the morning, which is what time it is now.

I take off Dafydd and get into the shower. I lather my hair and it still feels like a stranger's hair. But I'm getting used to it. I put on some of my actual clothes. A pair of jeans and a blue button-down. I look in the mirror and decide to keep my crooked sideburns for another day.

I go into Biji's room and she is still going full force with prayers. Biji has the entire thing memorized and has started crocheting with her eyes closed, something I don't think I'll ever have the guts to do.

I envy her nonchalance, the absolute calmness of her face as she nimbly moves the needles and the yarn. I'm constantly so worried about messing up a stitch that I won't even attempt anything I don't have a pattern for.

I feel my eyebrows knit together. And realize I'm not just thinking about a crochet stitch. Mindii would have a look on her face right now. I can imagine her clasping her hands like a therapist and being all, "I think we have a breakthrough" in a German accent.

Okay, she probably wouldn't do an accent. Would she? I can't believe I just left her at the donut shop. She probably got back on her bike, though. Right?

Biji pauses to squint at me as she puts on her fat-rimmed signature brown glasses. Then takes the teeth sitting in a glass on the kitchen counter and places them into her mouth, making the wrinkles in her face firm up, her face a little smoother.

She steadies herself with the walker, then moves toward our craft room, our cosplay store space in the back hall, and starts examining some of the wool. I really wish I was more organized with the wool. I have so many boxes and labels, and watch a lot, like a LOT of YouTube tutorials on organizing. I tried Marie Kondo, but every bit of yarn and needles and thread and wool sparks joy.

Biji wears a tattered parandi around her neck. One year I tried buying her a new, fancy, multicolored parandi from the Indian store, but she hated it and just wanted the old one back for a sense of familiarity. I move closer to Biji and loosen the parandi and start rebraiding it into her silver-white hair. Her natural hair is strong, probably from years of massaging warmed-up Amla oil into her scalp before taking a balti shower. I guess it shouldn't be called a shower. Not a bath either. It's just a balti filled with warm water, the way she grew up doing in India. A bucket.

I decide I'm going to create something new to post to my Loom the Fandom Instagram store. I gather up my crochet needles and yarn. I shut my eyes and start creating.

I feel exhilarated and after fifteen minutes with my eyes closed I take a look.

And it's a lumpy mess. I make another one. Another even lumpier mess. I rush outside and pluck a few petals of the Raat di Rani—night jasmine petals—then come back inside and arrange it artfully on a colorful blanket for the backdrop. I rush to my iPad and take a photo, then upload immediately to my Loom the Fandom Instagram store.

"Unfinished Crocheted Apology Sock with night jasmine. For the right person. Reasonable price of eight hundred fifty dollars. Make me an offer."

CHAPTER 22

AND THEN WE BEGIN AGAIN

I get a notification on my iPad. I look at the screen and my face lights up. A response to my Unfinished Crocheted Apology Sock on Instagram. I open the app.

thevangsterwrapper: This doesn't look like a sock.

loomthefandom: It's unfinished

thevangsterwrapper: Something to consider: Socks MAYBE should be the one thing that are not a rash decision?

thevangsterwrapper: Is material Best Material?

loomthefandom: The finest polyester in all the land

thevangsterwrapper: [worried emoji]

loomthefandom: Only kidding. Wool!

thevangsterwrapper: [heart eyes emoji]

thevangsterwrapper: I'll trade you a poem

I abruptly close my iPad and grab the Unfinished Apology Sock, kiss Biji, and scurry into the living room to grab the keys to the Toyota. Where am I going?

Of course. The makhi mandi.

I turn the knob and am outside. I look up at the sky. That strange time when it's still dark, but light has started to meld into it, the stars are out, but the sun is on its way.

I feel the cool breeze on my face and am ready.

The aroma of the Raat di Rani wafts toward me. I hear a rumble near the tree and my heart sings as Mindii slowly putters toward me on her Yamaha.

"Were you on the way to come find me and make a grand romantic gesture?" She gets off the bike.

"Kinda. A little. A-and to t-tell you some . . . uh . . . things," I say, looking sheepishly at her.

She looks right at me, like there's something bright and shiny beaming from within me. I'm starting to see it too. She touches my cheek, then sniffs me. "You smell nice," she says.

"I'm s-sorry about leaving you."

Mindii grabs my face. "It's okay. Sometimes you need to figure your shit out. Anyway, I'm not going anywhere," she says.

"Except France."

She smiles at me. "Don't think so literally all the time. Come on. Tell me where you were planning on finding me."

I grin and put on my helmet and just like that we're on the open road again.

There is a lot of activity happening at the makhi mandi. The farmers are starting to set up their fruit and vegetable stalls.

We get a dragonfruit smoothie, head over to the grounds where her niam tais's stall is.

"Thank you for being here," Mindii says, taking a sip of the smoothie. We look across at the stalls and I realize someone else is setting up Niam Tais's stall. An old woman is loading little glass jars.

Mindii looks on and smiles.

"It was time," Mindii says. "It is time."

We walk over to the stall and see the jars the woman is lining up. Pickles.

Mindii laughs at all the pickles. "Zaub qaub was Niam Tais's favorite."

I take a closer look. "Mustard greens?" I say.

"Sour greens."

I buy a jar and give it to Mindii. She talks to the woman in Hmong and they hug.

We stroll through the makhi mandi holding hands, her other hand clasping the jar of pickles. Her phone dings.

"It's a new comment on the apology sock," Mindii says. She opens it.

Ngozi: This is shit.

"Can I use your phone?" I say.

"Thought you'd never ask."

I call Ngozi.

She picks up in two rings.

She starts fake laughing, a high-pitch squeal. "Oh. Em. Gee. You gotta hear this hilarious joke my new friends and I have been laughing about for hours. In medias res. It's Latin for, Sunny, you plonker." Then she fake laughs again.

"Okay, good one," I say.

"Well," she says. "This is mighty brash of you."

"You hungry?" I say.

"I could murder some sausages and eggs. Meet you in fifteen?"

She doesn't wait for a response and hangs up.

I feel a little giddy. Maybe things aren't as final as I imagined.

We arrive at Denny's. Evidence of the mayhem from the night before is still here. Bits of tinsel that couldn't get swept up, tired waitresses still going. Ngozi is already waiting for us at a table with Shirin and the two Georges. Me and Mindii smile at the group. Our table. The table we used to sit at for hours over the years talking, planning, scheming.

"Remember that time I forgot to bring the amp for our first Unkempt gig," I say, sitting down. "And you were all, 'Let's just . . .'"

"*Scream louder,*" she snorts, and we all laugh. "The crowd hated us."

"What was the name of the band then?" Mindii says.

"Loathsome Twosome," I say, laughing.

"We should totally do a reading one night of our first fanfictions," Shirin says.

"C-count me i-i-n," I say.

"Budge in," Ngozi says as we all squeeze together. Mindii's face is squashed next to mine. Ngozi extends her arm, angles her phone downward as we all huddle in for a selfie. I look at the boy in the camera. I still don't fully recognize him, but I'm getting more comfortable being him. At least for now. I grin, showing my teeth.

Ngozi takes the photo.

ACKNOWLEDGMENTS

First and foremost, a massive thank-you to my mum's delicious tari vala chicken and beetroot rotis. Her delicious cooking kept me fed during my deadlines like I was the Maharaja of Patiala, rather than my usual: injecting coffee and sugar and instant ramen into my veins, for I am a writer on perpetual deadline. As Daddly, my father-in-law, used to say, "Jab bhi dekho, deadline pe hota hai. Lifeline ke baare mein bhi socho zara." *Whenever we see you, you're always on deadline. Don't forget about your lifeline!*

I wrote *Sunny G's Series of Rash Decisions* for you, my lovely readers, and also for teenaged me! While this is loosely based on my own experiences (I wish I were a quarter as cool as Sunny), it is a tiny blip in a galaxy of stories. You all deserve to be represented in books, your experiences normalized, and to read stories filled with joy and hope. Maybe the next book on the shelf will be written by you!

Thank you for taking a chance on my debut novel, especially my fellow stutterers and brown boys who think they don't like reading (not true!). This adventure stars you. You will get to enter a dream that has been chiseled down, dismantled, reassembled, polished, and nurtured by the incredible Dana Chidiac, the editor of my dreams at Dial/Penguin. From our first conversation, she immediately understood Sunny and his nerdy jokes, knew the story I was trying to tell, as well as where it needed to go. When she called for massive changes to the plot or characters, my response was usually a cheerful "Fair enough." The hill I chose to die on is that *Bhangra* should be capitalized for no logical reason except "I like it."

Even though Dana moved on from Dial/Penguin before the publishing date, she will always be Team Sunny, and left me in the very capable hands of the lovely Jessica Garrison (Hi Jess!) and Rosie Ahmed.

It's a strange experience writing a book, an even stranger experience revising a book with a whole team of people who love it as much as you do. And thoroughly discombobulating when you're finished and have forgotten normal people don't want to hear about the titillating details of *Ranveer Singh's Abs,* the name of my sourdough starter.

This book would not exist without the love and support of a lot of people.

A huge thanks to the team at CAKE literary for opening the metaphoric door, to Dhonielle for always having my back even when she uses that stern teacher voice, to Clay for keeping me on schedule! To Sona for being my firecracker of a voti, to our endless conversations hashing out the plot, chatting about Bollywood drrrama, for sending me recipes and songs and productivity hacks on Insta (and now TikTok!), for knowing the answer is always chai (except in this book, it's cha!). For being an amazing mum, traveling companion, and the best life partner a bloke could have. Cue that song from *Hero: Tu Mera Jaanu hai*.

Thank you to Jo and Meredith and Jordan and the New Leaf team for staying on top of it all, and to the entire team at Penguin for making this experience a smooth one!

A shoutout to Michelle Lee for her great feedback on *Sunny*, Regina Castillo for ironing out the minute details and logistics scattered throughout the manuscript, and Lauri Hornik and Nancy Mercado for their support every step of the way. Cheers to Jessica Jenkins for designing the cover and Salini Perera for the wonderful final product.

Thank you to my amazing family for always being supportive, for nurturing my love for learning new things, even when I clearly have no talent in it. I can't imagine a situation where they would not support me and for that I am truly grateful. Even when my sister was excommunicated from the Punjabi community for not having ginger powder or actual ginger in her house and for uttering the phrase "I don't always add ginger to my cha," my parents still supported her. In all seriousness, my sister is a wonderful doctor, a great mum, the world's best big sister, and an amazing artist (follow her on Instagram @Poppyjasperarts), who constantly inspires me with her beautiful artwork. I'm not just saying that because she surprised me with gorgeous framed paintings of scenes from *Sunny G*. She was the first person I gave a homemade physical ARC to . . . with duct tape for binding because I am a professional.

A special thank-you to Kavya and Shaiyar for their amazing cover art on my birthday, which happened to be one of my favorite scenes from the novel! Kavya and Shaiyar are the reason this book is so nerdy with cosplay and fandoms galore. I became immersed in fandoms because of you both. I've been cosplaying with Kavya at New York Comic Con since she was four (she's eleven now!), and my son, Shaiyar, just thinks kids and adults cosplaying is a totally normal part of life, which it is! During quarantine our nerdiness has branched out to some tabletop Role Playing Games, which do also make cameos in *Sunny G.* I love how cosplaying has crept into other aspects of our lives too. Both of them decided to learn Japanese for fandom-related reasons. For Kavya it was so she could read Sailor Moon manga, and for Shaiyar because he is convinced Japan gets the best Yo-kai toys and there is a whole unreleased secret season that is only in Japanese. Super impressed they both learned the entire Hiragana alphabet, and love languages as much as I do. I will always read your fanfiction and can't wait for it to be in other languages.

Huge hugs to Biji for being almost 100, being a crochet master, doing paath really loudly at all times of day, for having a sweet tooth, and when she misplaces her one parandi, it is pure dramedy until it's found again because everybody is going to get accused of grand theft parandi. May you live for another 100 years.

Thank you, Pappari, for having books be a huge part of our childhood, for singing poetry at all times of the day, making sure I knew the difference between a nazm and a sher and a ghazal, for instilling a love of language, even though you did teach me the entire pronunciation of the Urdu alphabet for my first day of Arabic class in Dubai! To Mum for using literally anything as a planter, even my old car speakers! To you both for your adventurous spirit of leaving everything to go try your luck in so many different countries, and coming to America for us and your grandkids. Thank you both for your patience. Only kidding. Nobody in our family has the patience gene.

Much love to Joshvir and Seerit, who are their own unique brand of nerdy and I love that. To Simrit the most argumentative nerd I've ever met, haha, don't ever change.

To the rest of my family, a big thanks for constantly asking when my book is coming out and now asking how you can magically get a hold of it without actually buying it. I'll see you in the Whatsapp group with the million gifs.

Much love to the Charaipotras. Thank you, Nani-ma, for everything you do for us, to Meena for always being excited about our successes, Tarun for being there when it counts (Carpon-punctual!), Lisa for making sure Tarun is there, to Daddly for all the warmth, righteous indignation, great sense of fashion, the filmy dialogue and Jagjit Singh quotes.

Thank you, Jasmin Kaur, for taking the time to read through an early draft of my novel and give me really helpful feedback on the Sikh components, as well as some other areas that needed ironing out. You are a huge reason Goldy has actual conversations instead of walking around with a megaphone reciting articles from Wikipedia! Also, thank you Jer Xiong and Mai Neng Moua for helping with the Hmong pronunciation, and my high school friend Ue Vang for my late night texts to ask random things about Green vs White Hmong spellings! To Candice Iloh for the generous feedback!

Thanks Adib for writing your amazing books and for being the only one to reply to my tweet on my birthday where I was moaning about my lack of iron nuggets on Animal Crossing, and then you showed up on my island on your private jet with iron nuggets galore.

To my Punjabi community for being a constant presence no matter what country I'm in, for the music, for the food, for the conversations, for the chadh di kala spirit in the kisan movement. For Dr. Atamjit for making me systematically learn Punjabi grammar, to all my Sikh community and Sikh organizations I've been proud to have learned from and been a member of the sangat. Thanks, Jakara, and thank you, Sidak and Sikh Research Institute, particularly Harinder Singh and Inderjit Singh and my U.K. posse who would definitely not be watching *Only Fools and Horses,* innit. Thank you, Resham Singh, for your valuable insight on raag and Gurbani.

To my writing community in real life and on social media, especially VONA (Voices of Our Nation), one of the only places I felt truly able to express myself and have real conversations about the art that needs to happen on the page.

To book bloggers, booksellers, librarians, educators, and everyone who champions children's books every day, especially to the We Need Diverse Books team: Thank you for everything.

Thank you, stuttering organizations and speech therapists.

Thank you, everyone, for being Team Sunny.